SHAUN BAINES

Black Rock Manor

A Holly Fleet Mystery

First edition

Editing by Kristen Weber
Cover art by Matt Davis
Cover art by Littlehaven Art

This book was professionally typeset on Reedsy.
Find out more at reedsy.com

Contents

Prologue

"They'll never forgive us for this," he said into his phone.

His words were met with static and the man bit his lip, staring at the incline at his feet. Jamming the phone into his camouflaged rucksack, he began to ascend.

Caitloon Hill consisted of sheer rockfaces and stubs of ferns turned black by the harsh Northumberland winter. It had stood for thousands of years and with his help, would stand for a thousand more.

But only if he moved quickly.

Above him, matted sheep trotted gingerly along the ledges worn smooth by their ancestors. They were searching for something to eat, looking forlorn at the prospect as they made tentative steps toward a barren summit.

The man shielded his head when a stray hoof dislodged a cavalcade of stones the size of his fist. They missed him by inches and he whistled with relief. Injuries this far from help had a tendency to prove fatal.

He knew about the dangers roaming this hill. Not just this hill, but through the entirety of the Black Rock Estate. There were clumsy sheep, wandering cows and a myriad of other domesticated and non-domesticated animals. None of them were dangerous, except by accidental design.

No, there were other creatures out here with far worse intentions. He knew of the eyes that only opened at night. The footsteps only heard when they were least expected. He had learned of their nature from tales told to him by his father; a weak-minded man who never turned off the lights for fear of the dark.

The man climbed higher, searching out handholds and footholds in the cliff. His breath was laboured and his legs screamed under a blistering pace.

The sun was setting and shadows crept over the hill. Darkness descended and the man kept to the light as best he could, hoping he did not have to climb much further. The sheep had rounded a curve and disappeared from view.

He was on his own.

Pausing for breath, he leaned against a boulder when a black raven alighted by his feet. Its dark eyes watched him closely as it hopped within striking distance.

The man was tempted to kick out, to scare it away, but he recognised the raven. Its glassy eyes betrayed an intelligence that was unmistakable. This animal would not be frightened by him or any other human straying this far into its lair. Although the man knew the bird, he did not believe in it. He did not believe in any of the spirits of this place.

A voice called his name and he grew pale.

Keeping a wary eye on the raven, he reached into his rucksack to retrieve his phone.

"Can you hear me now?" he asked.

"I was yelling for you."

"I had to climb for better reception," the man said. "Did you hear what I told you?"

"Yes," the voice said down the line.

He had not crested Caitloon Hill, but he was able to see the lights of Little Belton village. Its residents would be settling down to their evening meals. Families would be bickering or supporting each other through their latest trials. Those who lived alone would be listening to the radio for company. Night would fall and they'd retire to their beds, unaware of the fate they were about to suffer.

"They'll thank us in the end," the voice said.

"Thank, maybe. Forgive, probably not."

The lights of the village began to die, blinking out one by one. If he did nothing, they'd stay that way.

"Okay," said the man. "I'm ready for whatever comes our way."

The raven took to the air, its sharp beak open, exposing a pink tongue. With its wings outstretched, their feathered tips looking like black hands, it sailed towards Little Belton with a caw that chilled the man's bones.

Chapter One

Holly Fleet counted the pens in her top pocket. Their number never changed, no matter how many times she checked. A notebook was tucked into her battered handbag, as was a back-up, just in case. She'd thought of bringing a third, but didn't want to overdo it.

This was her chance to save her family.

With a deep breath, Holly ducked under the village bunting and joined the happy crowds of Little Belton's Spring Fair.

Holly was forty-two years old with a wonky fringe she'd cut herself. Her jacket and trousers hung loosely from a thin body. She'd dropped a few dress sizes recently, though her stomach and bum had refused to notice. Apparently, stress was selective when it came to weight loss.

Pulling her clothing to her frame, Holly wandered around the fair with an open mouth. Wooden stalls were arranged around a green, their crafts and goods protected by striped awnings. A Northumbrian Pipe band played a local tune on the wrong side of screeching. Holly winced as she passed and stumbled into a cloud of smoke from a nearby hog roast. It made her hungry and choke at the same time.

An elderly man wearing a butcher's apron turned the spit by hand. The pig, which was whole from snout to curly tail, crackled seductively over hot coals.

Holly backed into a stall manned by a rosy-cheeked woman selling nettle wine. The woman gave her a sloppy grin. Holly half-remembered her as Mrs Threadle, who had taught her English at Little Belton Primary School.

"Buy yourself a treat?" Mrs Threadle asked with a slur. "They're going fast."

Holly glanced at the empty bottles at the teacher's feet and guessed exactly where they were going. She declined politely, heading to a quiet corner of the green to gather her thoughts.

"You'll be the new hack for the Little Belton Herald, then."

A man and woman stood shoulder to shoulder, blocking Holly's path. They wore chunky Aran sweaters, knitted from the same enormous ball of purple wool.

The man was balding with a paunch. He stepped forward, offering his hand. "The name's Iain Winnow and this is the wife, Judy. We own the village convenience store."

Mrs Winnow nudged her husband out of the way. Her blonde hair was piled onto her head and lacquered into place with something industrial. She wore glossy red lipstick, expertly applied and at odds with her ill-fitting sweater.

"Look at you," she said. "We're so excited you're here."

Holly shook their hands, scrutinising their beaming faces. "How did you know who I was?"

Mr Winnow tapped the side of his nose. "We have spies everywhere."

"Never mind him," Mrs Winnow said, pulling her husband away. "Your new boss Old Jack said you'd be down. He asked us to keep an eye out for you."

"Give you the welcome, like," Mr Winnow said with a grin. "Would you like to try our stall?"

Mr and Mrs Winnow parted to reveal a park bench covered in empty milk bottles. Above them were plastic bags of fish swinging from a rail.

They ushered Holly closer and she peered at the grey fish swimming in lazy circles. "Are your goldfish ill?"

"They're not goldfish, dear," Mrs Winnow said. "We're trying to make a little profit, after all. Goldfish cost money."

Mr Winnow produced a ping-pong ball from his pocket, picking off tufts of lint. "All you have to do is throw a ball into a milk bottle to win your own stickleback."

Holly cleared her throat. "They're an unusual prize."

"They're free. That's what they are," Mr Winnow said, tugging on his sweater. "Got them out of Knock Lake this morning so you know they're fresh."

"I'm sorry, but don't you think they should remain in their natural environment?" Holly asked. "It seems a little cruel."

Mr Winnow's cheeks coloured and he gave his wife a sideways glance.

"Old Jack said you'd spent some time down south," Mrs Winnow said, patting Holly on the arm. "He said you might have fancy views, but we weren't to hold that against you."

"My parents came from Little Belton, actually."

"I remember your Dad," Mr Winnow said. "Black lung took mine as well."

"Don't worry about any of that, dear," Mrs Winnow said. "Why don't you play our game? You win a stickleback and release it back in the lake. Only fifty pence."

"I'm paying for the opportunity to return a fish to its home?" Holly blanched at the rudeness of the question. It had escaped her before she'd had a chance to stop it.

"Great game, isn't it? And those that are left behind, go to make my supper tonight," Mr Winnow said, rubbing his stomach with a laugh.

A herd of children arrived with a whoosh. Hands sticky with candy floss, they offered their fifty pence pieces, faces painted in glee. There must have been a face-painting stall somewhere, thought Holly, because she was suddenly surrounded by *Spidermen* and creepy looking clowns.

3

Mr and Mrs Winnow rushed into action, handing out balls and taking in money.

Holly took the opportunity to slink away.

Things had certainly changed since she had last lived in Little Belton.

The village comprised of tightly packed streets and terraced housing. The roofs were made of slate and the chimneys were stained with smoke. Beyond the houses were cottages dotted around patchwork fields that blended into moorland known locally as the Estate. The population was small. Most of the young folk had moved to the cities for work, leaving ageing parents and those unwilling to abandon the place where they were born.

One house in particular had stood empty for over a decade.

And it wasn't the only one. The village green ran the length of the high street, which had once been the beating heart of Little Belton. As Holly stared over the For Sale signs and the boarded-up windows, she wondered what had happened to the place she had once called home.

Holly sat on a large boulder wedged in the ground, tugging on the camera around her neck. If she was going to get her first scoop for the Little Belton Herald, she had to be clever. Villages had secrets and they wouldn't readily be confessed to a journalist.

Keep your head down, she told herself, willing her stomach to settle. You can't afford to lose your job on the same day you were hired.

She raised the camera to capture the primary school teacher dancing to a song only she could hear. Her finger hovered over the button when Mrs Winnow appeared, lowering the camera with her hand.

"Bless her," she said. "No need to embarrass Mrs Threadle, is there? She hasn't been the same since she was fired."

"I need an article for the paper," Holly said. "It's my first one and I need to get it right."

Mrs Winnow linked her arm through Holly's and led her to a brightly painted bandstand with a domed roof. A lonely microphone stood on a stand, casting a long shadow.

"Where in the south have you come from?" Mrs Winnow asked.

"London."

"Oh, I'd love to go there one day. The West End. Oxford Street. I heard you can't walk a road without bumping into a film star."

Or get mugged, Holly thought.

Mrs Winnow jerked her thumb to the empty bandstand. "If you want a story, why don't you take a look at him? He should have been on stage half an hour ago."

The new owner of the empty house known as Black Rock Manor was due to open the Spring Fair. Holly hadn't been in the village long, but she'd already heard the rumours. Some of the residents said he was a Northumbrian, back to reclaim his family's estate. Others said, he was an Arabian prince taking advantage of falling land prices. A local fishmonger claimed the manor had been bought by that actor from *Coronation Street*.

Whoever he was, he owned the house, the estate and, some argued, the future of Little Belton.

The faces of the villagers were ruddy with good humour. Holly watched as they laughed and gossiped. They carried armfuls of pork rolls and cans of fizzing beer. The Spring Fair was a chance to celebrate a new year and with the purchase of Black Rock Manor, this year promised to be eventful.

But every once in a while, Holly would catch the villagers turning to the bandstand. Their smiles would slip and their eyes would turn to the horizon, glazing over for a second before they remembered the next line of their joke.

Mrs Winnow pressed her fingers into her perm, making it creak. "We're desperate for a man in the manor. This village needs some direction. It could really grow. Businesses could really take off."

"I don't know much about the owner," Holly said.

"I know he hasn't turned up," Mrs Winnow said. "He's a man of mystery, but my sister's window cleaner saw him once. Three villages over in Crockfoot."

"And what did she tell you?" Holly asked, reaching for her notebook and pen.

Mrs Winnow cupped a hand over her mouth and whispered. "Well, my sister's window cleaner says the new owner went into the ironmongers. Bought a spade. We stock spades. He could have bought a spade here in Little Belton. A spade from Crockfoot, I ask you?"

Holly wasn't sure what Mrs Winnow was asking. She let her eyes drift over the fair, finding a merry-go-round cranking into action. Tinny music came from hidden speakers; a slow drawl speeding up as it rotated.

"Now I'm not one for gossip," Mrs Winnow continued. "We hadn't long been here when the last owner moved out. Sir Charles Wentworth, that is. He stayed when the coal mine closed down. His family owned it before it was nationalised. Anyway, he went bankrupt or something. Some say he left due to a scandal, but I'll never believe that. The estate has been going to ruin ever since. This new man should be turning things around and he should be here to open the fair. It's tradition. This village is relying on him."

"Do you know why he hasn't shown up?" Holly asked.

"I don't know, but there is something very suspicious about a man who buys his spades in Crockfoot," Mrs Winnow said, raising her voice against the sound of the merry-go-round. Her eyes narrowed at the dwindling crowd of children at her stall. "Tell me you'll look into him, won't you?"

The face-painted children abandoned the stickleback stall in favour of the new ride. Mrs Winnow rushed at them, cajoling them to stay, but it was like holding water in an open hand. The children flowed by and waited for their chance to spin in a circle on top of a unicorn.

The merry-go-round had a generator rumbling in protest, belching out black diesel fumes as it coughed into action. The smoke stung Holly's eyes. The notes in her book grew watery and indistinct. She realised too late she didn't know the new owner's name or how to find him.

Holly cursed. What kind of journalist was she? She should have asked for more details. It was her first lead and she had let it slip away.

A headache bloomed in the front half of her head, partly from frustration, partly from the fumes. She covered her nose and mouth, watching the children spin through an acrid fog, like the hog roast on its spit.

The rest of the crowd seemed oblivious to the harm their children were in. Dejected, Mr and Mrs Winnow hung more sticklebacks to their stall, but there were plenty of parents, plenty of people who should be appalled by the flagrant breach of Health and Safety.

And then it occurred to Holly that the opportunity to impress her boss wasn't over yet. If the crowds at the Spring Fair weren't interested, she bet her readers would be. It was a scandal. Someone could go to jail over this.

Brushing a wonky fringe from her eyes, Holly raised her camera.

Chapter Two

By the afternoon, Holly was back in the office with her headache following closely behind.

The Little Belton Herald was a newspaper run beneath the Newcastle to Edinburgh rail line. When the trains thundered past, Holly was forced to hold onto her computer to prevent it from vibrating off her desk. She was the only employee. Her employer, Old Jack, had a separate office constructed of walls made from wooden pallets. A paisley curtain riddled with holes hung from a horizontal pole acting as his door.

Holly heard Old Jack groaning as he stretched.

Picking up the phone, she called another number.

"Is that Mr Slattern?" Holly asked when the line was answered.

"Yes, lass," came Mr Slattern's voice. "Are you Old Jack's new man then?"

"I am, sir," Holly answered, rolling her eyes. "I'm calling to inquire if you would like to continue running your advert in the Little Belton Herald. It's for a dog grooming business, isn't it?"

She heard a laugh and removed the phone from her ear when it turned into a hacking cough. The cough died and Holly hoped Mr Slattern had not.

"For all the good that advert does me," Mr Slattern said. "That newspaper has a worse circulation than I do, but go on, then. Give me another six months."

"Thank you very much for your continued business, Mr – "

The phone line went dead and Holly typed up the advert. She had a list of sixteen companies to call. It was what Old Jack called the lifeline of the Herald. Without the advertising money, there'd be no newspaper and it was part of Holly's job to generate as much income as possible. Added to that was administration, delivering the Herald to three key outlets and cleaning the office.

Holly still referred to herself as a journalist, though.

She rubbed her throbbing temples before reaching into her desk for a Thank You card. Old Jack was the first person to give her a chance. It wasn't easy finding an office job in a small village and with everything going on at home, Holly knew how lucky she'd been. She hurriedly wrote out a message and sealed the card inside its envelope.

Just as she did, the curtains to Old Jack's office swished open and he stood with her Spring Fair story in his hand.

"We'll be needing a cup of tea, pet," he said. "No sugar, was it?"

Holly nodded and studied Old Jack's back as he bent over an ironing board where he kept the kettle and tea mugs. There was no telling how old he was. His skin was like a piece of gnarled bark, his spine as bent as a broken bough. He could have been a thousand years old, except for his flashing blue eyes giving him the look of a younger man.

When he turned to face her, Old Jack's smile was broad, showing the ivory of his false teeth. "It's not good news, I'm afraid."

The breath left Holly's body and she stared at the ground.

Old Jack perched on the side of her desk with a wobble, handing Holly her tea.

"How are you finding your place?" he asked. "By Knock Lake, is it?"

Her parents' old cottage sat on a hill overlooking a small lake. In the evening, the water turned to steel. As a child, it had frightened Holly as her imagination took her under its surface to where monsters lurked.

Even as an adult, she could only appreciate the lake when it was lit by sunshine.

"It's good to be back," she said. The tea was too hot to hold and she put it on her desk. "We like it. Me and my husband, I mean. Well, I do. It's just..."

Holly trailed off when she realised Old Jack wasn't listening.

"Grand, grand," he said, sipping from his mug. "Did you know I set this paper up? I've been running it for decades and the village hasn't changed a single bit in all that time."

Holly thought of the struggling shops and the unkempt buildings. To her, it seemed like there'd been a lot of changes, but she wasn't ready to start an argument with the boss on her first day.

She picked up a pen and dropped it back in its place. "Was there something about my article, Jack?"

His frown was an imperceptible movement of leathery skin. "I heard you met the Winnows."

"News travels fast around here," she said.

Old Jack tapped her desk with a finger. "It was nice to meet them, wasn't it? Little Belton is nice. Our news is nice."

"What do you mean?"

"I think you took the wrong angle with the Spring Fair," Old Jack said.

"But the generator? The fumes. It looked dangerous."

"Do you think those folk at the fair would stand around if it was?" Old Jack shook his head. "A year or so back, I came down with a bug. Bedridden and on my own. Then the Winnows called round with a trout. Mr Winnow caught it. Mrs Winnow cleaned it and they cooked it right in front of me. Good people. Do you understand?"

Holly nodded slowly, not understanding at all.

Old Jack stood with a smile. "Living in a village means living cheek by jowl and we watch out for one another. There are no mysteries in

Little Belton, pet."

"What about the new owner of Black Rock Manor?" Holly asked. "He didn't open the fair. No one knows where he is."

The desk creaked under Old Jack's buttocks. "Perhaps he got lost or perhaps, as a successful man, he had more important matters to contend with."

"You sound like you know who he is."

"All I know is that we are small people who like to make a big fuss every now and again. Trust me, pet. There is nothing lurking in the shadows of Little Belton."

Holly's shoulders sank and she blinked away the moisture gathering in her eyes. "I'm sorry, Jack. I meant to do a good job."

"And so you did. I saw your photos. There's a belter of the funny-looking vegetable stall." Old Jack took another sip from his tea, his blue eyes glowing. "That's front news stuff."

"You're not going to fire me?" Holly asked, glancing at the Thank You card.

"Of course not. You've only just turned up."

"Okay, then. I'm on it," Holly said, her cheeks flushing. "I'll write something about the carrots."

"Not right now you won't," Old Jack said. "Haven't you got somewhere else to be?"

Checking her watch, Holly scrambled from her chair. She considered drinking the tea Old Jack had made her. She didn't want to appear discourteous, but neither did she want to scald her mouth.

"I'll be back first thing in the morning," she shouted over her shoulder as she ran to the door.

Perhaps her tea would be cool enough to drink by then.

Chapter Three

The Travelling Star was the only pub in the village. Inside its double doors, the wallpaper was a deep red and the seats were a cracked green leather. An oil painting of a black raven was pitched over a fruit machine. A fire burned in the grate. The Travelling Star was a place where the locals swapped tales with tourists and the air was filled with clinking glasses and the hum of constant chatter.

Standing behind the bar was Big Gregg, his large hands nimbly changing the optics. He moved lightly for a man of his size; a fact made more amazing considering his false leg. Big Gregg was in his late forties with a mass of ginger curls tucked behind car door ears.

"That's how you switch the optics over," he said, dispensing an empty whisky bottle into a hidden bin. "And you'll need to learn fast. This lot go through two a night."

Holly adjusted her polyester uniform, making the hairs on her arm crackle with static.

"Working men need a dram to fuel the legs." The call came from a man wearing a stained shirt and a tartan kilt. He sat at the far end of the bar. Judging by the glazed look in his eyes, Holly guessed his legs had enough fuel for a marathon.

"That's Mr MacFarlene," Big Gregg whispered into her ear. "My best customer, though I worry for his liver at times."

"What does he do?" Holly asked, studying the small man with a large white beard and bloodshot eyes.

"His farm is on the outskirts of the estate. Used to be a profitable bit of land."

Mr MacFarlene swayed on his stool. He reached for his whisky tumbler and missed, knocking over a dish of peanuts instead.

"Perhaps I should get him a cup of coffee," Holly said.

"He lost his wife," Big Gregg said by way of explanation. "I think he deserves a drink or two."

Holly shrunk into her polyester uniform, deciding to keep her assumptions to herself.

"Thanks for giving me this chance, Mr Onstead," she said. "I'm a fast learner. I promise I won't let you down."

"Don't you worry. Old Jack recommended you." He threw a damp bar cloth over his shoulder and gave her a wink. "And call me Big Gregg. It's good for my self-esteem."

For the next hour, Holly dropped glasses and spilled drinks. The orders came with machine gun speed until she felt like ducking for cover under the bar, but she forced herself to gain ground. Soon, for every order she got wrong, she got two right and beamed at Big Gregg for approval. He would wink and point toward another thirsty customer. Wiping her brow with her own damp bar cloth, Holly launched back into the throng. She pulled pints, drained optics and felt her feet pulsate with pain.

The job at the Herald was great or would be when she learned how to be a journalist, but Old Jack couldn't afford to pay her much. So he'd found her a second job at The Travelling Star. There were problems at home and Holly would need to keep both if she expected to pay her bills every month.

As it neared eight o'clock, two women entered the bar. They wore ankle-length dresses and knitted shawls. Their faces were thin with oval eyes and hooked noses. They'd been beauties in their day, but a long life had taken its toll.

The drunken crowd parted to let the women through and they sat in a corner nearest to the fire.

"The Foxglove sisters drop by from time to time," Big Gregg said, suddenly at Holly's side. "They're our last food order of the night. Go see what they want."

Holly detected something in her other boss' face.

"What's the matter with them?" she asked.

Stepping around her like a light breeze, Big Gregg was at the gin optic, pouring himself a measure.

"There's nothing wrong with them," he said, draining his glass.

The colour returned to his cheeks, but the landlord remained quiet. His eyes flitted around the bar, settling on anything but the sisters.

Holly grabbed an order pad and waded through the undulating crowd to the table by the fire. "Evening, ladies. What will you have to eat tonight?"

The sisters both turned and there was something in their laser-like scrutiny that made Holly swallow.

"You'll be the new southerner, then?" the one on the right said. "My name is Nancy and this is Regina."

"Pleasure to meet you," Holly said, shivering despite the near fire. "Kitchen's closing soon. Can I take your order?"

Regina waved her hand. "Oh, they'll wait for us, dear. We hear you're up by Murder Lake."

A finger traced the back of Holly's neck and she turned to see who had touched her, but there was no-one about. There was only a space where other patrons feared to tread. When she returned her attention to the Foxgloves, she saw they were smiling.

"You're mistaken," Holly said, rubbing her neck. "I live next to Knock Lake."

"But did you know it used to be called Murder Lake?" Nancy asked.

The name shot a bolt through Holly's heart and the chatter of the bar dimmed.

"Why was that?" Holly asked, the order pad in her hand transforming into the notebook of a journalist.

"Why do you think?" Regina peered at the menu, eyes squinting in the dim light. "Back in the day, they used Murder Lake to dunk witches. All those women drowning because silly men were afraid of them."

"And those who didn't drown were burned," Nancy said, staring into the fire.

"We used to play there as kids," Regina said. "My sister and I. Old Jack, too."

"Course, he was known as Jack the Lad back then," Nancy added.

Holly jumped as a crackling log collapsed into the fire, spitting embers onto the hearth. They blazed briefly and withered to ash.

"Mince and dumplings," Regina said, tapping the menu in front of her. "Twice, please, dear. With a pot of tea."

The noise of the bar grew louder and Holly found herself gathering the menus and nodding at the sisters.

As she made to go, Nancy grabbed her arm. "We heard you're working for Old Jack. If that's the case, you'll be looking for a story."

"Leave her alone," Regina said, her face paling.

"She needs to know."

"I mainly write about vegetables," Holly said.

"Come see us," Nancy said. "We know all about the new owner of Black Rock Manor. You'll want to know, too. Especially if you want to write about a scandal."

Regina reached for her shawl, gripping it tightly.

Nancy released her hold on Holly and smiled through her gapped teeth. "Now how about those dumplings, dear."

Chapter Four

The car juddered up the incline to her cottage. Holly still hadn't grown used to the blackness of Little Belton nights. There were no street lamps, no radiant halo from a nearby town. Her headlights lanced through the dark. Every tree or boulder was captured in the white, ghostly skeletons of their daytime existence.

Nancy and Regina had left an impression on Holly and not necessarily a good one. After she'd served their meal, Holly had returned to the bar to continue serving the Star's other customers. Every now and again, she'd find the Foxgloves staring at her and where most people might be inclined to look away, Nancy and Regina did not.

As Holly journeyed home, she could still feel their gaze upon her.

Up ahead came two pinpricks of green by the side of the road. They were joined by others. Soon there was a host of floating green orbs. Her headlights swung over them to reveal a herd of deer watching her approach. They grew agitated, not by Holly's presence, but by a giant stag pushing his way through. He cantered onto the road and faced her, baring a chest twisted with scars.

Holly slowed, but she couldn't stop. The car was old with questionable mechanics. Stopping risked an uncertain slide down the hill.

"Get out of the way," she shouted, tooting her horn.

The stag rattled his vast antlers.

"For God's sake." Holly slowed further, but she was still gaining too much ground. Holly's stomach lurched at the thought of an accident and gritted her teeth.

A screech split the air, startling the stag and the deer. They bolted into the darkness, replaced by a shape flying into the light of Holly's headlamps. A large bird with talons stretched out to kill.

In shock, Holly's foot jammed on the accelerator. The car reared, scrambling forward. There was a thump. Feathers billowed in the air and Holly winced at the sound of the bird's body rumbling over the roof of her car.

Her heart raced as fast as the vehicle. Gripping the steering wheel, Holly took control, breathing deeply and slowing them both down. Her eyes searched the rearview mirror, hoping to see the bird flying off into the dim moonlight, but it was lost to the night.

By the time, she reached home, Holly was wet with sweat and chewing on her thumbnail. Her house keys slipped from her hand twice. Fumbling on the doorstep, she found them again and staggered through the door.

The house was quiet with the faint smell of damp she remembered from her childhood. Holly crept through the echoing rooms, not wanting to disturb her husband in bed. After a long day and her terrifying trip home, Holly needed a drink and she'd prefer to do it alone.

She tip-toed into the sitting room, her hand groping for the light switch on the wall. With a click, the room flooded with light and Holly jumped at the form on the sofa.

Derek was face down in the cushions, fully dressed and snoring. His shirt had ridden over his round stomach and his auburn hair was glued to the side of his face.

Their only bottle of wine was empty on the table beside him. There was no glass and she assumed he had drunk straight from the neck. Again.

Her fists clenched, anger replacing her exhaustion. It wasn't fair. Her feet were swollen and her back was aching. She'd been forced to work as many jobs as she could to support them both. All she wanted to do was relax.

Holly marched over to Derek, ready to shake him awake, but stopped when she saw the letter addressed from Micklewhite and Sons, an estate agent in Penrith. With a worried glance at her husband, she picked it up.

'We regret we will not be taking your application for the post of Manager any further. Good luck in your future career.'

That was it. Two lines and a bottle of wine.

She sighed, massaging her taught muscles. It wasn't easy for Derek. He was used to working, used to being in charge. Bankruptcy had loomed and Derek had crumpled. Her parents' cottage had been vacant for months. When it came to running from their problems, it was the obvious place to start again. Holly was beginning to suspect it might have been a backwards step.

There was no point in waking Derek, even if she could. He'd be too tired and too upset to talk.

And Holly felt the same. She slunk to the hallway cupboard, pulling out a thick, woollen blanket. She tucked it around her husband, smoothing hair from his face.

It would be another night sleeping alone.

Chapter Five

A week had passed before Holly had found the opportunity to visit the Foxglove sisters. She'd picked up two extra shifts at The Travelling Star. Her skills as a barmaid were either improving or entertaining enough for continued employment and Holly needed the money.

Old Jack had also made plans for her. While there was little actual journalism to do, the floors needed to be steam cleaned and invoices needed to be filed. The urgency of these tasks seemed suspicious, given neither had been done in years. Holly had done as she was told, but the lingering impression of the sisters had never left her.

There was no road to the Foxglove's home. Holly navigated a single-track lane tracing the outskirts of a conifer plantation. Peering through the pine trunks, the daylight gave way to dankness. Holly shivered, her imagination suggesting a list of dangerous animals just out of view.

She drove slowly, remembering the bird she had accidentally killed and not wanting to repeat the incident. As she turned a corner, a police car hurtled toward her and she swerved into a ditch to avoid a crash. The officer was decked in a luminous yellow vest and lifted a finger of acknowledgement before driving on.

Holly's tyres bit into the mud on the fourth attempt. Cursing, she righted herself onto the track and continued past a rusting telephone box to a grey brick house called Bellcraig Stack where the Foxgloves lived. The windows were small and few, their wooden frames decorated with peeling paint. Twists of smoke drifted from the chimney.

In the front garden was a tan coloured goat lying on its stomach. It was tethered to a gnarled apple tree. The goat made no effort to move as Holly walked by. Its baleful eyes followed her from the gate to the house before closing in a lack of interest.

Purple spired flowers filled the borders, swaying under the weight of cotton-tailed bumble bees.

The house's front door was shut, but warmth bled through gaps in the frame.

"Is anybody home?" Holly shouted, rapping her knuckles on the door.

A rustle came from inside and Regina appeared, a scarf tightened around her head. "If you're selling pegs, gypsy girl, we don't need any."

Holly cleared her throat. "You said to pop by. I'm Holly Fleet from the Little Belton Herald."

Regina's eyes narrowed as a memory dawned on her. "The barmaid, you mean?"

A cry came from the conifer forest. An animal or bird sounding as if it was panicked. Regina peered over Holly's shoulder, waiting for another shriek, but none came and Regina seemed to relax.

"That'll be Black Eye Bobby," she said. "I'm not surprised he's about. The scoundrel."

"I don't think I know him," Holly said.

"And you don't want to, neither," Regina said, her fingers curling around the door's edge. "It's not a good time, right now. Come back again."

"What about your sister? Is she around?"

Regina looked to the forest again. "I don't know," she said, the skin around her eyes contracting. She took a moment before forcing a smile. "Perhaps you should come in, after all."

Holly followed Regina into the house and found herself in a large room with low ceilings. It was lit by candles and a roaring fire. The heat was oppressive and Holly immediately shrugged off her coat.

"Best to keep that on," Regina said. "You don't want to catch a cold." Not wanting to seem impolite, Holly put the coat back on, but undid her collar button in the desperate hope she wouldn't pass out.

"You'll want a bite to eat, then?" Regina asked and disappeared into the kitchen without waiting for an answer.

Holly retreated from the heat of the fire and looked about the room. Two armchairs faced the hearth, each with their own side table covered in shabby paperbacks. A radio gathered dust in the corner. There were several demijohns filled with red or white fluid. Home-brew, she surmised, listening to the airlocks pop as the fluid fermented. Threadbare rugs hung from the walls, but there were none on the floor, which was made of stone slabs.

A painting of a black raven was nailed to the ceiling.

"There you are now," Regina said, returning to the room with a tray. "Let's warm our bones by the fire."

Holly groaned inwardly, taking a seat while sweat collected under her armpits. The tray was thrust into her lap and Regina sat opposite, stretching out her feet so that they were inches from the flames.

On the tray was a sandwich and a glass of liquid. Holly turned up a corner of the bread to reveal a thick layer of butter and sliced tomatoes.

Regina pulled a blanket over her thin legs. "We grow those ourselves and that's parsnip wine you've got there. Only bring it out for special occasions, mind you."

"That's very kind of you, but I'm not that hungry, Ms Foxglove. It is Ms, isn't it?"

"Neither of us had time for that marriage nonsense." Regina's eyes fell on the sandwich. "We don't like waste in this house, Mrs Fleet."

The sandwich loomed up at Holly like some creature from a horror film. Moisture trickled down her spine. Who on earth ate tomato and butter sandwiches? Even if she wasn't boiling from the inside out, she'd struggle to eat such a concoction. Holly felt Regina's gaze upon her and picked up the sandwich, offering a small smile. She took a bite, working it around her mouth. The bread was claggy with tomato juice and quickly turned to mush.

Fighting her gag reflex, Holly swallowed. The bite was gone, but the taste remained. She reached for the parsnip wine and rinsed her mouth, replacing one bad taste with another.

But Regina looked pleased and settled into her armchair. "We don't have many visitors, my sister and I. Can't say why."

Holly pointed to the painting on the ceiling. "Big Gregg has the same picture in his pub."

Regina nodded. "Most people have an image of Black Eye Bobby in their homes. They say, it keeps him from their door."

"Black Eye Bobby?" Holly asked. "Is that local folklore?"

"If you say so," Regina said. "He takes the form of a raven, but really he's a portent. He's a sign that evil is drawing close."

Recalling Regina's words at the door, it appeared Black Eye Bobby was more than folklore for her. As a village, Little Belton had survived as a farming community long before they discovered coal in the hills. The place was steeped in history. Holly wasn't surprised that some of that history had gone off track here and there.

"Where is Nancy?" she asked, picking a tomato seed from between her teeth.

"Whose story have you come for?" Regina asked. "Mine or my sister's?"

Holly considered her answer. She wasn't sure why she was here at all and judging by the scowl on Regina's face, she was wondering why she would stay.

"I'm happy to listen to anything you have to say," Holly said.

"You're not very bright, dear. I think Old Jack was wrong about you."
The comment made Holly feel ill, though it could have been the
tomato sandwich churning inside her. "That's not kind, Ms Foxglove."
Holly removed the tray from her lap, attempting to place it on the
floor as she stood. The heat made her woozy and she stumbled. The
tray clattered to the stone floor. The tomato sandwich skidded into the
fire and hissed in the heat.

"Oh, what a mess you've made," Regina said, wringing her hands.

"Perhaps I'll come back when you're feeling more sociable," Holly
said. "I'm sorry to have disturbed you."

"No, I'm sorry, dear. It's not you who's disturbing me."

"What's the matter?" Holly asked, wiping sweat from her face. "Is
it Black Eye Bobby?"

Regina pointed to the closed door. "The police. You must have seen
them."

As Holly stared at her, Regina's veneer cracked. She wasn't the
woman parting crowds at The Travelling Star. She was a woman trying
to ask for help.

Regina's hand went to her mouth, her fingers teasing out her lips.

"Where's Nancy?" Holly asked again.

"She could be anywhere, but I feel certain she is going to die."

Chapter Six

"I got suspicious when Nancy didn't take her goat," Regina said.

The fire was a carpet of red embers. Regina reached down the side of her armchair and retrieved a poker, jabbing it into the fire. She let it rest there, turning it in her hand, watching the tip glow white hot. "I like to stay by the fire. The furthest I go is to tend my vegetables or for a warm meal at The Travelling Star, but Nancy? She is a wanderer and Little Belton is no place to wander on your own. She couldn't leave well enough alone."

The room held onto its heat like a jealous lover and Holly steadied herself, wafting her notebook in front of her red face. "Did Nancy go for a walk? Did she get lost?"

"Aren't you listening to me?" Regina banged the poker against the fireplace and swung it in Holly's direction. "My sister is troubled. Her obsession was turning her mad."

"What was she obsessed about?" Holly was surprised by the question, popping out of her mouth as it did. She should be running for the door, but she watched the poker cool and waited for an answer.

The hardness slipped from Regina's face. She lowered the poker and pitched it into the fire. Her hands trembled as she tightened the scarf knot under her chin.

"I'm sorry," Regina said. "It's like missing every second beat of your heart."

"I understand," Holly said, but she didn't. She didn't understand this woman at all.

Regina pulled her feet from the fire and crossed them at the ankles. "My sister didn't want the new owner of Black Rock Manor taking over the estate."

"But no one knows who he is."

"You've lived here long enough to know we have our ways of finding out."

Despite the heat, Holly felt a chill.

"There were too many rumours to ignore," Regina continued. "My sister believed the estate had been bought by an outsider. Someone with more money than sense."

"Would that be such a bad thing?" Holly asked.

Regina snorted. "To some, no, but to my sister, yes. She wanted a Wentworth in there. One of the old families. Someone who understood the land and its ways."

"That seems sensible." Holly had nothing to commit to her notebook and drew a sad face instead. "It's important to keep with tradition."

"Nancy kept a file. It's a box filled with newspaper clippings and nonsense about the new owner."

"Why?" Holly asked.

"She sensed something was coming our way," Regina said. "Something bad."

Holly wiped the sweat from her upper lip. "Can I see it? The file?"

Regina uncrossed her ankles and tapped her feet on the floor. "The file has gone, too."

Anger crackled in Regina's voice, sounding like the logs in the fire and Holly strolled around the room, pretending to examine the rugs. She came across a framed black and white photograph and paused.

Holly inspected the blurry faces, recognising Regina and Nancy, looking like mirror images of each other. There was a small boy next to them, trying to look taller than he was. It might have been Old Jack as a boy. He had the same glint in his eyes he did now.

When Holly turned to Regina, she jumped. The sister stood behind her, her movement soft and unheard.

"She left her goat," Regina said, her breath smelling like sour tomatoes. "When she goes for a walk, she always takes her goat."

"Where exactly does she go?" Holly asked.

Pulling the scarf tighter around her neck, Regina tucked a stray hair under the material. "She never said and I never asked."

"Do you believe Nancy may have been meeting with the new owner? Perhaps to confront him with her findings?"

"It's the sort of thing the silly old girl would do."

"What did the police say about it all?" Holly asked.

"They'll file a missing person's report, but they said there was no need to worry yet." Regina grabbed Holly's hands and squeezed them tightly. "But I am worried. She's been gone for two days. The weather around here is unpredictable. Mark my words, this place will kill you if you give it half a chance."

Holly tried to free her hands, but they were trapped in Regina's iron clasp.

"You don't believe that, do you?" Holly asked.

Regina shook her head. "If what Old Jack says about you is true, I believe in you, Mrs Fleet."

***

Holly left Regina by the fire and stepped outside to find a signal on her mobile phone. She held it aloft, stumbling through the garden in search of higher ground. Her phone stayed blank and useless in the barren landscape of Bellcraig Stack. Holly jammed it into her pocket and looked to the red telephone box.

26

The door moved reluctantly, groaning in protest and Holly shouldered it open. Inside were two metal buckets containing tomato plants standing four foot high. The lower fruits were red and glistening, similar to the tomatoes she'd been forced to eat. The top fruits were green and hard.

A sign had been taped to a pane of glass.

'Use the phone. Leave the tomatoes. N+R'

Nothing went to waste. Even the telephone box had been turned into a greenhouse.

She eased around the plants, careful not to damage them. Picking up the phone, she heard a tone and dialled.

Old Jack answered the phone with a cough. "Little Belton Herald," he said, eventually.

"I've got a problem," Holly said.

Over the next five minutes, she recounted her time with Regina. There was no need to consult her notebook. The weirdness of the meeting was burnished onto Holly's brain. When she finished, her mouth was dry and the sweat on her back had turned cold.

"You should have seen her, Jack. She was sick with worry and maybe something else. Panic or guilt? You don't think she's involved in her sister's disappearance, do you?"

Holly listened to static on the line until Old Jack decided to speak. "They got lost once. The Foxgloves. In the middle of a blizzard. They were nought but twenty, the pair of them. After three days, we gave them up for dead, but you can't keep good women down."

Holly wiped the cooling sweat from her brow. If she'd been lost in a storm, maybe she would have opted to live in an oven of a house.

"Where had they been?" she asked.

Jack sighed. "They never said, pet, but they retired to that house of theirs and were never the same again. We suspected they'd grown afraid of the cold. After a while, we just let them be. No social calls, nothing."

"Didn't anyone check on them?"

"I tried, believe me. You see, I was sweet on Nancy." Holly heard rustling and wondered if Old Jack was using a handkerchief. "I wanted to marry her one day."

Holly didn't know what to say. She rubbed a tomato with the pad of her thumb, careful not to leave a bruise.

"They're not bad people," Old Jack continued. "They're country folk. They have a hard exterior, but that's only the outside of them. That's why you have to find Nancy. There's no way she would abandon everything without a good reason. She might not have married me, but she was married to that house."

Feeding another coin into the machine, Holly looked at the dark hills and the conifers blowing in the breeze. The landscape was breathtaking, but it was also bleak and threatening. If Nancy was out there, Holly couldn't see how she could survive.

Gathering her thoughts, Holly's eyes followed the line of conifers, pausing on the last tree.

She jumped.

On the top branch, seemingly waiting to be noticed, perched a sleek raven. It cawed and the wind blew in response, lifting it into the air. The raven swooped to the ground, hopping into the darkness of the forest.

"Find Callum Acres," Old Jack said. "He's the gamekeeper of the Black Rock Estate. There isn't a blade of grass moves on that land he doesn't know about."

"And then what?" Holly asked, tearing her gaze from the trees.

There was more rustling and Old Jack's voice grew faint.

"And then find the only woman I ever loved."

Chapter Seven

The driveway to Holly's cottage was blocked by a flatbed truck. It was hand-painted in olive green. Rivulets of paint had dried before being brushed smooth and hung like unripened grapes. The truck blended into the landscape and would have been lost except for the pink teddy bear strapped to its grill.

Mr Winnow appeared, swinging a plastic bag in his hand. His face split into a grin when he saw her.

"There you are now, Mrs Fleet," he said. "Just making your delivery."

He opened the bag and invited her to take a look.

Holly peered inside to be greeted by a wet trout staring back at her.

"That's a big truck to be delivering such a small fish," Holly said.

The door to the cottage opened and Derek leapt from the front step, waving a wad of banknotes in the air.

"I knew we had this somewhere, Mr Winnow. Three hundred, you said?" Derek thumbed through the money, coming to a standstill when he saw his wife.

Holly's mouth dropped open, mirroring that of the trout. "Three hundred pounds for a fish?"

Derek's eyes darted from Mr Winnow to the truck. "I didn't know you'd be back so soon."

"I came to collect my walking boots."

"Oh, are you taking to the hills, then?" Mr Winnow asked. "You should head for the Faerie Ring by Arden Wood. Beautiful views if the fog is thin enough."

Holly's fingers were twitching and her jaw tightened. She ignored Mr Winnow's walking advice and focused entirely on her husband.

"Why are you spending so much money, Derek?"

"I'm buying a shed."

Mr Winnow shuffled on his feet, looking away as he spoke. "Delivered it in my truck, Mrs Fleet. The trout was my way of a thank you for the extra business."

"May I have a word with my husband, please?" Holly asked, steaming toward Derek and stopping inches from his pallid face.

"Do you understand what we're doing here?" she asked, the words hissing from her like an over-boiling kettle. "We're barely hanging on, that's what. You don't have your own business anymore. You don't have a job anymore."

"We said we needed a shed," Derek said, the money quivering in his hands.

"Eventually. Maybe after I've scraped enough money together to keep the lights on."

"You want me to send him away?" Derek asked. "That's embarrassing, hun."

Holly flicked the fringe from her face and stared down the barrel of her nose. "You know, what? It's fine. Spend the money. Do what you want. I'm in a hurry and I need to get away from you."

"I can return it," Mr Winnow said from a distance, his hearing clearly better than his diplomatic skills.

"No, thank you," Holly said. "You know this area pretty well, do you?"

Mr Winnow nodded, the sun catching his bald spot.

"Good, then I need you to drive me as far into the Black Rock Estate as you can. We can take your truck now that it's free."

"Wait. Where are you going?" Derek asked.

But Holly pushed past her husband in search of her walking boots and a map. She sincerely hoped Derek would enjoy building his new shed because there was a real chance he'd be sleeping in it tonight.

***

The truck rumbled along a tarmacked road, its engine growling. Steep hills rose on either side, towering so high Holly was forced to crane her neck to see their tops. Green ferns dressed the boulders in frilly skirts. Above the boulders were frozen cascades of scree waiting for the right animal to set off a landslide.

The noise of the truck bounced off the hillsides, burrowing into Holly's skull as she twisted her wedding ring around her finger.

"Could we have the radio on please?" she asked.

"It doesn't work," Mr Winnow said, pressing the radio buttons to prove he was telling the truth, "but I have a spoken word tape. I like to listen to them while I make my deliveries. Would you like to hear it?"

Holly nodded and he slid a tape into an ancient deck. She recognised the book instantly. It was from the *Harry Potter* series by JK Rowling, though she was unsure which one. The voice sounded familiar, too. It was a female with a strong Northumberland accent.

"The lady reading the book sounds like your wife," she said.

Mr Winnow smiled. "That's our Judy, alright. I get her to record herself while she's reading. We sell them in the shop if you're interested?"

He indicated left, taking a smaller road cutting through the hills. They plunged into a valley toward the glitter of the North Sea.

"The truck will only get you as far as the Hanging Tree," Mr Winnow said.

Holly grasped her neck. "Don't tell me that's where they hung

31

witches?"

"No, it's where the women folk used to dry their washing."

"Not as magical as I thought it would be," Holly said, feeling foolish.

"Don't be so sure," Mr Winnow said. The truck hit a pothole and they bounced in their seats. "I'll give you directions to Acres' cottage from the Tree, but he's not likely to be in. Spends his days roaming the estate. They say he's half feral. They say he doesn't know how to speak. What do you want with him anyway?"

There was no point in disguising her plans. Old Jack had probably informed most of the village already so she told Mr Winnow about the missing Foxglove sister and his face grew grave.

"Maybe I'll come with you," he said. "Help with the search."

"I'm sure we can manage. Honestly, she's probably back home by now."

And Holly had almost convinced herself of it. Sitting in the truck, listening to Harry win his latest Quidditch game, she had examined the facts. Nancy was an experienced walker and although she was old, she seemed to be in full health. That she hadn't taken her goat with her was hardly a conclusive worry. Most importantly, the Police weren't concerned and that was their job.

But nagging doubts wriggled their way through the holes of Holly's logic. Why was Nancy keeping a file on a stranger? Why had she taken it with her? Had her supposed obsession turned into something darker?

Holly and Mr Winnow stopped at the foot of the Hanging Tree and Holly picked up her waterproof bag. Inside was a map, a compass, a spare coat and socks. She had even managed to find a piece of Kendal Mint Cake in case things got desperate. It was three years out of date, but she suspected that didn't matter.

"Are you sure you don't want me to come with you?" Mr Winnow asked.

"I won't be long," Holly said, climbing from the truck.

"I'll swing by and see Regina, then. Take her a nice bit of trout."

Mr Winnow proceeded to give Holly the directions to Acres' cottage. "Oh, and Mrs Fleet?" he added.

Holly looked up from the buttons on her coat she was struggling to fasten. "Yes?"

"It could be dangerous. You should have told your husband where you were going," Mr Winnow said. "He'll be worried."

The wind came directly from the sea. It was bitter and nipped at her cheeks. Holly shrugged and slapped the side of the truck.

"Thank you for the ride," she said and ducked under the branches of the Hanging Tree, following a stony path into the estate.

Chapter Eight

According to Mr Winnow, Holly was to continue on the path until she reached a tarn. From there she was to go south-west, cutting through spring bracken and up an incline to a cairn on Lambshield's Point. It was Mr MacFarlene's farmland around there and although he was personable after a drink or two, he didn't take kindly to strangers on his land.

"Be careful he doesn't catch you. He'll have words," Mr Winnow had said. "Or worse still, he'll tell you one of his stories."

Lambshield's Point was a look-out and from there, she should be able to see Acres' cottage.

Holly's heavy feet tramped along the path. Her walking boots were an old pair of her mother's. They didn't quite fit and rubbed painfully on her heels. The steel sky grew darker. There was weather coming, as the locals were fond of saying. Despite the cold, the walk warmed her and a rare feeling of joy crept under her many layers of clothing.

There were sheep in the distance, small splats of white on straw coloured grass. Trees budded into life, dancing in the clean wind. Holly felt like the only human on the planet. There was no Travelling Star pub or Little Belton Herald. No money troubles or drunken husbands. No thoughts of a final demand letter from a faceless bank. There was the sound of her feet and the breath in her lungs. It was all she needed.

Holly reached the tarn with an unexpected smile on her face. She consulted her map, the edges fluttering in her fingers. Mr Winnow had said to turn south-west, but the map said otherwise. She looked in a westerly direction toward a wire fence. Beyond it was a faint track, providing a swifter route to the cairn. She would be cutting across Mr MacFarlene's land, but he would never know. Her feet were hurting. The weather was worsening and Holly was buoyed with a sense of adventure. Why not, she asked herself and tucked the map away.

She scrambled under the loose wire, hurrying through a bank of damp grass. A bird of prey passed over her, a dark cross on a darkening sky. It was a hawk, playing on the breeze. It swooped toward the cairn and Holly hastened after it, hoping it might be the same bird she'd hit on her journey home.

The hawk was joined by two ravens, their flapping wings like black shrouds. They flew underneath Holly's bird, forcing it off course and a dog fight of snapping beaks commenced.

If one of the ravens was Black Eye Bobby, Holly didn't care. She hurled a stone at them, but they were too high and too belligerent to care. More ravens appeared, joining in the feathered hunt. They drove the hawk into the horizon, each bird disappearing into baying specks in the sky.

"Leave it alone," Holly shouted.

There was a panicked clatter of hooves and a head rose from the tall grass. It belonged to a sheep, its long face and glassy eyes turning upon her. Another head appeared. And another.

Holly hadn't noticed them as she'd tailed the hawk, but as the sheep made their presence known, she realised she was surrounded. Their blank stares unnerved her and her heart fluttered in panic. Telling herself to calm down, she continued on her way.

But the sheep decided to follow.

Holly knew there was nothing to fear, but she was having trouble convincing her legs. The cairn was in sight, perched on a plateau above a spillage of grey scree. The sheep wouldn't chase her up there, she thought and she doubled her pace, determined not to look behind her. When she did, the sheep gnashed their teeth close enough for Holly to hear.

Ignoring the blisters rubbing against her boots, Holly bolted.

The wind pushed her forward, causing her to stumble. The sheep formed into a woolly unit, advancing toward her in a mass of speckled white. Holly jumped to her feet, scrambling up the scree.

Her lungs burned and her legs were wooden. The cairn was near, but the sheep were ascending fast.

Holly crested the hill's summit and saw Acre's cottage in the valley. It was about a mile away. Holly was too exhausted to make it. With nowhere else to go, she climbed the cairn, a circular structure of stacked stone, rising two metres into the air. It wasn't much, but with her feet already digging into the gaps of the stone, it would have to do.

She sat on the top, exposed to the wind. The first spots of rain fell like silver bells, bursting open on a coat she hoped was waterproof.

The sheep gathered around her, baa-ing, jostling to get closer.

"What do you want?" Holly shouted.

There was a firelight in the cottage window below and wood smoke pumping from the chimney. Holly had almost reached it. Why did everything have to fall apart? She was just trying to help.

"It's not fair," she said into the wind.

"What's not fair?" The voice came from a patch of green ferns where a man appeared. A boy, really. Somewhere in his early twenties. He wore moleskin trousers and a white shirt. Soaked with the rain, it clung to his broad chest. His long hair trailed in the wind and his green eyes sparkled.

He was carrying a wet hessian sack over his shoulder peppered with seaweed strands. Dropping it to the ground, whatever was inside clunked its disapproval.

"I'm stuck," Holly said, trying to hide her embarrassment. "These sheep won't stop following me."

"They think you're here to feed them."

"Do I look like a farmer to you?"

"You look like someone who shouldn't be up here in this weather." The man waded through the sheep, forcing them aside with his knees. They baa-ed in response, refilling the gaps he'd created as he passed. Stretching to the cairn, he took Holly's hand.

His skin was rough, but his touch was warm.

"Sheep think with their stomachs on account of having nothing in their heads. Do you have a piece on you?"

Holly pulled her hand free and clutched her chest. "A piece? You mean, a gun?"

The man smiled and Holly stared at his lips. They were full and mesmerising. She looked away after five, maybe ten seconds. Despite the cold, Holly was heating up.

"This isn't the city," he said. "I mean, do you have a piece? Sandwiches? A packed lunch? The sheep can smell food on you."

"No, I don't have a piece. I don't have – " Holly stopped mid-sentence and grabbed her bag. Foraging through the maps and spare socks, she found the Kendal Mint Cake and held it forth.

The sheep baa-d loudly, pushing forward, making the man unsteady on his feet.

"Tastes like baked toothpaste to me, miss," he said, "but it's animating the locals. Why don't you pitch it down the slope?"

Holly threw the mint cake into the distance, falling short of where she intended it to land.

The sheep hurtled after it, emitting excited farts as they went. The last of them disappeared and Holly climbed from the cairn, snapping her bag closed in frustration.

The man brushed strands of wool from his trousers. "What are you doing here anyway?" he asked. "It's not the weather for a ramble, miss."

"Could you stop calling me 'miss'? My name is Holly Fleet. Are you Callum Acres' son?"

He shook his head and stared into the sky. His eyes closed to slits and his face hardened. A cloud raced toward the hill. It was the colour of pewter and shaped like the head of a wolf.

She studied the man who had turned to stone and her hand strayed to a loose rock. "Who are you?" she asked, her voice sounding small.

The wolf cloud answered with a fork of lightning and the man went from a standing start to a move so fast Holly was unable to prevent it. He grabbed her arm and pulled her into the murk of the valley.

Chapter Nine

The rain rattled the single pane windows of the cottage. A wind whisked through the eaves, but Holly wasn't cold. The weather thundered outside and she stared into a smoky fire dancing in the fireplace, scenting the air with peat. The wooden floor was thick with animal skins of differing sizes and colours. Carcasses of what appeared to be rabbits swung from the ceiling. Candles lit the cottage with an orange glimmer. Their flames flickered, causing the shadows to dance.

The man's hessian sack sat on the only table in the cottage.

Holly caressed her upper arm where a bruise was beginning to show.

"I'm sorry about that," the man said without looking at her. He busied himself around a metal stove, stirring a bubbling pot. "It's dangerous to be out there in weather like this. We had to be quick."

"You could have just asked me to come with you," Holly said.

"Dad always said women shouldn't go anywhere with strangers." The man rubbed the back of his neck, massaging bunched muscles. "I thought it'd be best not to start an argument."

"Your Dad?" Holly asked. "So you are Callum Acres' son? This is his home, isn't it?"

"No, this is mine. I'm Callum Acres."

He turned from the stove. The heat had brought a shine to his eyes. Steam wafted from his wet clothes as they dried, enveloping Callum in a mist.

Holly saw the outline of his body through his shirt and tried to focus on something else. "You don't look old enough to vote, never mind be a gamekeeper. How old are you?"

"Twenty-three, I think," Callum said, pointing at the pot. "Rabbit stew? It'll warm your bones."

Her stomach rumbled. She hadn't eaten since her ill-fated tomato sandwich with Regina Foxglove, but her gnawing hunger wasn't enough to pick up a spoon. Images of bunny rabbits and *Watership Down* scampered through her mind. No matter how hungry she was, she wouldn't eat Hazel and his friends.

"No, thank you," she said. "I'll have something when I get home."

Dropping a ladle into the pot, Callum left it there and sat in a battered armchair.

"It's not my thing," Holly said. "Please don't let me stop you from eating."

"It's not that. It's just that I can't let you go home."

The rabbit stew took on a curdled smell. Holly glanced at the door, remembering how Callum had locked it. Outside of the windows, there was nothing but black, as if someone had thrown a blanket over the world, obscuring it from view.

"I have a husband. He'll be expecting me back." Holly got to her feet and went to the door. She expected Callum to stop her, but he remained in the armchair, tugging threads from the material.

Holly undid the locks and the door blew open, knocking her to the ground. A cold wind whirled around them, extinguishing the candles and worrying the flames in the fireplace.

Callum jumped up, forcing his shoulder to the door and wedging it shut. "I bumped into Mr Winnow. He told me you were on the estate and why you might need my help. As soon as the weather passes, we'll get going."

He extended a hand and lifted Holly from the ground. "You can have my bed tonight," he said. "I'll sleep by the fire. What's left of it."

The red ash had spilled from the grate and Callum pushed it into place with his foot. He fed dried grass onto the embers, blowing on them to get a flame. When it caught, he quickly loaded it with twigs and branches and smiled when the flames began to build.

Holly palmed down her hair, which the wind had whipped into candy floss. "Where is your father?" she asked.

"He has his own place out the back of the cottage."

Holly hoped it was somewhere warm.

"Can I take your coat?" Callum asked.

It was bunched in a soggy pile by the corner. Holly had peeled it from her damp skin the moment she'd got inside. It was not as waterproof as it purported to be.

Callum hung it by the fire to dry. "Mr Winnow said you were trying to find Nancy Foxglove. Are you good at that sort of thing? Working out problems?" Callum asked, moving to the table with a solitary chair at its head. His hand strayed to the hessian sack and he picked off a strand of seaweed.

The answer was no. Holly had never searched for a missing person before. There were some days when she couldn't even find her house keys, but Old Jack had asked for her help.

How could she refuse?

"Yeah, I'm pretty good," she said quietly.

Callum worried his lip. "Can I show you something weird? I was out mending a fence down by the beach. There was an inlet and I found these."

He took the hessian sack and turned it upside down. A waft of salty air hit Holly as red tins spilled onto the table with a clatter. Their surface was mottled with rust, but Holly could clearly see each one sported a picture of a fish.

She raised her eyebrows at Callum.

"They're tins of salmon," he said, answering her silent question.

"I can see that. Where did you find them?"

"They were washed ashore," Callum said. "People shouldn't be dumping things where they don't belong. Especially not tins of salmon. Why would someone do that?"

"Maybe a ship ran aground?" Holly offered. "Spilled its cargo."

Callum scraped rust from one of the tins. "There was no shipwreck."

Her eyes glazed as she stared at the tinned salmon. They melted into a blur, the fish appearing to swim in front of her eyes.

"Someone threw away some salmon," she said, sitting on Callum's bed. "Have you opened any?"

Callum pushed back his shoulders. "Of course not. They're not mine, are they?"

Kicking off her boots, she lay on the bed, slipping into the indent left by Callum's body. It was comfortable, more comfortable than her bed and Holly's eyelids grew heavy.

"There are forty-one tins. I counted them. That's a lot to throw away," Callum said.

A thought roused her and Holly sat up in bed.

"What about Nancy Foxglove?" She pointed to the window and the darkness beyond. "She's out there all alone."

"I'll find her," Callum said. "I promise, but what about these tins? Who do they belong to?"

Pollution was a problem everywhere. Can't afford to dispose of something properly? Dump it by the roadside. Don't have a refuse licence? Dump it in the sea.

Callum was a sweet man. He'd rescued her from the storm and he'd given up his bed. Holly tried not to think about how handsome he was. Or how young. Right now, Holly's main concern was finding Nancy before the weather claimed her for itself.

"Don't worry about it," she said with a yawn. Her long and fraught day was catching up with her. "I'm sure it's not a big deal."

Closing her eyes, Holly listened to Callum heave a sigh before she drifted off to sleep.

She woke in the middle of the night, struggling to remember where she was. A blanket at the foot of the bed had been placed over her. The cairn, the sheep and the surprising appearance of Callum flashed through her mind. Holly rolled onto her side to see him asleep in the armchair. He was lit by the pulsing embers of the fire. His hands were tucked under his armpits and his chin was tucked into his chest as he shivered in his sleep.

As quietly as she could, she crept toward him, dragging the blanket behind her. Holly draped it over him and retreated back to bed, stopping at the pile of salmon tins.

Inspecting them in the struggling light, Holly wasn't surprised to find they looked like all the other tins of salmon she'd ever seen. The picture was of a fish leaping in the air. The brand was called Wesson Brothers. It wasn't one she'd heard of, but that wasn't unusual in itself. Turning the tin over, she read the list of ingredients. Salmon, obviously. Spring water, some salt and a few e-numbers. Again, nothing unusual.

Weary and feeling the cold, Holly decided to forget the whole thing when her stomach growled so loudly, she feared it would wake up Callum. She wasn't a fan of tinned fish, but it was better than rabbit stew and the tins came with their own key.

She snuck into bed, feeling like a child again, having purloined a midnight feast. Holly opened the tin and wrinkled her nose at the smell. There was something wrong with it. It smelled earthy. It smelled of soil and when she angled it to the fading light, she saw why. The contents did not match the promise on the tin.

Holly drew a deep breath. She wasn't hungry anymore. She was nervous because opening the tin had opened up a world of possibilities with only one clear conclusion.

Those tins weren't as harmless as she'd first thought.

Chapter Ten

"And you didn't open any of them?" Holly asked.

Callum shook his head as they hurried to his yellow Defender jeep. "Should I have?"

Holly wasn't sure.

"What's in them?" Callum asked.

"I think they're bulbs or something."

"Plant bulbs? That doesn't seem so bad. I'm not sure why you're panicking so much."

Callum opened the rear door to his Defender and Holly threw in an armful of the tins, returning to the cottage for more. Callum trailed after her.

"Someone has hidden plant bulbs in salmon tins," she said, catching her breath between words. "That implies they didn't want the bulbs to be found and what did you do?"

Callum stared at his muddy boots. "I found them."

"Exactly. Why they hid them that way, I don't know. Maybe they're valuable. Maybe they're dangerous. Either way, you don't go through all that trouble to forget about them when they go missing." Holly balanced the last of the salmon in the crook of her arm while she surveyed the cottage. "We need to get them out of here. Someone could come looking for them. Unless you're happy with strangers coming to your door asking why you have their secret bulbs?"

Callum pulled a rifle from under his bed. He shucked the bolt and his face grew hard. As the rifle clunked into place, the sound echoed around the cottage.

Holly had received his message loud and clear. "You're not the Lone Ranger, Callum."

"Who?"

God, he was so young, Holly thought. "I might be overreacting, but if I'm right, we don't want this situation to get out of hand, do we?"

"I guess not," Callum said, lowering his rifle.

Holly tossed the tins into the back of the jeep and brushed her hands clean. "We can lose them in the estate somewhere until we figure out what to do."

"I know a place."

"Great. The estate is big enough to lose anything and that includes Nancy. She's our priority today, okay?"

"Wait," Callum said. "You don't think the two things are linked, do you? Nancy and the bulbs?"

Holly considered the question. Had Nancy got involved in some sort of weird bulb smuggling operation? Had she discovered the bulbs before Callum, only to come to harm when their owners returned? It was a possibility, but then everything was a possibility when there was no supporting evidence.

"Let's just get going," she said.

Callum disposed of his rifle and they climbed into the front seats.

"So where are we going?" he asked.

"Pardon?"

The engine idled and Callum shifted in his seat. "We can't just drive around and hope we spot her. Nancy could be anywhere."

Holly tapped a fingernail against her front teeth. Through a rain-stained windscreen, she saw the hills and the moorland. The storm had abated and the estate had survived its onslaught like it had many times before. The landscape dropped into hidden valleys and ran to forests capable of hiding the entire village, never mind a single elderly woman. An indistinct shape moved in the distance.

Could be Nancy, Holly thought. Could be a cow.

Scratching at her chin, she cast her mind back to the conversation she'd had with Regina, wishing she'd made more notes. What was it she'd said?

"There's a track from the Foxglove sisters' house to Knock Lake," Callum said, slipping the Defender into gear. "If she took a lot of walks, that's the most obvious place to start."

Holly grabbed Callum's hand. "No, wait. Nancy was obsessed with the new owner of Black Rock Manor. She was keeping a file on him. It's missing and I think she took it with her."

"To Knock Lake?"

"No, to the manor."

"The owner isn't there. No one's heard anything from him."

"Mrs Winnow said he'd been spotted in Crockfoot and maybe Nancy knew that. I think Nancy believed he was hiding in the manor and went to confront him."

"Over what?"

"Whatever was in her file."

Callum picked lint from his trousers, staring at it between his fingers. "It's more likely that she went for a walk. If she slipped and fell, she could be lying in a ditch waiting for help. With the weather we've been having, she won't have long."

"If she was out for a casual stroll, she would have taken her goat, but she left it behind." Holly cringed at the words. It was a weak argument and she knew it.

The Defender roared to life and Callum joined the track at the end of his driveway. "Well, you seem certain," he said. "Black Rock Manor, it is."

Realising her hand was still on his, Holly withdrew it, closing it into a fist.

If she was wrong, Holly was putting Nancy in mortal danger, but following Callum's suggestion was an emotional response. A voice in Holly's head told her to be logical. Isn't that what good journalists did?

The fields were wet with rain, glistening in the sunlight breaking through the clouds. "What's that?" she asked, gazing out of the window.

Callum slowed the jeep. Running along the track was more wire fencing. A twisted skeleton lay with its legs trapped in the top line, its skull submerged under brackish water.

"It's a deer," Callum said. "Most of the time they can jump over the fences. Sometimes they can't. Looks like this one drowned."

"In a ditch," Holly said, forcing the lump from her throat.

"I'm sure you're right and Nancy is at the manor," Callum said and they drove on in silence.

The track widened into two lanes of broken tarmac. It rumbled beneath them, providing a soundtrack to Holly's growing doubts. She nipped the side of her cheek with her teeth. She appreciated the fact that Callum trusted her, but her own faith was waning.

The road took them over a small bridge and through thinning trees to open ground. In the distance stood an imposing building surrounded by overgrown gardens.

"Welcome to Black Rock Manor," Callum said in hushed tones.

Chapter Eleven

"Where did it get its name?" Holly asked as they stopped by the entrance. "It sounds like a haunted house."

"It was built with coal. Black Rock. Not literally, but I guess that's why. The Wentworths made their money from mining and spent some of it building the manor."

Holly followed Callum as he climbed from the Defender. The manor was a cube with chimneys at every corner. The roof rose in a pyramidal peak at the centre. Lower windows were made of stained glass depicting various saints while the upper windows were lead-lined in grids. In the centre of the manor was a large door with an ornate knocker in the style of Northumberland's county flower – the bloody cranesbill.

Holly reached for it, ready to announce their presence.

"I told you, there's no one home," Callum said.

She knocked twice and they listened to the sound reverberate through the empty rooms of the manor.

"It was worth a try," Holly said, going for the door handle.

"The door is locked," Callum said. "Why don't we look around the grounds?"

Holly tried the handle and the latch gave. The door swung open with a haunted house creak.

"That's impossible," Callum said, pushing in front of her. "It should be locked. No-one has the keys, except the owner. Not even me."

Beyond was a small lobby with clay tiles on the floor. Stepping inside, Holly and Callum were faced with a second door. It was engraved with the Wentworth coat of arms, which was a lion cresting the side of a mountain. Dust piled like snowdrifts in the grooves.

"If the door is open, someone could be inside," Holly said. "It must be the new owner and maybe Nancy is with them."

She made to push at the door, but Callum grabbed her arm, gently, but firmly.

"We can't go in," he said.

"Why not?"

"It's not ours. We don't have permission to enter."

Holly pulled her arm away. "What if the new owner is in there? What if he has something to do with Nancy's disappearance? Nancy might be trapped in a cupboard or something."

The questions tumbled out. Holly's curiosity was piqued and she didn't understand why Callum was being so reluctant.

"You don't have to be afraid," she said, half-jokingly. "I'll protect you."

The muscles in Callum's jaw bunched. "I ignored my instincts and followed you here because you seemed to know what you were talking about. That doesn't give you the right to barge into my employer's house, whether he is in there or not."

"But you said you'd help me. What's wrong? What have I done?"

"You trespassed on Mr MacFarlene's land. Don't deny it. I saw you. You put yourself in danger by stumbling around in a storm. You run me out of my own home because you're convinced some bulb smuggling mafia are out to get me. And now you're not listening to what I'm saying."

Callum's face was puckered in frustration and Holly turned away from him. He was right to be annoyed.

"I'm asking a lot of you," Holly said. "I'm sorry. If you don't want to go inside, then why did you bring me here?"

"Because," Callum said, smoothing out a crease in his shirt, "you asked me to and I can't - "

Holly had raised her hand, interrupting Callum's speech. Her ears were trained to the rasps and groans of the house. "I can hear something."

Callum let out a sigh. "You're just saying that."

"I'm not. I promise."

Together, they listened to the house. Callum leaned in, bringing his face close to hers.

"Intruders," he said, taking the lead. "There is someone inside."

"Let's hope it's Nancy and not a ghost."

They crept into the manor and found themselves in a wide space with high ceilings. The walls were decorated in peeling murals. Dust sheets were thrown over hidden furniture. The sun beamed through a stained-glass window of Saint George throttling a dragon. The muted image was projected at their feet.

"This is the Reception room," Callum whispered. "When the Wentworths held their balls or banquets, they'd stand here and greet their guests as they entered."

"You seem to know a lot about it."

"Dad told me. He was invited once. He told me all about it when I was a kid."

"Your father attended one of the Wentworths' events? They must have thought highly of him."

Callum nodded, puffing out his chest. "It wasn't long after the mine closed. They had to dismiss a lot of staff. Dad stepped in as an under-butler."

He turned to the murals above him, a smile playing on his lips.

Holly understood Callum then, or rather the reason she had upset him. Holly had once been the wife of a wealthy London estate agent and was now a journalist at a failing newspaper and a part-time barmaid. She may not have much, but it gifted her a unique perspective.

Holly gave him a playful nudge with her shoulder. "Just because they have money doesn't make them better than you, Callum. You don't have to doff your cap anymore."

He looked at her, confusion in his eyes. "Sure I do."

They walked from room to room, pausing, listening and then moving on. Most of the remaining furniture was covered in shrouds and her earlier comments of Black Rock being haunted gave Holly the chills. It was cold in the manor, but filled with an old-world majesty. It was easy to see how Callum had been seduced by Black Rock's splendour.

Some of the rooms were oak-panelled, retaining the scent of beeswax candles. Others had velveteen wallpaper and chandeliers that had been converted from using candles, to gas and finally to electricity.

Holly climbed a spiral staircase to the upper rooms with Callum in tow. The kaleidoscopic tints of the stained-glass windows were gone. Upstairs, the light was stark as if designed to replicate the Northumberland winter. There were more dust sheets, more dust and the floorboards groaned with every step.

"There are footprints everywhere," Callum said, dropping to his haunches. "They're going this way."

They continued down the corridor, coming to a closed door.

"Be careful," she whispered and swung it open.

Behind the door was a bedroom without a bed. Dust sheets had been pulled to the floor, exposing the glossy wood of wardrobes. In the middle were an inflatable mattress and an open sleeping bag, looking like a large, discarded sock. There was a gas stove for cooking and slips of silver packaging.

Callum picked up one of them. "Camping food. This one is curried prawns."

"They smell as bad as your rabbit stew."

"Someone is staying here," Callum said. "Who? Is it Nancy?"

A washing line hung by the window. Holly unpegged a pair of large Y-fronts and held them in front of Callum.

"Not unless Nancy has a secret," she said.

"They're big enough to use as sails," Callum said. "You could cross the Atlantic with those."

Holly dropped the underwear, kicking them aside and wiping her hands on her trousers. "Whoever is living here, it's not Nancy and it's not the owner of Black Rock."

"I understand it's not Nancy, but why not the owner?"

"Because anyone who can afford this place won't be camping in it."

"But only the owner has access to Black Rock." Callum stooped to a pile of dirty outdoor clothes and pulled out a set of keys, jangling them in front of Holly. A wooden duck keyring swung in his hand.

"These are the keys to the manor," Callum said.

"Could they have been stolen?"

Callum slipped them into his pocket. "They don't belong here, that's for certain."

"Well, if they weren't stolen before, they are now," Holly said.

Callum opened his mouth to speak and stopped. Slowly, he raised a finger to his lips and pointed to the ceiling. Holly froze, her eyes following the direction of his finger. The air was still. Callum was still. And Holly couldn't hear a thing.

"Is anybody there?" Callum shouted.

A floorboard creaked, sending a shudder down Holly's spine.

"Nancy?" she asked.

A clattering noise came from the room above.

Callum bolted to the door with Holly in pursuit.

"It's the servants' quarters," Callum shouted over his shoulder. "Quickly. Through here."

Holly struggled to keep up, her breath coming in gulps. She bounced off the walls, knocking dust sheets and vases to the floor. She pretended not to hear them smashing as she stumbled up a second staircase, her lungs burning.

Callum took the stairs three at a time while Holly cursed the day she'd given up using her Stairmaster.

They stopped at a half-open door. Callum hid behind it, looking like he'd done no more than a light jog. Holly arrived, wiping sweaty hair from her brow. He pulled her in beside him and she tried not to touch him with her slick skin.

"They're inside that room," he whispered. "I want you to stay here until it's safe."

"I...can...take...care of...myself," Holly said between pants.

Shucking off his wax coat, Callum dropped it on the floor. He rolled up his sleeves, exposing forearms like twisted metal. "I don't want you to get hurt."

"What are you going to do? Knock his block off? We need to ask him some questions."

"This won't take long," Callum said.

Holly didn't doubt it. Callum seemed more than capable of subduing the type of man who wore Y-fronts, but Holly hadn't come this far to lose her only lead.

She launched from their hiding place before Callum could stop her, his jacket entangling itself around her feet. Running into the room, it clamped around her ankles. She fell with a thump with no time to scream. Open-mouthed, Holly skidded along the floor before crumpling into a heap. She was winded, hoping the ground would take mercy on her and swallow her whole.

The curtains were drawn and the room was in darkness. As her eyes became accustomed to the gloom, she saw a shape standing in the corner.

"What are you doing here?" Holly asked.

Chapter Twelve

"Are you okay?" Callum asked.

His presence startled the shape in the corner and it charged at them. Callum flung himself on top of Holly, rolling her to one side. The shape missed them, leaping onto a battered table before jumping through the doorway.

Callum watched it canter out of the room. "Was that a goat?"

Its hooves clattered down the staircase to the floor below.

"It belongs to Nancy," Holly said, propping herself up on her elbow. "I saw it back at Bellcraig Stack, but it was tied to a tree. It must have chewed through the rope."

"How did it get in here?" Callum asked. "The doors were closed and I doubt it used the keys."

Holly dusted herself down. "At least we know who was making all the noise."

Callum stared through the doorway. "We have to catch it."

"What for?"

"A goat will chew anything. Not just rope. It will eat tapestries, paintings, Y-fronts. It might even break a vase or two."

Holly rubbed the side of her face. "You heard me do that, did you?"

"I can't leave a goat in here to damage the manor. Come on."

They sneaked down the narrow staircase to the second floor.

"I think I can hear it," Callum said.

"Me, too. It's in one of the bedrooms."

A crash of something breaking came from the far end of the corridor.

They hurried along to the last room. The door was open and they peered inside. A writing desk was lying on the floor in front of a family portrait hanging on the wall.

The goat was on its hind legs, nibbling at a corner of the painting.

"Take that out of your mouth right now," shouted Callum.

Startled, the goat charged at them again.

But Callum was ready. He crouched, holding out his arms, ready to make the catch.

The goat bounded toward him. With a flick of its hind quarters, it sailed over him and onto his back. It leapt to safety and escaped down the winding staircase to the lower ground.

"I hope you're are a better gamekeeper than you are a shepherd," Holly said, grabbing a dust sheet from the fallen writer's table. "We need to get it out of the manor. We worry about getting it back to Bellcraig Stack later, right?"

Rubbing his lower spine where the goat had trodden on him, Callum gave her a nod.

"Then follow me," Holly said.

The goat was pacing the Reception room when they descended the final staircase.

"Open the front door," Holly said.

Callum edged around the goat, giving it as much space as possible. He reached the door and opened it. A cool wind blew in, stirring the dust on the floor into tiny tornados.

The goat raised its head and sniffed the air.

Holding a corner of the dust sheet in each hand, Holly widened her arms. The sheeting billowed with the breeze and she ran at the goat, like a matador. The goat bucked and ran for the exit, swerving at the last moment. It barrelled through a door in the oak panelling and

Callum sprang forward, snapping it shut.

"Where did it go?" Holly asked.

"It's trapped in the pantry," he said with a smile. "There's nothing in there for it to chew on."

"How ironic," Holly said. "What are we going to do now?"

Callum stared at the ground, pinching his shoulders. "I could always fetch my rifle."

"No," Holly said. "It's not a wild animal. It's a pet."

"It'll starve to death. That's worse in my book."

Holly sucked air over her teeth. "Well, you'll have to go in there and get it," she said, pushing Callum toward the pantry.

"Why me?"

"Because you're a gamekeeper." Holly handed him the dust sheet. "Catch it in this. Throw it outside."

Callum raised an eyebrow.

"Trust me. It will work," Holly said.

The gamekeeper didn't look convinced.

Holly stood by the pantry door, ready to fling it open.

"Ready?" she asked.

"Does it matter?"

With a crank of the handle, Callum rushed into the darkness with Holly quickly shutting him inside. There were a series of bangs and the odd expletive. After a while, the pantry fell silent.

"Callum?" Holly asked. "Have you got it?"

"It's gone," Callum's muffled voice answered.

Holly inched open the door, squinting inside. "What did you say?"

The pantry was long and narrow with shelves down either side. The food had long been eaten, except for a lonely jar of pickled cucumbers nobody wanted.

Callum marched to the far end. "It's gone," he repeated, patting the walls as if to assure himself they were there. "I don't understand."

Frustrated, Holly left him in his search and went to the front door. The wind cooled her face and she sat on the step, propping her elbows on her knees.

She listened to Callum's angry mutterings as he thrashed around the pantry. What was going on, she thought? She'd felt sure Nancy would be waiting for them at the manor. It was the most obvious place to hide.

But was she hiding? Perhaps she was on the run. Nancy might have met the new owner. Perhaps the meeting had gone badly and she'd been forced to flee the estate.

Or maybe Callum was right and Nancy was in a ditch somewhere, waiting to be discovered.

Holly lowered her spinning head when it jerked to attention at something moving through the tall grass.

"Callum," she hissed.

More banging. A litany of swear words and then it went quiet.

"What the chuff is that?" Callum asked from the pantry.

Holding her breath, Holly's eyes were trained on the grounds. She took her time in standing, wincing as her boots scraped the ground.

The goat ambled through the grass, churning a green dock leaf around its mouth.

This time Holly was determined to capture it.

"Hey, there was a hidden door," Callum said, suddenly appearing in front of her.

The goat took off, carving a path through the garden. It bounced through the air, kicking out its legs. The goat was enjoying this too much, she thought and turned to Callum with a frown.

"Sorry about that," he said to his shoes.

Holly sighed. "How did it get into the manor?"

"Goats are as dumb as sheep, but they're curious creatures. They butt their heads against stuff they don't understand."

"Sounds familiar," Holly said.

"Probably rammed the secret door open from the outside," Callum said. "Did the same to get out. The hinge was spring loaded so the door snapped shut right after."

They watched the goat run giddy circles. It drew closer to the border, threatening to disappear through a row of rhododendrons.

"You want to go and catch it?" Callum asked without enthusiasm.

Holly cupped her weary face and stared at the yellow Defender instead. "Let's walk along the path to Knock Lake. I think you were right all along."

As if it had heard her, the goat stopped its capering. It backed away from the border and glanced in their direction.

"What's it doing?" Holly asked. "Has it smelled something?"

Callum tucked his long hair behind his ears. "Something has spooked it."

He started a slow walk toward the bushes. Holly expected the goat to run, but it remained stationary, stamping its hooves into the ground.

Callum approached in a zig-zag fashion and Holly followed his footsteps through the grass.

"Why isn't it running?" she asked when she reached him.

"I told you, they're curious animals," he said. "I guess it's found something."

As they approached, the goat's nostrils flared, its shaggy legs dancing, ready to bolt, but it didn't go far. It trotted to a flattened plain of grass and dropped to its knobbly knees, braying softly.

"It sounds like it's crying," Holly said.

Moving slowly, they reached the border when Holly's blood ran cold. She saw the feet first. The legs were hidden under an ankle length dress. The body was wrapped in layers of wool and the head was covered with a shawl stained with blood.

Holly pressed fingers to her open mouth and they shook against her lips.

"We were too late," she said.

Callum placed an arm around her shoulders. "But we found her."

Shrugging off Callum's hold, Holly inched toward the body, fear building with every tentative step. Gritting her teeth, she tugged the shawl from the face.

"No, we didn't," she said. "It's not Nancy. This is Regina, her sister."

Chapter Thirteen

Wansbeck General Hospital was on the outskirts of Ashington, an ex-mining town near the north-east coast. Like all hospitals, it smelled of anti-bacterial soap and illness. It was a hive of medical practitioners rushing from one bed to another. There was the rattle of rolling trolleys and the bark of insistent voices.

But the ward that housed Regina's unconscious form was hushed in quiet.

Holly stood shoulder to shoulder with Derek. Her husband had insisted on using the car to pick up his daily newspaper from Little Belton. Unable to reach the hospital by other means, Holly made Derek drive them to the hospital.

They were listening to Reverend Applecroft whispering a prayer over Regina's bed. Mr MacFarlene stood in the corner, his fingers playing with the clasps of his sporran. Big Gregg stood next to him, tapping his false leg against the wall. The Winnows had brought flowers, stationing them on every flat surface they could find. Old Jack stood alone, disguising his despair with a muted smile.

After discovering Regina and her shallow breathing, Holly had attempted to call for an ambulance. Her signal was weak and she marched the overgrown lawns with her phone held in the air. As she climbed a tree, searching for one bar, an ambulance miraculously appeared. It hurtled past her in a disco of flashing lights and she tumbled from the full two feet she had managed to climb.

Callum explained what had happened and the paramedics called the police. Both Holly and Callum had been interviewed about their involvement. Statements were signed and fingerprints were taken. The manor had been searched for the mysterious squatter after Callum demanded it be done.

The police found neither the squatter nor any of his belongings.

It led to further questions and more time in the interview room. When the officer in charge seemed satisfied that Holly and Callum hadn't attacked Regina, or had any motivation to do so, they were released under a cloud of suspicion.

In the hospital, Holly stared at Regina's bandaged head and let her eyes travel around the room.

Derek squeezed her hand so hard it made her jump.

"Who are you looking for?" he asked.

"No one."

The Reverend's monologue mutated into the Lord's prayer and the occupants of the room mumbled along.

"Really? Because you seem to be spending a lot of time with *no one* recently."

"Leave it be," Holly said.

Derek stiffened. "The whole village has come to see Regan," he said, picking dirt from under his fingernails, "and your new boyfriend hasn't even shown up."

"Her name is Regina," Holly said.

"Whatever."

Holly sniffed loudly. "What's that supposed to mean?"

Old Jack raised his head, his blue eyes searching their faces, but Derek didn't seem to notice.

"What am I supposed to think?" he hissed. "You spent the night with him. I thought you'd been in an accident. I was worried sick."

The door to the room was open. Outside were more villagers waiting to pay their respects. Some had flowers, others had brought baked goods, but none of them was Callum.

"And what's worse," Derek continued, "is that I found my wife had spent the night with a gamekeeper from one of the busy-bodies in the village. That drunken farmer over there. He collared me. Oh, he couldn't wait to let me know. Do you know how humiliating that was?"

"You read the *Daily Mail*, Derek. You deserve to be humiliated."

"That's right. Make fun of me," Derek said, throwing his arms into the air. "Make fun of your stupid, worthless husband who can't even get a job."

"If you spent more time looking for one instead of building that bloody shed, I wouldn't mind. And I've told you, over and over again, we were trapped by a storm."

When she stopped shouting, her voice had been replaced by the soft shuffling of feet.

The Reverend's white knuckles gripped his Bible. "Perhaps you would like to take your dispute away from the injured."

Holly caught Old Jack pointing toward the door.

"Sorry," she said to the crowd. She looked to her husband, about to apologise, but he had already slipped away. The gap he had left was filled by a newcomer taking the opportunity to offer both their condolences and their homemade brandy snaps.

The Reverend cleared his throat and continued with his prayers. By the time he had finished, Holly was halfway to Callum's cottage.

***

It was dark by the time she arrived. The cottage glowed from the inside, looking cheerful and welcoming, but Holly was guided by a light behind the building.

Callum sat in a weathered deckchair, its stripes washed away by the weather. A fire danced at his feet and he poked it with a stick, tracing the burning end through the air, painting in circles of light.

"How did it go?" he asked without turning around.

Holly sat cross-legged by his side, the fire warming her face. "How do you do that? How did you know it was me?"

"Spent more time with you than I have most other people," he said with a sad smile.

They stared into the fire.

"No one likes hospitals," Holly said. "You'd be pretty weird if you did, but you should have been there."

The fire lit the surrounding area in a yellow halo and Holly made out the outline of a headstone in the distance.

"When my Dad died," Callum said, "I was the only person there."

"Your Dad is..." Holly didn't finish the sentence, realising her mistake. When Callum had said his father was out back, she had assumed he lived behind the cottage somewhere. Callum was young. His father should still be alive, but if Regina's attack proved anything, it was that danger came unannounced.

"I'm sorry to hear that," she said. "Was he unwell?"

"Mam wasn't around. It was always just me and him." Callum kicked at a stone, sending it into the flames. "It was right that it was only me at the end."

"What happened?"

The glowing tip of his charred stick died. Callum licked his fingers and extinguished the last of the heat. "When the Wentworths left, he was out of work. The mines were gone. There were no jobs anywhere. There was nothing for him. That rifle I use? That was his. A father should hold onto his son in his final moments. My Dad held onto that rifle."

The words dried in Holly's mouth.

"Giving your life in service of others..." Callum said with a pause, "... when they leave, there's no one to replace them. Dad couldn't let go.

He was loyal to the end."

"You're living that same life," Holly said.

The air was warm, but Callum shuddered. "It's not hospitals, I mind. I knew the whole village would be there for Regina. They're good like that. The best thing I can do for them is to remember what my Dad taught me. He always said, never burden the people you love. That's what I would have been if I'd turned up."

Holly tightened her coat. "Sometimes they want to be burdened."

"Why are you here?" Callum asked. "It's late."

"I had an argument with my husband." Holly swallowed, fighting a lump in her throat. "He's under so much pressure and I'm making it worse. I'm never around."

"What did he do in London?"

"He was an estate agent, a successful one, but the market slumped. People stopped buying houses. I did his books. I saw it all in black and white. Derek blamed housing trends. He blamed Brexit. He blamed himself. It was all those things, I suppose. We became a sinking ship. We laid off staff. We moved to smaller premises. We jettisoned everything to stay afloat, but it didn't matter. We sank anyway.

"I persuaded him we needed a new start. My parents came from here. The house had been empty since they died."

Holly glanced at her wedding band as it glowed in the firelight. "My parents...they met in their teens. Never spent more than a night apart in over fifty-two years. That means something, doesn't it? A marriage like that?"

"Devotion like that is rare," Callum said.

"I thought Little Belton was the answer," Holly said. "I thought some of that magic might rub off on Derek and me. For all the blame he threw around, I never blamed him, but now, I kinda do. He doesn't talk to anyone, least of all me. He's either drunk or playing with his new shed. If he made more of an effort...I know it's difficult coming to a new place, but if he got to know people, he'd find they're decent. They could help, like they helped me."

"It sounds like his fault," Callum said, the fire dying by his boots. "Not yours."

"I should never have stayed here last night."

Callum shifted in his chair. "Nothing happened."

The road by Callum's cottage was lost to the night. His driveway led into the unknown. There were no guiding lights, except for the stars. They blinked into existence, like lightbulbs switched on by unknown hands. Holly gazed up at them, hoping to find a way home.

"I take it you won't be staying again?" Callum asked,

The question was loaded and they both knew it. His voice was low. Its vibrations hummed in Holly's bones. It was the voice of a man saying one thing and meaning another.

She had no doubt what would happen if she stayed.

Looking to the cottage, Holly saw the door was invitingly open. She imagined the heat from the fireplace and the comfort of the candlelight.

Holly got to her feet. Callum stood too and she stepped away, pulling a torch from her pocket. She shone it down the driveway and saw the road to Little Belton.

Back to her home and back to her husband.

"I came prepared this time," she said, waving the torch.

"Of course, yeah."

Holly rested her hand on Callum's chest.

"Thank you," she said. "For listening to me."

Callum smiled and jerked his head to the cottage. "Actually, I would like you to come inside. I have something to show you."

"Don't make me be blunt with you, Callum."

He took her hand. "It's not like that. This one has me baffled."

Callum led her to the cottage where moments ago Holly had considered staying and they stood over his kitchen sink.

"I went back to the manor hoping to find that squatter," Callum said. "The police did what they could, but I tore that place upside down. He wasn't there. When I'm stalking through the estate, there isn't an animal alive that doesn't leave some trace that it's been there."

"What did you find?"

Callum pointed into a sink filled with water. The light was poor and Holly struggled to see what was concerning him. A silver flash cut through the water and she peered closer.

"I found them swimming in the toilet bowl," Callum said. "I think he tried to flush them away."

"You really did look everywhere, didn't you?" Holly asked. "So you fished these out of the toilet?"

"I'm not proud of it, but it seemed weird."

There were three fish in total, small and fierce, their spines erect as they chased each other through the kitchen sink.

"Were there any bags about?" she asked.

"Plastic bags? Yeah. Lying on the cistern."

Sticklebacks, thought Holly and she knew how to find more.

Chapter Fourteen

Early the following morning, Holly and Callum met by a beach on the north-east coast. They crested a hill together, leaning into a wind whipping off the sea.

The tide was out on Ratkin Bay, exposing black rocks crusted with limpets. A small rowing boat was tethered to the shoreline. Its owner was walking through the waves.

"They think I don't know about their poaching," Callum said, "but I know. They're here at the same time every day."

Holly and Callum skidded down the slope, stepping onto white sand the consistency of sherbet.

"How's it going?" Callum shouted at the unsuspecting figure in the water.

Mrs Winnow turned in fright, her feet slipping underneath her. She was subsumed and her shriek was lost beneath the salty surface. Holly went to help, but Callum held her back.

"She deserves a dunking," he said.

A second passed before Mrs Winnow reappeared and staggered to the beach.

"You bloody fool," she shouted.

Her hair hung in ropes down her face. Lipstick carefully applied that morning now made her look like *The Joker*.

Mrs Winnow dragged herself toward them, coughing and spluttering.

"What did you do that for?" she asked, shaking her hands and feet like a wet dog. "Here I am minding my own business and you do something like that."

Callum braced his hands on his hips. "Catch much today?"

Her mouth dropped open and she glanced sideways to the rowing boat. "I don't know what you mean, dear. I was merely out for...a constitutional."

"Where's your husband?" Holly asked.

"Tending the shop as always. Can't have a day off in this game."

Callum walked to the rowing boat and found crab nets wet with sea water. Captured inside were a gang of grey crabs, waving their pincers in protest. "Mr and Mrs Winnow are poachers," he called back to Holly.

"Such an ugly word," Mrs Winnow said, wringing her hair dry between her hands.

"They can buy fish at Amble," Callum said, "and sell them in their shop, but there's more profit if you cut out the middle man."

The rowing boat was made of fibreglass and chequered with bitumen patches where it had been made watertight. The bow was dented. The oars were spindly and ready to break.

"Where's the big one?" Callum asked Mrs Winnow. "Where's the Sea Cucumber?"

"I had that in a restaurant once," Holly said, not following the conversation. "It was like chewing out-of-date glue."

"The Sea Cucumber is the Winnows' old Plymouth Pilot boat," Callum said. "Hand-painted in olive green. I watched it cruising the waterline in search of fish for ages, wondering who was behind the wheel. It was only when Mr Winnow once delivered some winter coal for me that I noticed his flatbed truck was the exact same colour as the boat. I suspect they got a deal on surplus paint."

"The Cucumber is in Amble shipyard, as it happens," Mrs Winnow said, ruffling her collar. "Trouble with the engine. It's too large to be brought this close to shore anyway."

"Well, I can't let you go out to sea in this," Callum said, pointing at the crumbling rowing boat. "It's a death trap. If you answer some of our questions, I'll give you a lift in the Defender to wherever you're going."

Mrs Winnow winked at Holly. "He's a lovely boy, really. Knows we're not any harm. Hey, wait. What are you doing?"

Callum emptied the crab nets into a rock pool. "Don't push your luck," he said. "This is still my land to look after."

The brief victory slipped from Mrs Winnow's face. "What questions?" she asked Holly.

"We're still trying to find Nancy," Holly said. "It's the least we can do after what happened to her sister."

Mrs Winnow bit her lip to stop it from trembling. "Those poor sisters. You wouldn't wish it on your worst enemy, would you?"

Holly explained about the squatter and Mrs Winnow nodded along, her eyes glazing over. Holly suspected she already knew. The whole village knew when the Reverend hung his washing out to dry. A juicy titbit like a squatter was unlikely to go amiss, but Mrs Winnow's expression changed when Holly told her about the sticklebacks.

"We think the squatter came to your stall," she said. "At the Spring Fair."

"And he hurt poor Regina?"

"We're not saying that, but he's involved somehow."

The tide had changed and Mrs Winnow stepped away from the waves rushing in at her feet.

"People came from all over," she said. "We made a lot of money. I can't remember everyone."

"Did you see anyone suspicious? Someone looking shifty? Or someone who looked like they didn't belong?"

Mrs Winnow shrugged, her face twisted with vague recollections.

70

"I'm sorry, dear."

The sea wind bit hard and Holly pulled up the zip on her coat.

"Hang on a sec," Mrs Winnow said, raising a finger in the air. "There was a man. It was a warm day and his coat was zipped up to his neck. That's odd, I thought. People from around here are used to the cold."

Holly's heart drummed in her chest. "Can you describe him?"

Mrs Winnow shook her head. "No, but I remember he was only interested in the fish. He bought three without tossing a single ball."

"Was he tall? Short? Fat? Thin?"

"I can't remember."

"What about his hair? Black? Brown? Bald?"

"Stop it, dear. You're confusing me." Mrs Winnow wrung her hands, tracing a wet foot through the sand. "It's too much."

Holly clamped her mouth shut. The squatter was the closest thing they had to a lead. They had to find him because if he wasn't Regina's attacker, he might know who was.

"I'm sorry for pressing so hard," Holly said.

"I know. I know. Poor Regina." Mrs Winnow linked arms with Holly and they walked along the beach. The wind blew their footprints into dust. When they turned, their tracks were buried in sand. No-one would have guessed they'd been there at all.

Holly stopped and gave Mrs Winnow a smile.

"I have an idea," she said.

Chapter Fifteen

A damp Mrs Winnow insisted on returning to her shop for a change of clothes. Her husband stood behind the counter, serving a customer. He mouthed, "Where are the crabs?" as Mrs Winnow bustled past him, but she had no time to answer.

Holly and Callum lingered by the entrance, pretending to browse the shelves.

Mrs Winnow reappeared moments later in a new outfit with make-up freshly applied.

Callum drove them to the newspaper office and they crowded around the flickering images on the screen.

"You're so clever, dear," Mrs Winnow said, stooping over the computer on Holly's desk.

Holly's first day as a journalist had been a disappointment, but it hadn't been wasted. She'd taken random, thoughtless pictures of the crowd at the Spring Fair. At the time, they had meant nothing to her. Now, they might prove crucial in finding Regina Foxglove's assailant.

Some of the pictures were blurred. Others were hidden behind a stray thumb. Holly whistled through them. On the whole, however, the pictures captured the Spring Fair in all its chaos, including the faces of several strangers.

"There's Mrs Threadle on the nettle wine again," Callum said. "The biggest sting is in the hangover."

Mrs Winnow pointed at the screen with a smile. "That's me. The Pilates is really working, isn't it?"

The pictures rolled on and Holly pinched her shoulders, hoping to ease the tension from her neck. It didn't work. Neither did filtering out the gossip flying between Mrs Winnow and Callum.

The door to the office creaked open and Old Jack paused before entering.

"How are you, Jack?" Holly asked.

His blue eyes scanned the room. "What are you doing here, pet? The office is closed."

"Oh, I'm sorry," Holly said. "I didn't know."

"It's closed."

She got from her seat and approached him. Up close, Jack's blue eyes were pink and Holly smelled alcohol. Her hand itched to touch him, to offer some comfort, but he was her boss and Holly was practically a stranger to him.

"How have you been? You know, since visiting Regina in the hospital?" she asked.

Old Jack's leathery hand slipped into hers.

"Have you found her yet?" he asked. "Have you found Nancy?"

"We will," Holly said, hoping to sound convincing.

"That's him," Mrs Winnow said. "That's the man asking about the sticklebacks."

Holly rushed back to the computer. The face on the screen was of an ordinary man somewhere in his fifties. He was a little dour and his skin was mottled, but he didn't look the type to hurt anyone.

"Are you sure that's him?" Callum asked, hitching up the cuffs of his coat to expose sinewy forearms. He seemed to double in size, looking like an animal whose hackles were raised at the sight of danger.

Callum walked purposely to the door, his legs cantering, ready to break into a run. "The customer Mr Winnow was serving when we went to the store," he said through a clenched jaw. "It's the same man."

Old Jack stepped to one side and Holly launched after Callum.

He was a blur, cutting over the village green, leaping over the boulders in the grass. His coat flapped behind him like wings.

Adrenaline fuelled Holly's legs, but she couldn't catch Callum, who raced on ahead. She hadn't noticed the customer in the store. Her mind was on catching the man in the manor. It hadn't occurred to her that they were one and the same.

By the time she reached the store, Callum was pacing the cobbled pavement. Mr Winnow was on his doorstep, ashen-faced and leaning on an upturned yard brush.

"We missed him," Callum shouted.

Holly slowed to a stop and steadied her hands on her knees.

Mr Winnow rubbed a purple bruise on his cheek.

"Are you alright?" he asked Holly.

"Never mind me," she said between gulps of air. "What about you?"

"Man, I didn't see that coming," Mr Winnow said. "The guy just flipped."

"What happened?"

Mr Winnow held tightly to his yard brush. "I recognised him from the Spring Fair, but didn't mention it in case he wanted to return his fish. They were sold in good faith, after all."

"Why was he so interested in sticklebacks?" Holly asked.

"I'm not sure. He asked where I got them from. What I was doing with them. I didn't tell him, though. He might have been a competitor. This is a cutthroat business."

Callum pointed at the bruise on Mr Winnow's cheek. "Is that when he gave you that?"

Mr Winnow shuddered. "He said, I was being evasive. That I didn't understand."

"Understand what?" Holly asked.

But Mr Winnow shrugged. "Then, he said he'd seen me and Judy on the estate. That we had to stop."

Holly had recovered sufficiently to inspect Mr Winnow's wounds. His bruise was glowing and his eye was shrinking under the swelling.

"Was he threatening you?" she asked.

"I told him, I didn't know what he was blethering on about. We live by the letter of the law around here."

Callum coughed into the back of his hand. "I guess he was talking about the poaching, Mr Winnow."

The purple bruise was masked by the store owner's reddening cheeks. He turned and began sweeping the pavement.

"Why would he care about you poaching?" she asked.

"I haven't confirmed or denied we do that, by the way," Mr Winnow said. "So, I asked him to leave and that's when all the argy-bargy kicked off."

"Did you see which way he went?" Callum asked, scanning the high street for tracks.

"Too busy seeing stars, mate."

Callum muttered under his breath. To Holly, it sounded like a growl.

The high street was as quiet as usual. There were no witnesses, no-one out there to help. It was her and Callum and failure again.

She watched Mr Winnow push his brush around the pavement. He may not have been *Gordon Gecko*, but for him, business never slept. Not even in Little Belton.

"If it helps," Mr Winnow said, sweeping an empty crisp packet further down the street, "he left his bag in the shop."

Chapter Sixteen

Holly rushed down the hallway, frantically pressing her unruly hair into shape. The doorbell sounded again and she heard Derek stir in the sitting room.

"Don't worry," she said. "I've got it."

She opened the front door to find Callum waiting on the other side, wiping his muddy boots on the doorstep. In his hand was a bouquet of wild flowers. He looked up and smiled.

"Dad always said to bring a gift when you visit a stranger's home."

"But we're not strangers, you dope," Holly said, returning his smile.

"Who's a dope?" Derek called from behind her.

The fumes from his alcoholic breath reached her before he did. Derek held a wine glass in one hand and planted the other on Holly's shoulder as he peered at Callum.

"You must be Mr Fleet," Callum said, extending his hand in greeting.

Derek drained his glass dry, watching Callum over the stained rim. "And you're the gamekeeper? I'm surprised you're here. I'd heard your cottage is much cosier than mine."

Callum dropped his hand, casting his gaze to the ground.

Holly wriggled from under Derek's grasp. He was usually asleep on the sofa by now.

"Why don't you go back into the sitting room?" she asked her husband.

Without her shoulder to support him, Derek swayed in the hallway, pitching like a ship lost in a storm.

"You'd like that, wouldn't you?" he asked, slurring his words. "Keep me locked up while you entertain your fancy man."

Holly noticed Callum stiffen, the flicker of a frown on his forehead. She caught his eye and gave a small shake of her head. Callum appeared to relax at her command, though the wild flowers suffered under his tightened grip.

"Are those for me?" Derek asked, the question loaded with sarcasm.

Holly turned to her husband. "I told you Callum was coming. We have something to discuss. Would you allow him to come inside please?"

Derek snorted, but stumbled out of the way.

Holly hoped Callum could see the apology in her eyes. "Go to the kitchen, Callum. I'll be right there."

Callum nodded and made to cross the threshold.

But he was barred by Derek's hand.

"Shoes off, please," Derek said.

"Stop being such a pain," Holly said.

Callum backed away. "Maybe we could speak outside?"

"Oh, no. My wife has put on quite the spread," Derek said. "My wife wants you in the kitchen."

Holly actually wanted to cry. The embarrassment was killing her. She bit down a sob as her fury blazed.

Derek dragged his finger around the rim of his glass, creating a high pitched keen. "I don't want you here, but my opinion counts for nothing. However, I insist on keeping my carpets clean."

"That's enough," Holly said.

Callum hovered on the doorstep, his eyes flitting from Holly to Derek. Slowly, he heeled off his boots and kicked them to the ground.

Derek smirked. "No-one home to do your darning?"

Callum's big toe jutted through a hole in the thin material of his socks. "Haven't got around to doing it myself."

"I'm sure there are plenty of women out there aching to do it for you." Derek lifted the glass to his lips before realising it was empty. "I better leave you two alone then."

His shoulder collided with Callum as he pushed past, weaving his way to the new shed.

Holly and Callum watched him fumble with the lock before he fell inside. Derek swore as he hit the floor and he kicked the door shut behind him.

"Through here," Holly said, retreating down the hallway.

"What's all this?" Callum asked as he followed her into the kitchen.

The room consisted of pale coloured cupboards and a stone floor. It was tired, but functional. The wooden counter ran around three-quarters of the room and one quarter was laden with food. Sausage rolls. Sandwiches. Salad in a Tupperware bowl.

Holly took the flowers from Callum and placed them in a vase. She uncorked a bottle of wine.

"I just wanted to make an effort," she said.

"No, I mean that," Callum said, pointing at the kitchen table buried under a pile of paper.

Holly leaned against a kitchen counter and folded her arms. "That's what I found in our mystery man's bag and I don't think they're his."

Pulling a chair loose, Callum sat by the table.

"Would you like some wine?" Holly asked.

Callum selected a sheaf of curled paper and studied pencil drawings of the estate from various angles.

"That's Angel's Basin," he said, tapping his finger on the first picture. "I recognise this other one, too. It's nowhere. A boulder run down to Aker's Bay. I heard rumours of wildcats living there a few years back, but other than that, it's a blank bit of map."

"Do you recognise anything else?" Holly asked.

"All of it." Callum rubbed his temple. "There's no connection other than they're locations within the estate. What's this?"

He held up a clipping from an American newspaper. Holly placed the wine bottle back on the kitchen counter and took the clipping from his hand.

"I'm not sure. The ink has run and it is difficult to read, but it's an article about gun control in a rural town called Eureka. And there's this." Holly shook free a page from a tattered glossy magazine. "It's a rich list. I can't tell where it's from. The page is damaged and water-stained, as if it's been read in all sorts of weathers. All I know for certain is there are no journalists on there."

She waited while Callum scanned the list comprising of industrialists, retail kings and tech giants. The poorest of them all had an estimated worth of two-hundred-and-nine million pounds.

"Aren't many gamekeepers, either," Callum said as he finished. "We appear to be the lowest of the low, especially in Derek's eyes."

A breath caught in Holly's throat and she struggled to swallow. "My husband isn't well."

"Funny," Callum said. "He looked drunk to me."

Holly backed into the kitchen counter, disturbing a pile of cheese sandwiches. They tumbled to the floor and she hurried to gather them up.

Callum slipped from his chair to his knees, scooping cheese slices into his hands.

"This is a lot of food for two people," he said.

"I went overboard," Holly said, tossing dishevelled sandwiches into the kitchen bin. "Stupid, really. Who's going to eat it all? Derek is on a liquid diet at the moment."

"That liquid being wine?" Callum asked.

With the kitchen floor cleared, Holly stood and turned to the sink. She washed her hands, watching the water pour through her fingers.

"We never have guests here," she said. "We used to entertain all the time in London. We'd have dinner parties and bloody cocktail parties, but not now. I know us two working together is a bit weird, but can't it be normal? Can't I feel okay for a bit?"

Callum climbed to his feet. She could sense him standing behind her, almost feel his breath on the back of her neck. It was wrong and she told herself she didn't like it, but right now, it was all she had.

"You want normal?" Callum asked.

More than anything, Holly thought, turning to face him. Her eyes roamed to the kitchen table and the papers from the squatter's bag.

Callum followed her gaze and smiled. "So let's get back to why we're here then."

Returning to his seat, he picked up the rich list and waved it at her. "Why would Nancy keep this?"

"She was searching for the owner of Black Rock," Holly said. "She was using this list to figure out who he was."

"Did she find him?" Callum asked.

Holly ran a finger down the page, finding a section that hadn't been touched. "Most of the names have been crossed out, but there are a few that haven't. Perhaps she suspected them."

Pouring herself some wine, Holly pinged her fingernail against the glass. Callum had purposely steered her back to work. He wasn't always so intuitive, but his gamble had paid off and Holly raised her glass to him.

"Thank you for being so understanding," she said.

Callum glanced at the hole in his sock. "Derek is lucky to have you."

"I'm not sure about that," Holly said. "I can be pretty sharp with him at times."

"Well, he was lucky today. He made me look like a right idiot. If you hadn't been there to protect him, he might have found himself in trouble."

Although Callum was smiling, there was something about it that made Holly feel nervous. Now it was her turn to steer them back to work.

"I think Nancy found out who the owner was and that's why she went missing," she said.

"Doubtful. I mean, whoever the new owner is, it's not a secret, is it? They'll show up eventually and it's not worth killing an old woman over."

"We don't know Nancy is dead," Holly said.

"I've lived in Little Belton all my life. The last scandalous thing to happen was Mr MacFarlene cheating at last year's Spring Fair. There was no way he grew that leek." Callum drummed his fingers on the table. "One sister is missing. The other was assaulted. It has to be connected and I suspect its worse than we think."

Holly sipped her wine. "We need to find the squatter. This is Nancy's file. He took it from her so maybe he knows where she is."

"Maybe he did something to her that he doesn't want us to know about." Callum pushed the papers around the table. "And how do we know these even belong to Nancy?"

Holly strode to the table and showed Callum a letter she'd found among the papers.

"The squatter took Nancy's notes, doing God knows what to get them," Holly said. "Find him and we find Nancy."

Callum turned his eyes to the letter, but Holly was already halfway out of the door.

Chapter Seventeen

It had taken an hour's drive to reach Crockfoot. Holly and Callum sat in silence while they corkscrewed through country lanes. Occasionally, Callum would brake to avoid a sheep or crumbling pothole. Otherwise, they kept to a steady, monotonous pace.

Holly stared out of the passenger window, supporting her chin in a hand. The scenery was a muddle of greens and browns. This was big sky country, she thought. The landscape was a rugged sliver under a vast steel bell.

"I called the hospital," Holly said, "to check on Regina's condition."

Callum fumbled with the clutch, his teeth grinding with the gears. "Whoever hit her, hit her hard."

"She's stable, but unresponsive. The doctor said, she'd have been a lot worse if the paramedics hadn't arrived so quickly."

"Which was pretty strange, if you think about it? You didn't call the paramedics because you couldn't get a signal. How come they happened to be passing at just the right moment?" Callum asked.

Holly was about to answer when she saw the sign for Crockfoot. The village was bigger than Little Belton. The high street was longer. The shops were more expensive. It started at the top of one hill, sinking into a trough before rising again on the other side. The road was a smile drawn in tarmac. There were art galleries, artisan craft makers and a music shop. There was even a vegan café; something Holly hadn't seen since leaving London.

As Callum parked, he took in the high street through narrowed eyes.

"They think they're so great because they've got a Starbucks," he muttered.

He held onto the letter Holly had given him as they searched the high street for door numbers. Callum refused to acknowledge the designer clothes store or the restaurant boasting of a Michelin star.

Salting Building Surveyors was a single-storey building with a pitched roof and gutters blocked with weeds. The buildings on either side were three storeys high, dwarfing their companion in the middle. It looked like a hobbit hole set into a cliff. The shop window had yellowing blinds and a collection of dead flies on the sill.

A sun-bleached sign read – 'Building a Better Future Tomorrow.'

"Why would Nancy be involved with a place like this?" Callum asked.

Inside was what Holly supposed was a reception area, but it looked more like a taxidermist's shop. Stag heads, fox heads and badgers were mounted on wooden plaques on the wall. A stuffed stoat was posed on a branch, his head tilted as if sensing danger. A little too late, it seemed to Holly. She was drawn to a glass case on a counter where dead mice stood around a table playing poker.

Beside it was a picture of two men outside the same shop Holly and Callum had entered. They were shaking hands and grinning.

"Recognise anyone?" Callum asked.

And Holly did. One of the men was the person they were looking for. She lifted her nose and sniffed the air, like the unfortunate stoat.

"Can you smell a barbeque?" she asked.

A second door creaked open and a head popped through the gap. It was a man in his late forties with round cheeks and a patch over one eye.

"Are you the two bods from The Crockfoot Mail?" he asked.

The floorboards groaned under Callum's shifting weight.

"Little Belton Herald," Holly said, stepping forward.

"Little Belters, eh? I can't remember inviting you," the man said. His single eye drank them in. "Well, I suppose you'll do until the real journos turn up. After all, it affects you most of all. Come on through."

The man disappeared and Holly and Callum followed, finding themselves in a walled garden filled with the scent of burning meat. This was less like a hobbit hole, thought Holly and more like Alice's decent into Wonderland.

"Don't act so cool," the man said. "I was bowled over when we discovered this building had its own garden. Only one in the high street, mind. That's why we never extended the shop. It gets the sun from 1.30pm to 2.00pm and you're right on time. I'm Brian Salting and I'll be your host."

Drystone walls acted as a climbing frame for honeysuckle as it strained toward a chink of light. There were topiary bushes shaped into various animals, giving the impression the garden was a petting zoo. Flowers spilled over the lips of raised beds like tongues and the area was filled with the faint hum of insects.

"You did all this?" Holly asked.

Mr Salting stood by a smoking barbeque, poking the coals with a pair of tongs. "No, no. If I were to have green fingers, I'd go and see a doctor. No, this is the work of my brother, Arnold."

"The man in the photograph on your desk?" Callum asked.

"The very same."

"Will Arnold be joining us?" Holly asked.

Mr Salting may have been standing in his half-hour of sun, but his features clouded over. "This barbeque is about ready. What'll you care for? Sausage or burger?"

They selected a burger each, admiring the black crust encasing the meat like a hard shell. Holly picked at the charred flakes to reveal a pinkness underneath. It was like every barbeque she'd ever been to.

Holly scoured the garden for somewhere to stash it, silently apologising to a nearby Hosta when she slid the burger between its leaves.

Meanwhile, Callum had finished his and was accepting a second.

"This is quite the celebration, Mr Salting," Holly said, producing her notebook and pen. "Can you tell our readers why?"

"Ah, Little Belton. You're all about to become important," Mr Salting said. "All the letters have been sent and the authorities have been alerted, but I'm getting ahead of myself. The residents of Crockfoot are well versed in Salting Brothers' lore. I suspect the tom-tom drums have yet to reach the deserted plains of Little Belton so let me enlighten you."

Holly cursed inwardly. There was a soliloquy coming and Mr Salting looked like his might be both lengthy and numbing. She saw Callum rolling his eyes. At least, they were in this together.

Mr Salting broadened his stance and placed a hand on his chest. "My brother and I are known for being a small company with a long reach. The sign says building surveyors, but we are also estate agents, land valuers and development entrepreneurs." He paused to glance at Holly and her notebook. "You are writing this down, aren't you?"

So far, Holly had drawn a horse's arse, but decided she better comply. "Of course," she said and began to scribble.

"Today is the culmination of three years hard work," Mr Salting said. "Our customers are distinguished and wealthy. The Salting Brothers trade on their good name and their discretion, but today I can reveal we have completed Phase One of a development putting Northumberland on the map."

"What exactly is this development?" Holly asked. "Is it yours?"

Mr Salting waved her away. "We were merely facilitators and the individual investor doesn't wish his name to be made public until the folk at Little Belton have read their letters. What I can say is he is extremely wealthy and only wants the best for the little people."

Holly cast her mind back to Nancy's Rich List, feeling surer than ever that the investor's name was on it. "This investor? He's the new owner of Black Rock Manor, isn't he? He owns the estate."

Mr Salting smiled coquettishly. "I couldn't say, but Little Belton will never be the same again. In a good way, of course."

"What are these letters you're talking about?" Callum looked a little green around the neck. Even for a man used to eating rabbit stew, Mr Salting's raw burgers appeared to have been a step too far.

"Is it the same as this one?" Callum asked, producing Nancy's letter from his coat pocket.

"No, my man," said Mr Salting. "I don't know what that is, but the letters for Little Belton will be dropped on them tomorrow."

Callum approached Mr Salting, waving the paper in his hand. "This was found in your brother's possession, but it's addressed to Nancy Foxglove. Can you explain that?"

Mr Salting's visible eye swivelled in its socket. "I don't know what you're insinuating, young man."

"The letter is threatening Nancy Foxglove with legal action," Callum said. "You posted it to her a few weeks ago. We have the date mark and envelope to prove it."

The hand dropped from Mr Salting's chest and his lips clamped shut, but he didn't need to speak. Holly could see he recognised Nancy's name. It was all over the letter they'd found in Arnold Salting's bag and all over his brother's face.

"Why were you threatening to take away her home?" Holly asked. "What was she to you?"

"You're not here for the celebration, are you?" Mr Salting asked them, stepping in front of the barbeque. The smoke from the coals rose above his shoulders like dark wings.

Holly forgot about writing and held her pen like a sword, cutting a swathe through the smoke. "Nancy Foxglove is missing. Her sister is in hospital. We have a menacing letter from you and Arnold stole a file Nancy was keeping on your wealthy client."

"Not to mention your brother was in the vicinity when Regina was attacked," Callum said.

"Arnold is on a sabbatical." Mr Salting's puffed chest deflated and his single eye was wide and wary. "He would never hurt anyone or anything. He simply detests my hunting trophies in the reception area. He called me a monster because of it."

"He assaulted a Little Belton shop owner," Holly said.

"Do you have proof?" Mr Salting asked.

Callum batted away a cloud of barbeque smoke. "There's something you're not telling us, but I think you're as worried about your brother as we are."

Mr Salting's eye went from Callum to Holly and he licked his dry lips. With a sigh, he reached to his patch and flipped it to his forehead.

"I've been telling everyone it's conjunctivitis," he said.

But it wasn't. It was a black eye with swollen lids lined with a nasty cut.

"Arnold did that to you?" Holly asked. "Because of a stuffed stoat."

"We were acting on behalf of our client," Mr Salting said. "Ms Foxglove wrote several letters to us. Came to our offices a number of times. Always angry. Always accusing us of selling Northumberland to the highest bidder, but we weren't."

Mr Salting returned a trembling hand on his heart. This time he looked sincere. "My brother and I grew up here. Our parents grew up here, but this area isn't what it used to be. Once the mine closed, the jobs went and the people went with them. Our project was about regeneration. About bringing people back into the area."

"Your letter makes it sound like you were trying to run Nancy out of town," Holly said.

"I can't speak about that."

"Who is the new owner?" Callum asked.

"I can't tell you," Mr Salting said.

"What has your brother got to do with this?" Holly asked.

"He was one hundred percent behind regenerating the area. When the owner revealed his true plans, Arnold said, we'd gone too far. He hit me and stole the keys for the manor. I didn't report it because a scandal would derail the project."

"These keys?" Callum asked, swinging them from his finger.

Mr Salting gave him a doleful look. "May I have them back, please? They don't belong to me."

Callum gripped them tightly, strangling the wooden duck keyring.

"They don't belong to you, either," Holly said to Callum, shooting him a look.

His shoulders slumped and Callum dropped the keys into Mr Salting's waiting hand.

Holly returned her idle pen to her pocket and laid an arm around Mr Salting's shoulder.

"What are the plans that got Arnold so riled?" she asked.

Mr Salting hung his head, but kept quiet.

"This is serious," Holly said. "Your brother could be in danger. He might be a danger to others. We have to tell the police."

Mr Salting leaned into her. "I want you to know I never hid a thing from the police."

"What do you mean?"

"I heard about what happened to Ms Foxglove. I called the police because I was worried about what my brother might do in his present state of mind. But I swear that no matter how he feels about me or what we are doing to Little Belton, Arnold wouldn't harm a fly."

Holly didn't agree. Arnold Salting was violent and unstable. He had attacked both his own brother and Mr Winnow. He had been in the area when Regina was discovered and he had Nancy's file.

"You don't have to worry," Holly said. "All we want to do is ask him some questions."

As Holly spoke, they heard voices from Mr Salting's office. Two men stepped into the hidden garden, their mouths open in slack wondered smiles.

Mr Salting shrugged off Holly's arm and straightened his tie. "Gentlemen, you'll be the dear old Crockfoot Mail?" he asked, quickly flipping his eye patch back into place.

One of the men pushed his way through the greenery as if working his way through a jungle. "Mr Salting, I presume?" he asked.

"These people were just leaving," Mr Salting said, giving Holly a less than gentle shove.

She stumbled over a potted plant and Callum swooped to her side, taking hold of her waist.

"I only spoke to you because you seem to care about what happens to my brother," Mr Salting hissed. "If any of it makes it into that Little Belton rag, I shall sue."

He turned his back on Holly and Callum to address the newcomers. "Lovely to have some real journos here for a change. I have a stirring speech for you to quote from. Now, what will you have? Sausage or burger?"

Callum led Holly to the door, but she broke free and ran back to Mr Salting.

"What's in those letters? What is the conclusion of Phase One?" she asked.

Mr Salting handed over two burnt burgers to the Crockfoot journalists. They eyed them with dread and looked about the garden for a nearby Hosta.

Holly waited impatiently for an answer.

Mr Salting wiped his fingers on a serviette. When he was done, he folded it neatly into a square, tucking it into the breast pocket of his jacket.

With a long sigh, Mr Salting whispered his response into Holly's disbelieving ear.

Chapter Eighteen

It had been a long night for Holly. Leaving her husband to snore into his pillow, she took the blanket from the bottom of her bed. Holly went to the sitting room and wrapped it around her shoulders. Sleep had come in fitful bouts. Her dreams were pitted with images of trees reduced to splinters. She saw again the bird she had run over. It was larger than she remembered and wearing an eye patch. It glided over the estate, salting the earth with its shadow. Everything withered and Holly wept when it flew toward Callum's cottage.

When dawn broke, she was exhausted from pacing the kitchen floor, awaiting the arrival of the postman. He was late, his face soured by the inexplicable number of letters he'd been required to deliver.

Holly jigged on the spot as she accepted hers.

"I don't know who the Salting Brothers are," the postman said, "but I've a mind to send them my chiropractor's bill for all the backache they've given me."

The Salting Brothers' name was ink-stamped onto the envelope, together with their slogan - 'Building A Better Future Tomorrow.'

Holly tore open the envelope, speed reading the letter's contents. Words leapt out at random, but there was no sense to be had. Its contents were implausible. Mr Salting had revealed nothing in his hurried whisper, except to imply Little Belton was in for a shock. Reading the letter now, she had to agree.

Holly forced herself to calm down and read more slowly, her lips moving as she progressed. Reaching the end, her fingertips were numb from gripping the paper too hard.

This was it, Holly thought. This was Little Belton's Better Future. She had only just returned. The village was her fresh start and she'd arrived in time to see it die.

She needed to speak to someone. Derek was still asleep. He slept more and more these days and Holly wondered if it was a symptom of depression. Or the copious amounts of alcohol he swam in these days.

Callum was at home. Presumably. He'd been quiet on the drive home yesterday, merely wishing her goodnight when he dropped her off. He had smiled when he said it so perhaps things weren't so bad, but part of Holly wasn't convinced.

There was one place Holly wanted to go and she wasn't the only person to think so.

The village green was swamped with lost souls, each dragging their letter as if it was a boulder chained to their necks. Gaunt faces stared at each other. They huddled or stood open-mouthed at the timeless mountains framing their village.

Mr MacFarlene, unusually sober, conversed with the wine drinking Mrs Threadle, who was not. Old Jack consoled Reverend Applecroft, rubbing his back and repeating calming Psalms. The Winnows walked the green, arm in arm, their facial expressions resolute.

Holly approached and they waved their letter.

"It's terrible, dear," Mrs Winnow said, clutching her husband tighter. "It doesn't seem right."

Mr Winnow rubbed his wife's arm. "We're all for progress. We'd like Little Belton to grow. Maybe get as big as Crockfoot, but not like this. All we wanted was a Starbucks."

"How are you?" Mrs Winnow asked Holly. "I bet you wished you'd stayed in London now."

The whispering village green grew silent. All eyes were turned to a four-by-four with mirrored windows. It was a black Range Rover with a silver grill. The engine was silent as it circled the green.

"It looks like a shark," Mr Winnow said quietly.

The Rover stopped, the low hum of the engine throbbing in Holly's chest. The sound was cut dead and Little Belton held its collective breath.

"I followed them down the B725," Callum said. "I guess they're out-of-towners."

Holly jumped at Callum's sudden presence.

"Where did you spring from?" she asked.

"I told you. The B725. I was trying to work. Thought it might keep my mind off the letter, but then – "

"You needed to be with your friends?" Holly asked and without thinking or second-guessing herself, she slipped her hand into his. "So did we."

The door to the Rover opened and a pair of long shimmering legs appeared, followed by the woman who owned them. She was tall and slender, wearing a tight-fitting camouflage dress.

"I saw that dress in a magazine," Mrs Winnow said, yanking her waterproofs over an ill-fitting jumper. "It's a Harvey DuBec. They're worth thousands."

"Well, it looks a million bucks on her," Mr Winnow said, quickly regretting it when his wife flicked his ear.

The woman's face was thin. She had high cheekbones and lips fixed into a fashionable pout. She swung an expensive handbag and searched the sky.

The villagers shuffled toward her, drawn to her presence. No one spoke. No one looked at one another. They inched closer as the woman lifted her nose and looked away.

"Why are the newsagents closed?" Derek asked, fighting his way through the crowd to Holly. "I came for my paper."

Holly dropped Callum's hand, hoping her husband hadn't seen her. Callum stepped aside.

Derek's face was blank, staring around the village green. "Is there another Spring Fair?"

It didn't seem right to keep Derek in the dark, but Holly didn't know how to explain they might have to move again. He was fragile enough without dropping a bombshell like that. His relationship with Little Belton stopped at his morning paper and the occasional lottery ticket. He didn't know the village like Holly did, but leaving it might untether him further.

"Is that why you're here?" Derek asked, pointing into the sky.

Following his finger, Holly saw a black shape cutting through the clouds, its engine going from a hum to a growl as it approached.

"What is it?" Callum asked, jamming his hands on his hips.

Dark wings were silhouetted against a yellow sun. There was a sharpness to the creature, a danger. It reminded Holly of Black Eye Bobby or the bird who had haunted her dreams.

Mr Winnow rubbed his forehead, a red mark appearing above his eyebrows. "Whatever it is, it's making a hell of a racket."

"It's a microlight," Holly said. "I hired one on holiday once."

The villagers craned their necks, nudging each other with their elbows. The microlight swooped toward the village green. The fabric wings were black, flecked with yellow dots, looking like the cap of a deadly toadstool. The trike underneath was of a similar colouring, gleaming as it streaked toward them.

The pilot was crouched forward and waving at the crowd. With both hands.

Holly wondered how he was steering.

"It's going to crash," shouted the Reverend.

With a scream, the villagers ran for their doorways.

Holly watched the microlight loom closer, fearing the touch of its poisonous wings. She turned to see Derek and Callum cowering beside her.

"What are you waiting for?" she asked, grabbing them both and hauling them to the safety of a doorway.

The microlight's engines were cut. The air whistled under its wings, the toadstool fabric stretched taut against the updraft.

Classical music started playing from the Range Rover. Holly didn't recognise it, but there were heavy strings and resounding bass notes, lending cinematic drama to what was about to be a horrific crash.

The microlight reared, its back wheels hitting the ground, churning up the village green, spitting wet mud like bullets. The front wheel of the microlight landed with a bounce. It hurtled toward the Rover while the woman watched it with bored eyes.

The pilot applied the brakes and leapt from the vehicle, happy to watch it continue on its own. Its progress slowed, but not enough to stop without help from the Range Rover. There was a crunch and the microlight toppled to its side.

The pilot barrelled to his own stop, hopping into the air with his arms aloft. "Welcome to Black Rock Adventureland," he shouted.

Chapter Nineteen

"My name is Devron Masterly," the pilot said. "You may have heard of me."

Mr Masterly was around six foot with angular shoulders. His dyed blonde hair hung in curtains around a handsome face. When he smiled, his perfect teeth were unnaturally white.

"Come on, dudes," he said. "Don't be shy. I'm the new owner of the Black Rock Estate."

The villagers were skittish, their wide eyes seeking assurances from their neighbours. They inched toward Mr Masterly, but Callum strode through the herd, offering his hand.

"I'm Callum Acres. I'm your gamekeeper," he said, standing tall.

Mr Masterly grabbed Callum's hand, attempting an intricate greeting involving fist bumps and finger grips.

Unable to understand his boss' intentions, Callum abandoned the handshake in favour of an embarrassed pat on Mr Masterly's shoulder.

"My family have been working on the estate for generations," Callum said.

"Good to have you on board, Cal," Mr Masterly said, turning to the crowd. "Anyone else want to say hello?"

Holly detected a faint blush of pride in Callum's face and approached Mr Masterly.

"I've heard of you," she said. "You're based in California. You own

Arcadia Leisure."

"Yes, I do." Mr Masterly swept his blonde locks from his eyes and pointed to the woman by the car.

"And this is Sadie, my wife," Mr Masterly said.

Mrs Masterly cast her eyes over the crowd of people emerging from their hiding places. She glided toward the village green and took her place next to her husband. Where most objects appeared larger close-up, the thin frame of Mrs Masterly seemed to shrink.

Holly nodded a welcome while sucking in her stomach.

"You own a chain of theme parks," Holly said. "Treetop Mountain Range. Splashdown Waters. You're worldwide."

"And now we're here," Mr Masterly said.

Derek was at Holly's side, lowering his head in a bow. "I used to work in real estate myself. Nothing quite as grand as yourself, but I've always been an admirer. If I can be of service in any way, please don't hesitate to call."

"Not now, Derek," Holly whispered to herself.

Mr Masterly held up his hand for a high five. "That's the kind of welcome I'm looking for, dude."

Derek slapped Mr Masterly's hand and grinned.

Holly fumbled in her pocket for the letter they'd all received and read the opening paragraph. "Arcadia Leisure applied and was granted permitted development rights in the Little Belton area. As it was deemed the residents would not be directly affected, there was no public consultation, but a brief period will be held to hear any objections."

"But why would you object?" Mr Masterly asked the crowd. "We're building a massive theme park. It will draw millions of tourists. There will be jobs. There will be money. It will bring people to your tiny village."

"How many people?" Mr Winnow asked, rubbing his hands. "How

much money?"

"You'll be overrun with both."

"We should have been consulted," Old Jack shouted. "You can't do all this on our doorstep and expect us to roll over."

There were murmurs, but Holly didn't know if they were in agreement.

Mr Masterly picked at a grass stain on his trousers caused by his dramatic entry. "But it's not on your doorstep. It's mine. I own the Black Rock Estate and everything on it. This is what I do. I rejuvenate tired, forgotten places and you're welcome."

Callum cleared his throat. "You're getting rid of the estate? The land? The animals?"

"I'm making it better," Mr Masterly said, "but don't worry, dude. You're with me, right? There'll be a job waiting for you."

"Will there be jobs for everyone?" Derek asked.

"Absolutely. It's my top priority. Wherever I build my theme parks, the residents of the surrounding area always benefit. You're family to me now."

"The estate should be a national park," Old Jack said, "or a conservation area or something. This is our heritage."

The thin figure of Mrs Masterly stirred, roused by the vehemence in Old Jack's voice. She gave a sideways glance at her husband before settling her unflinching gaze on the crowd.

"Adventureland is sympathetic to the environment," she said. "Given the economic benefit to the area, the council waived such concerns aside."

"Money was slipped under the table, you mean," Old Jack said, his blue eyes flashing. "I've turned a blind eye to this sort of thing for too long. Regina Foxglove is in hospital. Nancy...my Nancy...is still missing. If you ask me, your arrival is too much of a coincidence."

A cloud tumbled over the horizon and Mr Masterly held up his hands for calm. "I don't understand. I'm here to help. Are you dudes saying you don't want me here?"

"Of course, we do," Derek said.

Old Jack stamped his foot, too furious to speak.

"Our research stated Little Belton was in poverty," Mr Masterly said, teasing out a strand of his blonde hair. "What about the jobs and money?"

"It's not always about that," Holly said.

Derek puffed out his chest. "It is to those of us who don't have any."

Holly's face went crimson and she turned it from the crowd. "We're getting by," she hissed at her husband.

"You're getting by," Derek said. "I'm getting left behind."

Mrs Masterly glided to the car, the villagers parting for her as she sashayed past. She slipped inside the Rover and slammed the door shut.

Holly pressed closer to Old Jack. "There's something not right about all of this," she said to him. "It's too rushed. Too forced."

"Business has to move fast," Mr Masterly said, over-hearing.

"So fast, you ignore the people you should be listening to," Holly said.

"I am listening. I'm here, aren't I?"

"You intimidated Nancy Foxglove," Holly shouted. "She knew all about you and your plans. Now she's missing."

The crowd gave a low moan, the sound rattling around the village green like the chains of a ghost. Holly felt Old Jack's hand grip her forearm.

"I've never heard of this Nancy woman," Mr Masterly said, strolling to his car.

"You directed the Salting Brothers to keep her quiet," Holly said.

"Little Belton has the right to object," he said.

"Who's going to listen to us?" Holly asked. "Men like you stack the deck long before you play your hand. That's what this was about. You turn up here, falling out of the sky like the Second Coming and expect us to worship at your feet because we have no other choice. Well, we do."

"No, you don't," Mr Masterly said. His face burned red and his unnatural teeth ground together. The engine of his car growled and Mr Masterly patted the bonnet. The Californian sun was washed from his face and his eyes darkened.

"What if I leave and take my investment with me?" Mr Masterly asked. "The estate will go to ruin and Black Rock Manor will fall down brick by brick. This little village will starve and you'll starve with it."

Mr Masterly dropped into the car and the Rover navigated around the debris of the microlight. The villagers watched it disappear around a bend, unsure of themselves, unsure if anything had been resolved.

One by one they drifted away, back to their homes and an uncertain future.

But Derek stayed, staring at the crumpled microlight, idly kicking a buckled wheel.

"This is our home," Holly said, wandering to his side. "I can't let him turn it into a bloody log flume. I had to say something."

"I'm barely hanging on," Derek said. "I need this."

Bent over, Derek reached into the cockpit, pulling out a brochure from a pile on the floor. He offered it to Holly who flicked through the pages. It was filled with pictures of theme parks Arcadia Leisure had built. Smiling families enjoyed cable car rides while shiny-faced employees laughed for the camera.

"Everyone has something here worth staying for," Derek said, "but you've taken away my last reason."

"I can make this better," Holly said, a lump in her throat.

"I saw you holding hands with the gamekeeper."

The cloud on the horizon grew into a curling mass promising rain.

Holly couldn't take her eyes off it. The cloud was dense and heavy. If she turned from it and looked into the face of her husband, Holly would cry.

"Me and Callum," she said quietly. "It's not what you think."

"How would you know?" Derek asked. "Whenever we talk, we shout. You don't know what I think."

The first drops of rain parachuted to the ground, pinging against the broken aircraft.

"Have you ever wondered about Callum?" Derek continued. "The estate has been empty for years. Who's paying him to stay? Where is he getting his money from?"

"He works on the estate out of loyalty," Holly said.

"And who's bought that loyalty?" Derek asked, shoving his hands into his pockets. "Because we all have to live somehow."

Kicking his heels, Derek began a slow march back home without looking back.

Holly wrung the glossy brochure in her hands, making the pages squeak. She needed to chase after him, but didn't move past the wreckage. What would she say if she caught up? That she and Callum were friends? They were. That holding hands was a friendly gesture of solidarity? It was. Holly loved Derek, but the cracks in their marriage were widening.

Callum was there for her. He was kind and supportive. She searched the village green and found him leaning on a lamppost, his arms folded. The crowd had all but gone and he had remained, watching her with careful eyes.

Derek's questions came back to her and Holly began to wonder.

How had Callum survived all these years?

Chapter Twenty

The cloud that had gathered over Little Belton delivered on its promise. Rain pattered against the windscreen of Holly's car and her wipers danced left and right to shoo it aside. The road drummed under her rolling wheels. She sat straight, two hands on the wheel, listening to one of Mrs Winnow's spoken word tapes, but it did little to distract her.

At first, she had looked for Derek, scanning the side of the road, hoping to find him before he got too wet. She'd wanted to give him a lift home, to talk with him over the kitchen table. Her stomach churned as she'd recalled their argument and she'd wondered how to put it right. Deciding they probably needed some space before they commenced Round Two, Holly gave up her search and urged her car down a rugged dirt track.

Derek hadn't disappeared from her thoughts entirely. His parting shot about Callum still rung in her ears. How had Callum survived without an income? It was a valid question. Holly didn't feel comfortable contemplating it. The people of Little Belton did what they could to survive and Callum would be no different.

"It's none of my business," Holly said, chewing on a fingernail.

She indicated left and slid her car along the ruts of a waterlogged road. There were bigger questions to consider, Holly thought as she splashed through brackish water. She brought the car to a stop under a sycamore tree, switching off Mrs Winnow mid-sentence. Alone, pressing into her seat, she stared into the face of Black Rock Manor.

It was the Masterlys who commanded the majority of her brain space. They were planning to take over the village. The crashing microlight was a spectacle designed to dazzle the residents, to seduce them into silence. Holly had been there to ask questions and it had quickly become apparent the Masterlys weren't prepared for them.

Holly folded her arms. She almost felt justified in spying on their new home.

A movement caught her eye and she squinted through the rain-washed windscreen. Unable to see, Holly quietly opened the car door and stepped outside. Water ran in rivulets down her face.

She pulled up the collar of her coat and waited.

There. In the window. A shadow.

She treaded carefully through the overgrown grass. Her boots squelched through the mud as she made her way to the door. Holly paused, her fingers grazing the handle.

Holly needed to find the returning squatter, but what if the Masterlys had decided on an inspection of the manor? She peered around the grounds. There were no vehicles. While Mr Masterly seemed the outdoor type, Mrs Masterly did not. Holly couldn't imagine her trekking through the rain to spend time in a house without heat or electricity.

Holly straightened. What if it was Nancy who was inside the manor? She could be hurt. She could be trapped. She could have been kidnapped.

Sucking in a breath, Holly slowly turned the handle. It was locked, clunking to a stop. She froze, hoping the noise hadn't alerted the intruder to her presence. Minutes ticked by to the sound of Holly's heart thudding in her chest, but no one came to the door.

Callum had returned the keys to Mr Salting. Whoever was in there had used a different means and Holly decided to do the same.

She edged along the wall to the secret entrance Callum had discovered on his last visit. With a shove, the door clicked open and swung toward her on a spring. Holly climbed inside, finding herself in the pantry. Light spilled through a gap in the door at the other side and she inched closer.

The hallway was filled with dust and echoes. Holly entered on her tiptoes, every rustle of her clothing sounding as if they were made from crisp packets. With weather like this, the squatter would have been forced to seek shelter. This could be her chance to find out what had happened to Nancy.

Her face froze at the sight of the manor keys hanging from the lock of the main door. The wooden duck keyring was clearly visible. The only people Mr Salting would have given them to was...

Holly heard Mr Masterly's voice from a room up ahead.

"They don't want us here," he shouted.

"They're scared of change." It was Mrs Masterly, her voice like silk, warm and soothing.

"Everywhere we go, it's the same," her husband said. "We have to drag them kicking and screaming into the future."

"I'll take care of it, darling."

"The wheels have already started spinning," Mr Masterly said. "They'll be crushed by them if they get in the way. It will be another Eureka moment."

Holly's confusion was matched by the ice in her veins. The Masterlys were about to reveal their real intentions in coming to Little Belton. They might even reveal what they did to Nancy. She doubted they'd take kindly to her eavesdropping, but it was up to Holly to find out the truth.

As quietly as she could, Holly rummaged through her coat for a notebook, but her movement attracted attention.

Nancy's goat appeared from the shadows. It wore a studded leather collar and a lead frayed at one end. The goat wagged its tail, trotting toward her, its gnarled teeth arranged into a smile.

"Not now," Holly whispered.

The goat cantered in a circle.

"Be quiet," Holly said, pressing a finger to her lips.

The goat raised its head to bray.

"No, no, no," Holly said and ran to the pantry. She couldn't be seen by the new owners, but neither could she leave the goat to wreak further damage. Callum would never forgive her. Searching the shelves, Holly found the last remaining food item. She twisted off the lid from the pickled cucumbers, her eyes watering at the odour. With a finger and thumb, she fished out a grey lump and waved it at the goat, whose nostrils twitched at the tang.

"Let's take you back to Old Jack, eh?" Holly said through gritted teeth. "Maybe find a chain to keep you from wandering off."

The hum of conversation in the far room stopped and Holly worried at her lip. Backing further into the pantry, she wiggled the cucumber enticingly.

"Come on, you stupid thing," she said. "I'll see you in a pie if you get us caught."

Holly counted the goat's hesitant steps toward her.

The smell from the pickle jar was over-powering and Holly wished she'd closed the lid, but Nancy's goat seemed to like it. Its lower jaw worked in circles, anticipating its ugly meal.

The goat wedged its head into the dark room.

One more step, Holly thought. Just one more.

The goat scuttled inside and Holly yanked the door closed. The goat hollered, kicking out its hind legs, banging on the door. Holly launched forward, snatching the frayed lead as the goat thundered past her. It threw itself through the secret entrance and she staggered after it.

A gloom had settled over the manor grounds. Holly and the goat froze at the sight of the Rover. The Masterlys' driver was hidden behind tinted windows, but the Rover's headlights illuminated the grounds in a cutting arc.

Hurrying to the undergrowth, Holly and the goat crawled through the waxy leaves of a rhododendron, finding a space to hide.

The Masterlys left the manor, jogging to the warmth of their car. Their faces were stern and Mr Masterly spoke rapidly into his mobile phone. He jumped inside, but Mrs Masterly hovered by the door. Raindrops flattened her hair and soaked her designer clothes, but she seemed in no mood to rush. Her eyes scanned the overgrown garden, settling briefly on Holly's hiding spot.

There was no way Mrs Masterly could see her, but Holly eased further into the darkness just in case.

With a flick of her hair, Mrs Masterly abandoned her search and climbed into the car.

Holly waited until they had driven out of sight before she broke cover, dragging the goat with her. The mud was sodden and treacherous, and she was careful not to fall. The goat put up no resistance and Holly secured it on the back seat.

The goat settled immediately, closing its yellow eyes to sleep.

Holly jumped behind the wheel and reversed out of her hiding spot by the tree.

There was something about how Mrs Masterly had consoled her husband that made Holly want to speak to Callum. The Lady of the Manor appeared as cool as a pickled cucumber and Holly wondered where the true power lay. Mr Masterly lacked the unwavering presence of his wife and his wife worried Holly.

Spinning the car into the right direction, she ploughed it through a puddled ditch and onto a tarmacked road, running the Masterlys' conversation through her head.

One part stood out.

They'll be crushed if they get in the way, Mr Masterly had said and Holly's knuckles blanched white on the steering wheel.

Chapter Twenty-One

"Why are we heading to Amble?" Holly asked from the passenger seat.

"You'll see," Callum said.

Holly had recounted her adventure at the manor the moment she'd leapt into Callum's Defender. He'd listened patiently, but aside from the odd nod, there was no indication the words were sinking in.

He was driving with narrowed eyes fixed to the road.

"Aren't you going to say anything?" Holly asked.

"You know what I'm going to say," Callum said. "I'm going to say, you shouldn't have gone on your own. That you should have waited for me and then, you're going to say, I don't need a chaperone and I'll say, there are unknown dangers and then we'll bicker about it for the next five miles. So why don't we pretend we've already had the argument and simply enjoy our journey?"

Holly glanced at Callum from the corner of her eye. "Spoilsport. At least say something about what I discovered."

Callum steered them around a tractor, holding his nose against the smell. "That goat keeps on showing up, doesn't it?"

"I took it back to Old Jack," Holly said. "He's in a bad way. His outburst at the village green was so out of character."

A road sign told them Amble was three miles away, seemingly galvanising Callum's thoughts.

"When Nancy takes her goat for a walk," he said, "I think she takes it to the manor. As dumb as goats are, they can be pretty smart. It's learned how to get there through repetition."

"It's an empty house," Holly said, keen to discuss what had happened at the manor. "I don't see the appeal."

Callum shrugged. "It's beautiful in its own way and it has a lot of history."

Holly remembered her parents talking about the manor when she was a child. There had been midnight dances and fundraising raffles. It had hosted the annual Burning of the Dancing Man, a local tradition similar to Guy Fawkes night with fewer fireworks and more flat beer. The manor had been a focal point for the village, but when the Wentworths left, it wasn't theirs any more. It was a painful reminder of what they once had.

"There's a link between Nancy and Black Rock Manor," Holly said, watching the scenery shrink into town buildings, "but I don't know what. Amble seems like a day trip we don't need right now."

"It's the closest library to Little Belton. If there's any kind of link to be found, we'll find it there."

Amble had grown around a port in the North Sea where the region's coal had been shipped to the rest of the UK. When that died, Amble reinvented itself. A few fishing boats remained to stock Amble's seafood restaurants and by sheer willpower, a tourist industry was born.

Holly stood outside of the Defender by a wind-swept beach. A family of three were being sandblasted as they ate a picnic on the dunes. The mother protected her young child under a Visit Britain beach towel while the father gamely picked grit out of his ham sandwiches.

"It's no wonder Mr Masterly is as rich as he is," Holly said, folding her arms. "If you can persuade tourists to a place like this, imagine what you can do with a rollercoaster?"

Holly and Callum walked along the town's narrow pavements,

stepping into the road whenever the path became blocked. The air tasted of salt from the sea and vinegar from the fish shops. They passed a wool shop with yellow cellophane over the window. A man stood in the doorway of an empty ironmongers, smoking a cigarette, watching them through puffs of blue smoke.

Holly nodded at him as they passed and he gave her a wave.

The Amble Library and Salon were on Haddock Street. It was a red brick building with a glass revolving door as an entrance. Inside the foyer, Holly stood with her hands on her hips, reading the signs taped to the wall. One arrow pointed to the library.

The other pointed in the opposite direction.

"Why is there a hairdresser in a library building?" she asked.

"Because the sandwich shop went bust," Callum said. "It's a way of generating enough money to keep the library open."

The smell of peroxide made Holly's nose twitch. "Maybe it's time you got all that hair cut off," she said.

Callum's hands went to his head in fright and he scurried into the library. Holly picked up a price list for later.

The library was as quiet as she expected. An elderly librarian was bent over a desk, half-moon glasses perched on his bulbous nose. He was too engrossed in a book to acknowledge their presence, but pointedly turned a page at their entrance. There were no other books in the library and no shelves to put them on. They were greeted by a circular room edged with computers capable of accessing the internet.

"Where are all the books?" Holly asked.

"This is the new library," Callum said. "The old library is at the wool shop on Grafton Street."

Holly and Callum nudged their chairs together.

"I guess we start looking?" Callum asked.

Holly double clicked the mouse. "Yes, but for what?"

For the next hour, their heads buzzed with the hum of the computer.

It appeared Black Rock Manor had yet to enter the digital age. There was nothing on its history they couldn't have found by asking the Little Belton residents. Created with coal money, the manor had been standing for over a century and a half. Generations of Wentworths had passed through its doors, living there and governing the mines.

"I knew that," Callum said.

Holly chewed the inside of her cheek and searched the Wentworth name. She found them all over the globe, from the Wentworths of Kent who ran a costume hire business to a Wentworth in Melbourne, Australia whose Twitter handle was CrazyCatfish.

"Not much of a journalist, am I?" Holly typed on the keyboard, her fingers striking the keys so loudly, the librarian silenced her with a tut.

"You are a journalist," Callum said.

Holly held her head in her hands. "You don't have to try and make me feel better."

"No, I mean, you write for a newspaper," Callum said. "You must be able to search for old stories from the Herald."

"Of course. That's what they do in the movies, right? They search through clippings on microfilm."

After a brief enquiry with the librarian, Holly was assured they didn't have a microfilm reader and they weren't living in a movie, either.

She slumped back in her seat. "I'm so bad at this," she said into her chest.

Callum licked a fingertip and typed slowly, pausing between each letter as he searched for the next.

"Never used a keyboard before," he said. "What do I do now?"

Holly pressed Enter.

A search for the Little Belton Herald came up blank, but it gave Holly an idea and she looked for The Crockfoot Mail.

Three stories appeared on screen. The first discussed the closure of the mine, detailing the loss of jobs and its impact on the area. Years later came an article on the Wentworth family abandoning Black Rock Manor after failing to find a buyer. It came with a picture of the Wentworths standing outside their front door, side by side, showing a united front. The head of the family Charles clasped a crucifix hanging around his neck.

If Holly didn't know any better, she'd think the Mail was revelling in the bad luck of its neighbour. From her brief time on the Little Belton Herald, Holly knew they didn't deal in scandal so it was no wonder these stories weren't covered between their pages. It also explained the Herald's low circulation numbers.

The third article was dated from the 1960s. Most newspapers kept a copy of every paper printed. Holly suspected even Old Jack had done so, but The Crockfoot Mail had photographed theirs and placed them online. It was a difficult read, but Holly followed it because she'd heard a different version of the story from Old Jack.

It followed the disappearance of not two sisters, but one – Regina Foxglove. Being a sickly, but headstrong teenager, she'd been caught in a storm while exploring the estate. Stumbling into Black Rock Manor, Regina sought shelter and within hours showed the first signs of bronchitis. Being a Christian man, Charles Wentworth looked after her, sending word to her parents that Regina was safe with him. She stayed at Black Rock for three months, receiving daily visits from her sister Nancy.

"Is that how the goat learned its way to the manor?" Holly asked.

"Goats live for ten to twelve years," Callum answered. "I'm guessing the goat Nancy has now is around five years old."

"That means Nancy has been going there recently."

"The Wentworths have been gone for ages so who was she going to see?" Callum asked, his brows knitted into a frown.

Holly tapped her fingers on the desk. "It was Regina with the first link to the manor, but something inspired a life-long fascination for Nancy.

When her health returned, Regina was paranoid she'd become ill again and she locked herself away in Bellcraig Stack. Nancy continued to roam the estate on her own. The question isn't who Nancy was visiting, but why?"

"Didn't Old Jack tell you it was both sisters that went missing?"

"Yes," Holly said, "and I think I know why."

A shadow fell over them and they turned to find the elderly librarian standing uncomfortably near.

"We're closing," he said, his voice sounding like sandpaper scratching down glass.

Callum checked his watch. "It's only 2 pm."

"Closing early," the librarian said. "Going to get my hair cut next door."

Holly rustled in her handbag. "Five minutes?"

"Glenda doesn't like me to be late," the librarian said, returning to his desk with another loud tut.

"What's that?" Callum asked pointing at the brochure scrunched in Holly's hand.

"It's promotion for Mr Masterly's parks around the world." Holly flattened out the brochure and flicked through the pages. "Look at this. It's Mountain Safari Land in Nevada."

It was a double page spread with pictures of black bears and coyotes and other species indigenous to mountain deserts. Next to them were images of rollercoasters, go-karts and rows of shops selling Safari Land merchandise.

"Is that what he's going to do with Little Belton?" Callum asked.

Holly remembered the newspaper clipping featuring the town called Eureka and entered its name into a search engine. "All of these entries talk about how a town called Eureka went down the drain. Crime rates went up. Businesses closed and people moved away."

Callum slapped the desk with his hand. "Mr Masterly called it 'another Eureka moment.' This is what he meant."

Holly pointed at a map in the brochure. "The town is a few miles north of Mr Masterly's theme park in Nevada. The residents objected to its development."

"Like Little Belton," Callum said, "Well, some of us, anyway."

"Remember what we found in Nancy's file? There was an article about gun control in a place called Eureka. According to these websites, Eureka is a hunting town, or was, rather. It made its money from taking tourists out on shooting trips. The legislation was changed so only residents could have a gun permit. Visitors to the town couldn't get one and the tourism died overnight."

"Why would they do that?" Callum asked. "It sounds like suicide to me."

"Why wasn't Little Belton consulted about Mr Masterly's plans?" Holly asked. "Why is the window for our appeal process so small? It doesn't say anything on these websites about Mr Masterly being involved, but the legislation was changed. The town objected, but there wasn't anything they could do. The residents started to leave and building on Mountain Safari Land started two months later."

"Mr Masterly said Little Belton would benefit," Callum said, his face contracting to stone. "He lied and if we object to what he's doing, then he'll destroy us."

Holly closed the brochure, not wanting to see Mountain Safari Land any longer. She folded it in half, attempting to fold it again.

"When Old Jack and I shouted at Mr Masterly at the village green," Holly said, "I think that counted as an objection. Don't you get it? What comes next is because of me."

Chapter Twenty-Two

"Mr Masterly isn't going to go away, Callum. That's not how big business works. He's invested too much."

They trudged through the sand dunes opposite Amble Caravan Park. It appeared busy with every caravan having a car parked beside it. The sea wind howled around the park like a stray dog, tearing up the grass and banging on screen windows. The caravan occupants stayed inside, watching the same TV channels they could have watched from home.

While Holly and Callum walked, they cradled cartons of chips under their coats, fearful of them being peppered with sand. They dropped greasy potato wedges into their mouths whenever the wind died down.

"I thought it was going to be alright," Callum said. "I thought I had my job back."

Holly rubbed grease through her fingers. Her friend looked tired. Not unhappy, but overwrought by the corkscrewing of events, as if he'd ridden one of Mr Masterly's rollercoasters too far and for too long.

"Do you enjoy working on the estate?" she asked.

Finishing his chips, Callum crushed the carton in his hand. "It's my life."

The path along the dunes gave way to wooden boards and the sand crunched under Holly's feet. "Who pays you?"

"What?"

"Your Dad worked for the Wentworths," Holly said, "but you'd have been too young. They were gone by the time you took over from him."

"Who have you been talking to?"

Holly wasn't looking at Callum and Callum wasn't looking at her. She took the carton from him and dropped it into a nearby bin.

"No one," she lied. "I was wondering how you've survived out there on your own, that's all."

The wooden boards led to a pavement. They walked along it until they reached a disused car park. The tarmac was cracked and weeds grew through the gaps. Piles of windblown sand formed undulating waves, bringing the sea to their feet.

"I do what I have to," Callum said. "Dad was the last gamekeeper for Black Rock. I learned from him and when he died, it was natural I took over."

"But without any money?" Holly asked. "You could forage for food, hunt for it, but you can't buy petrol with rabbit stew. And you show such devotion to your job. Who are you showing that devotion to? You're on your own doing a job no one asked you to do."

Callum pressed his fingers into the frown on his face. "I'm not used to people asking so many questions about me."

"But they do. Just not to your face. Mr Winnow described you as half-feral. What do you think he meant by that?"

Callum dragged the tip of his boot through the sand, drawing a line. "Who's asking? Him or you?"

"I don't mean to pry, but – "

"But you're a journalist and it's your job to be nosey."

His answer stung, but Holly was ready to defend herself. She wasn't asking as a journalist. She wasn't probing for a story, but as the retort came to her lips, she wondered why she was asking. Because she was genuinely concerned for Callum? Or because Derek had put doubts in her head as a jealous husband? When she stared at Callum, what was she looking for?

"Maybe it's time we went home," Holly said, a queasiness in her stomach that had nothing to do with the chips she'd eaten.

Callum laid a hand on her arm. His grip was firm and warm.

"Pottery Boat Yard," he said, pointing along the shore.

She followed his gaze to a large building constructed from wooden slats. The roof was formed from rusted corrugated iron. At its entrance was a small pier leading into the calm waters of a bay. Boats in varying states of dishevelment either bobbed in the water or were beached by the building. One in particular stood out. It took dishevelment to a new level of sinkability. The front half of the hull was missing and jagged fibreglass protruded like British teeth. It was painted in thick olive-green paint. If Holly was a gambling woman, she'd put money on it containing lead.

"That's the Sea Cucumber. It belongs to the Winnows," Callum said. "Mrs Winnow told us it had engine trouble."

"You'd think she might have mentioned that massive hole," Holly said.

The gates to the boatyard were open and they were drawn to the scream of an angle-grinder. A man in his forties looked up as they approached. He was bare-chested with a pot belly damp with sweat. His trousers were black leather and his moustache was a patchwork of greys and nicotine yellow.

"Alright, Callum?" he asked, switching off the angle grinder. He flipped a cigarette into his mouth and lit it from the glowing blade.

"Alright, Mr Potts," Callum answered. "The Winnows sent me down. Asking about the Cucumber."

Holly caught the lie and said nothing, intently examining a coil of orange, nylon rope instead.

Mr Potts laid the grinder on the floor and reached for a moth-eaten shirt hanging from a nail. He dressed quickly, generating clouds of smoke from his cigarette.

"They've really done one this time," he said, taking Callum and Holly outside. "Tell them the price has gone up. It was more than a bloody bump in the ocean, this one."

"What did they do?" Holly asked.

Rolling the cigarette around his mouth, Mr Potts took a long draw. "They must have told you."

"Keeping it hush-hush," Callum said, tapping the side of his nose. "You know how they are."

Mr Potts nodded with a grimace. "I know exactly, but there's no hiding this. Don't get me wrong. They slip me the odd bit of mackerel, but if they think they can run a boat aground and not pay for it, they've got another thing coming."

"Where did they ground it?" Callum asked.

"I picked her up from Ratkin Bay."

"Wasn't that where we found Mrs Winnow collecting crabs?" Holly asked Callum.

"And it's the same place I found those salmon tins," Callum said.

"They're always down there," Mr Potts said, scratching at his chest. "That's where the best mackerel are, they say. Nothing like fresh fish."

Callum studied the Sea Cucumber, prodding the crumpled fibreglass with his finger. Part of it fell away. He picked up the remnant and examined it in the light. "There's an inlet down there."

"That's where I hauled her from," Potts said. "There's an extra fifty for that alone."

Callum walked around the boat, his hands searching the damage. Stooping low, his arm snaked through the hole. When he pulled it free, he showed a battered tin of salmon to Holly – the same type of tinned salmon Callum still had stacked in the back of his Defender.

"I should be grateful. It looks like they've given up poaching for a while," Callum said.

"Don't tell me they're selling that filth," Mr Potts said, clutching his throat. "Tinned fish?"

"Wait until you see what's inside," Holly said.

Chapter Twenty-Three

The brakes screeched on Callum's Defender as he lurched to a stop outside of Winnows' Conveniences. The frontage had been redecorated in a bunting Holly recognised from the Spring Fair. The triangular flags were weather-beaten. Some were torn and mended with tape. They whipped in a cool breeze, crackling as they fluttered.

Stepping from the jeep, Holly and Callum paused.

"What's that smell?" Callum asked.

Holly looked through the window to the store. Unusually, there was no-one behind the counter, but she saw the inside had been redecorated, too. There was a new range of products, including books on Northumberland history, a pile of Northumberland tartan scarves and tins of Northumberland shortbread.

"Follow me," Callum said, leading her down a cobbled side street. The smell grew more pungent, making Holly sneeze. They pushed through a latticed metal gate and into a concrete yard.

The faces of Mr and Mrs Winnow were hidden behind masks. They held spray cans in their hands and clouds of red mist floated in the air carrying the astringent taint of chemicals.

"What are you doing?" Holly asked.

Engrossed in their work, the couple hadn't seen Holly and Callum enter. They jerked to attention.

"Mymm thh bburrr," Mr Winnow said.

Holly pointed at the masks and then to her ear. "We can't hear you." Mr and Mrs Winnow tugged off their masks, leaving a clean mark around their mouths while the rest of their faces were stained in red.

"It's our new business," Mr Winnow said.

He stood to one side and revealed a line of wooden figures. They were about a foot tall with a round red nose and toothy grins. Their antlers were flecked with sequins.

"Are those Christmas reindeer decorations?" Holly asked.

Mr Winnow rattled his spray can at her. "Not after we're done with them," he said. "A little bit of paint and hey presto, you've got a herd of deer."

Holly examined one of the finished products. Rudolf had been painted red, together with most of the ground he stood on. The red paint had done little to disguise his inherent Christmas vibe.

"Why would you do that?" she asked.

"For the tourists," Mr Winnow said as if the answer was self-explanatory. "This new theme park is going to bring a lot of people to Little Belton and we have to be ready for them. There's no fighting people like the Masterlys so we're turning our place into a souvenir shop."

"Oh my lord," Mrs Winnow said, staring into her compact mirror. "Why didn't you tell me I look like Donald Trump?"

Hiding her face, she scuttled from the yard and Holly hid her smile.

"Maybe your deer will help pay for the damage to your boat," Callum said.

Mr Winnow rubbed his chest, wiping paint down his shirt. "Ah, Judy said she'd mentioned it. Engine trouble. Shouldn't be a problem."

"We've been to Amble," Holly said. "We saw the boat."

The cheeks of Mr Winnow's face turned redder than the paint spattered over it. "You went to the shipyard?"

Holly nodded, watching Mr Winnow skip from foot to foot.

"Hold on a second," he said. "Were you checking up on me? What were you doing at Amble?"

"It was a day trip," Callum said. "I was getting my haircut at the library."

Mr Winnow stopped jostling and cast an eye over Callum's long hair. "You need to go back for the rest."

"We weren't checking up on you," Holly said, "but we did see the boat."

She wasn't blaming Mr Winnow for trying to make money. Holly was guilty of the same thing. This was one hustler talking to another and her insides squirmed at the thought of interrogating him, but Mr Winnow was involved in this whole debacle. Holly needed to know to what degree.

Wringing his hands, Mr Winnow stared at the ground. "Please don't tell our Judy. She really does think its engine trouble. She's going to kill me when she sees the bill."

"We've already guessed part of the story," Callum said. "You ran aground trying to bring in something pretending to be tinned salmon."

Mr Winnow looked up, his eyes flitting between Holly and Callum. "What do you mean? 'Something pretending to be tinned salmon?'"

"You didn't look inside the tins?" Holly asked.

"They weren't mine to look into," Mr Winnow said. "I was asked to sail to the Port of Tyne and pick up a shipment of tinned salmon. I thought, that's a bit weird. You can pick up salmon anywhere. Why there? But then I thought, what's the harm? It's hardly illegal and I am in the delivery business, after all. Maybe it was special salmon."

"It was special, alright," Callum said.

"I bring it back here and the instructions were to take it to the manor, which is a helluva hike from the beach. Judy had the truck so I was going to have to carry the lot by hand. So I try to get a little closer using an inlet and...well, you know the rest. I run aground and spill my cargo.

I was too busy keeping the Sea Cucumber afloat to worry what had happened to the tinned salmon."

"Why didn't you ask Judy to meet you?" Holly asked. "Did you tell her what you were up to?"

"I didn't tell her any of it."

After Derek had been declared bankrupt, he didn't speak to Holly for a month. They chatted about the weather and what to have for dinner, but they didn't talk about losing the business or how long it would be before they lost their home. His silence had scared her. Not wishing to expose her troubles to friends, who had their own, Holly went to a counsellor. The session was confidential and they spoke of secrets between husbands and wives. Big secrets damaged a marriage. Small ones often protected it. Holly left thinking she understood the difference, but watching her marriage deteriorate, she realised there wasn't much difference at all.

"You didn't tell her because she'd have known there was something odd about that delivery," Holly said. "Judy would have questioned it. She would have stopped you from getting involved."

"Maybe," Mr Winnow said. "Maybe."

They heard running water coming from the flat above the shop. The bathroom window was open. Steam escaped in feathery wisps as Mrs Winnow showered.

Mr Winnow cocked his head, listening to the water gurgling down the drain. "I'm going to tell her, but in my own time. Not when you two are here."

"We don't want to cause trouble," Holly said. "Just tell us who paid for the delivery and we'll go."

"What's this all about?" Mr Winnow asked.

"Who was it?" Callum asked, pulling out the tinned salmon he found in the boat wreckage.

"I don't know. Honestly."

Taking the key, Callum delicately peeled back the metal lid. He tilted it in Mr Winnow's direction, exposing the plant bulbs for him to see.

Mr Winnow's eyes widened. "What are those?"

"That's what you delivered," Callum said.

Holly saw the wheels turning in Mr Winnow's mind, the cogs slotting into place. She saw him realise he'd been tricked and that he should have spoken to his wife.

Holly twisted the wedding band around her finger, feeling it loosen with every rotation.

Mr Winnow had been made to look like a fool and he knew it.

"Am I going to jail?" he asked through a clenched jaw.

"Don't worry," Callum said. "We'll keep you out of the big house."

Holly took the spray can from Mr Winnow, placing it on the ground. She took his hand, not caring that her own would be stained with paint. "You were misled. You're the victim, but if we don't figure this out, the whole village might be in danger."

"It was an email," Mr Winnow said, staring at his bodged reindeer. "I thought it was spam. I ignored it until the money arrived in my bank account the next day."

"Did you get the name of the person who sent it?" Callum asked.

Mr Winnow turned away and sniffed. "No."

"What about the email address? Did you recognise it?" Holly asked.

"There wasn't one," Mr Winnow said. "It said Origin Unknown."

Holly felt the pressure in her hand increase. Mr Winnow was squeezing too hard.

"I'm going to ask again," she said, "because this is very important. Did you get a name?"

The water falling in the bathroom stopped and Mrs Winnow began singing. Like her spoken word tapes, her voice was pleasant, carrying a warmth that was homely and inviting.

Mr Winnow's face crumpled.

"The only thing I know is where it came from," he said. "At the bottom of the email was the name of an internet café. It was called *Coffee and a Byte.*"

"I know that place," Callum said, staring at the horizon. "It's in Crockfoot."

Chapter Twenty-Four

The computer screen in the Herald office lit Holly's face. She watched the spinning wheel of her cursor blink blue before finally giving up on the creaky Internet. She retrieved a wad of paper from her handbag, consulting her research for the article she was writing on the local cattle mart.

Apart from the glow of her computer, the office was shrouded in a veil of darkness.

Holly had walked past the switch and slumped into her chair, unheedful of the shadows. She'd switched on her computer and blindly wrote her article. The words had tapped out of her without conscious thought and she had to re-read them twice to make sure she'd finished.

Old Jack had abandoned his work at the newspaper, but Holly felt a duty to keep the Herald afloat.

Adding her last full stop, her eyes were drawn to his makeshift office. Old Jack had lied about the Foxglove sisters' disappearance. She had her suspicions as to why, but perhaps she was wrong. Time could warp memory. Perhaps he'd simply been mistaken.

Guilt could do the same. Either way, her trust in him felt misplaced, like Mr Winnow's trust in the mysterious email.

The idea that someone in Crockfoot was shipping plant bulbs to Little Belton didn't fit with Holly. Their only interest in their neighbours was in watching their demise and that included the Salting brothers.

It made more sense to suspect a Little Belter. Faced with a terrible internet connection, a short trip to Crockfoot wasn't without question. But out of everyone Holly knew, who might have sent the email?

Holly left her seat, her heartbeat resounding in her ears as she crept into Old Jack's office. His computer was turned off and Holly guessed it hadn't been used in a while. His desk was littered with notebooks filled with spidery writing. Holly flicked through the pages, finding mentions of a fundraising raffle at a donkey sanctuary, a minor landslide on the B234a and a *John Nettles* look-alike competition. They were the typical scoops Holly had come to associate with the Herald.

The potential ruination of Little Belton was too controversial for Old Jack.

The drawers to his desk were unlocked and Holly searched through them, finding nothing more interesting than a packet of fruity chewing gum.

Snooping on her boss left her feeling ungrateful for a job she needed, but Old Jack had been acting oddly since Nancy had gone missing and Holly wanted to know more.

His Alnwick Castle mug contained a forest of chewed Biro pens. Holly decided to leave a note asking for a chat when he returned to the office. Grabbing a piece of paper, she snatched a pen. It caught on something lodged in the mug. Pens spilled onto the desk. The mug tipped over and Holly saw inside. There was a crushed ball of cardboard and she eased it free, flattening it out on the desk.

She recognised it immediately and ran a finger over her lips as she reread the cover. The cardboard was a sleeve for the anti-depressant Seroxat. Her husband had been taking them since the demise of his business. Now, it looked like Old Jack was using them too because the box was empty.

"Is anybody here?"

Holly jumped at the voice, spinning in her chair to face it. The office light was switched on and she blinked at the sudden illumination.

Mrs Masterly slinked into the room, wearing jeans so tight, Holly imagined her feet to be blue. On her arm was another expensive handbag, sparkling with golden threads.

"Can I help you?" Holly asked.

Her voice attracted Mrs Masterly's attention and she held onto her handbag like a shield. "I'm looking for Old Jack. I was told he works here."

"He's not in."

"Why are you in his office?" Mrs Masterly said, looking down her nose.

Holly hoped it was still too dark for Mrs Masterly to see her blush. She slipped the Seroxat packet up her sleeve. "This is my office. He works over there," she said, pointing at her own desk.

Mrs Masterly raised an eyebrow. "The one with the handbag on it?"

Why hadn't she left her tatty handbag in the car, Holly asked herself?

"That's right," she said. "That's his desk."

"I remember you from the village green," Mrs Masterly said. "You were very vocal on the new development."

"We have the right to ask questions."

"It felt more like a student demonstration. Aren't you too old for that?"

Holly skulked into the main office, her hands behind her back, hiding the fact they were bunched into fists. "Why do you want to see Old Jack?"

Mrs Masterly smiled. "We have another announcement to make. After you disturbed the last one, we thought it would be simpler if we placed it in the local press."

The way Mrs Masterly said the word 'press' set Holly's teeth on edge.

"I work here," she said. "I'll make sure it gets mentioned."

"Very well," Mrs Masterly said. "It's about the appeal process. There isn't going to be one."

Holly leaned on the ironing board where Old Jack kept the kettle. It wobbled under her shaking hand.

"Apparently, the council have reviewed their appeal policy and found it redundant," Mrs Masterly continued. "Arcadia Leisure are free to build their theme park as soon as logistically possible."

Holly swallowed repeatedly.

"You can't do that," she said, spitting out the words.

"My husband can be very persuasive."

"You must be proud of him," Holly said, releasing her grip on the ironing board. "Proud of everything he's done to villages like ours. Like he did to Eureka in Nevada."

For a moment, Mrs Masterly's smile slipped. "He's an adventurer and sportsman."

"And a millionaire," Holly said. "What attracted you to him first, I wonder?"

Mrs Masterly snapped open her handbag and retrieved a lipstick. She proceeded to apply another coat to her mouth.

"I'm not the only one attracted to him," Mrs Masterly said, finishing her paint job. "Your husband took a shine to him, too. That *was* your husband, wasn't it? Asking *my* husband for a job? He sounded hungry for it, poor soul."

Holly yanked her shirt away from her chest. She was suddenly too warm. "It's time for you to leave."

"We left Eureka how we found it. Little Belton will be the same. We rarely intrude unless we have to."

"And are you going to?" Holly asked. "Intrude into our lives, I mean?"

Mrs Masterly smacked her freshly rouged lips. She turned to the door and Holly wanted to follow, to physically and unnecessarily eject her from the premises, but her body was too stiff. Her muscles were bunched in anger. It wasn't Mrs Masterly's words that hurt, but the fact that they were right. Her fury transferred briefly to Derek. For his treachery and for giving this woman ammunition.

Holly was humiliated by his desperation.

"Tinned salmon," she shouted.

Mrs Masterly stumbled, holding onto the doorframe as she looked over her shoulder. "Excuse me?"

"You know what I'm talking about."

And Mrs Masterly did. Holly was sure of it and her mind raced, stitching thoughts together in rapid succession. She recalled what she'd discovered over the previous few days and like any good journalist, Holly constructed a story.

"Arcadia Leisure sabotaged Eureka when they raised objections to your theme park," she said, marching up to Mrs Masterly. "You did it in the most underhanded of ways. Getting someone else to restrict gun permits so you wouldn't get your hands dirty. It was subtle and devastating and you're doing the same thing here."

Mrs Masterly looked to the door.

"An anonymous source tricked one of our residents," Holly said, "playing on his weakness for an easy penny. He smuggled plant bulbs into Little Belton. They were destined to go to Black Rock Manor, which you now own. They were hidden inside tins of salmon."

"And what are these bulbs for?" Mrs Masterly asked.

Holly's galloping thoughts deserted her. Her mind dissolved and Holly found she had nothing to say.

Mrs Masterly smirked. "Are they an invasive species? Are they poisonous? Do they have something to do with a beanstalk?"

Holly bit her tongue, to stop it from talking further nonsense.

"Why would we put bulbs in tins of salmon?" Mrs Masterly asked.

"I told you," Holly said. "To hide them."

"For what reason? To hide them from whom?" Mrs Masterly

adjusted her handbag around the crook of a bent arm. "If you don't mind me asking, are you okay? You must be under a lot of stress. I imagine money must be an issue."

Mrs Masterly turned on her heels, but lingered by the doorway. "I suggest you spend more time at home before you lose that as well."

Old Jack's kettle called to Holly and she fantasised about bashing it over Mrs Masterly's head, but it was the only one in the office and Holly couldn't afford to replace it.

"By the way," Mrs Masterly said. "I found this pinned to the door. Let's hope it's not an eviction notice."

She slapped an envelope into Holly's hand and left in a haze of choking perfume.

In the battle of the handbags, Holly had lost. In terms of waistline and wealth, Holly was a loser there too. What had she been thinking? How could Holly defeat someone like Mrs Masterly?

A sigh escaped Holly's lips and she angrily tore open the envelope, wincing when she gave herself a papercut. The letter inside had been torn from an exercise book. It was frayed at the edges and slightly yellowed.

Holly's throat dried as she read what was on it.

The letter said, 'Follow The Star.'

Chapter Twenty-Five

Holly shoved open the doors of The Travelling Star with her shoulder. Her mind had been whirring since her encounter with Mrs Masterly. It had been so combative, but had ended so oddly that Holly couldn't conclude anything from it. As an answer flared in front of her, it raised a question to tamp it down.

The weather outside was mild, but the fire still blazed in the pub. Holly took off her jacket and headed to the bar.

Big Gregg raised a ham-sized hand into the air as she approached.

"Here comes the Little Belton warrior," he said. "Defender of the people."

"I'm not sure I did the right thing," Holly said, sitting by the bar.

"You said your piece," Big Gregg said, taking a clean glass from the shelf. "No one can blame you for that."

With a damp cloth, he polished the glass, smearing grime around the rim. "I'm on your side. To hell what other people say."

Holly gripped the bar. "What are they saying? Did they want me to leave Arcadia Leisure alone?"

Big Gregg grinned. "I've got something to show you."

He twirled on his heels, his huge frame like a feather caught in the breeze until he landed delicately in front of the till. "This is new. We'll have to train you up."

Straining over the bar, Holly saw the old till had been replaced with something that looked like it had been designed by NASA. It had a dark touch screen with hieroglyphics pulsing in yellow.

The previous till had been old enough to be housed in a museum, but at least Holly knew how to use it.

Big Gregg looked at her like a proud father. "Practically the same as the one before, but quicker and smarter. I place an order and it adjusts the stock so I know when to reorder. Not that I have to do that because it reorders for me. It does the bookkeeping, switches the lights on and off and changes the music in the bar."

"Does it pull pints, as well?" Holly asked.

"We still have to do that," Big Gregg said, "but do you like it?"

Holly rubbed her face with her hands. "How does it all work? You must need broadband or something for it to do all that."

Big Gregg pointed to the ceiling. "Got a satellite dish installed on the roof. Runs the till and it's free WiFi for every customer."

"How can you afford this?" Holly asked.

"It's an investment," Big Gregg said.

"For when the theme park is built and all the tourists come," Holly said.

She lowered her head, allowing her hair to cover her face. Poor Gregg, she thought. He'd been swept up in a tide of hope like the Winnows and Holly couldn't blame any of them. He might claim to support Holly's actions, but she saw where Big Gregg's dreams lay.

"Just wait until all the tourists come," he said. "This till will pay for itself in no time."

"I'm sorry," Holly said. "I had no right to speak for you on the village green. I had no right to voice an objection."

"This is your home. You had every right." Big Gregg's finger appeared under her chin and he gently lifted her face toward him. "I was proud of you, but this is an opportunity to bring this village back to life."

"What if it's not?" Holly asked. "What if it's all a lie?"

"Why would it be?" Big Gregg asked back. "We haven't done anything to Arcadia Leisure. Why would they betray us?"

Holly glanced at the new, space-age till. In her mind's eye, she saw the Winnows' freshly decorated souvenir shop. Behind every door in Little Belton, she imagined the excited residents preparing for a new future. Holly couldn't tell them their hope was false. Little Belton was about to share the same headstone as the forgotten town of Eureka.

"Cheer up," Big Gregg said, placing a shot of vodka by her. "In a couple of years, we'll be able to open another pub. You can manage this one for me."

Holly sipped her drink, noting how clean the glass was. "Is that how big business works?"

Nodding, Big Gregg gave her a grin. "It should."

"Have you seen Old Jack recently?" Holly asked.

Big Gregg wiped the bar with his cloth. "Poor sod," he said. "He was in earlier. Didn't seem like himself. Kinda dazed."

"I need to speak with him. Have you got his address?"

Writing on a beer mat, Big Gregg handed it over. The mat belonged to the bar and pictured a yellow star. Old Jack's address was written along one of the points.

Holly considered the note given to her by Mrs Masterly. Follow The Star. What had it meant? Did it mean The Travelling Star or something else?

The pub door opened and Mr MacFarlene entered. Holly expected him to take a seat, but he hovered by the entrance.

"You won't believe this," he said and returned outside.

Big Gregg scratched his head. "That's the first time he's left here sober."

Through the doors, Holly and Big Gregg joined a growing throng of people milling about the village green. Parked dead centre was an American-style campervan. It was polished aluminium, its sides looking like a shell. The tyres were thick and commanding, capable of carrying it over treacherous terrain. The windows were reflected glass and Holly noticed a beady eyed raven dancing on its roof.

Mr Masterly stood at the entrance with his arms wide open.

"Huddle up, dudes," he shouted, his teeth flashing white. "This is all for you."

Holly and Big Gregg were swept along by the crowd, finding themselves at the front.

Mr Masterly spotted Holly and his smile froze. His hands pressed together in a prayer sign. "Please hear me out this time."

He turned to the crowd with a bow. A few of the residents glanced at the sky, worried they were about to be bombarded by another microlight.

"This is your new information media hub," Mr Masterly announced. He paused for a round of applause, hiding his disappointment when it didn't arrive. "I know you're concerned about what I'm planning here. Some think I'm here to knock down your houses and chase you from your homes.

"Inside this RV is everything you need to know about Arcadia Leisure and Black Rock Adventureland. Our blueprints, proposals, mission statements. Inside is the answer to every question you have."

A murmur rippled through the crowd. Big Gregg put an arm around Holly's shoulder and gave her a squeeze.

"We believe in total transparency," Mr Masterly said, standing in front of the reflective windows. "We're here to help Little Belton and we want you on board. We want you to join us on this journey."

A solitary clap sounded, followed by another. It built into the applause Mr Masterly had been seeking.

Holly stared about the village green, listening to Little Belton voice their approval. She raised her hand, but lowered it before anyone noticed. Holly wanted to ask about the appeals process. Why had it been cancelled? Why were their objections now obsolete? But she didn't. Holly kept quiet because rocking the boat wasn't the Little Belton way.

Mr Masterly's eyes sparkled. "And there's one more thing."

Towering over Holly, Big Gregg whispered into her ear. "I told you. Everything is going to be okay. We're going to be rich."

"To show our appreciation for accepting us into your lives," Mr Masterly said, "our media hub will offer free drinks to every Little Belton resident."

The crowd cheered, their applause like thunder.

Mr Masterly waved his hands in the air. "And they will remain free until Adventureland is completed."

The crowd surged forward, moving as one, their faces lit up in anticipation.

The raven on the roof took to the sky, its shadow darkening Big Gregg's face.

"No," he said. "He can't. That's my business. It will bankrupt me."

Mr MacFarlene jostled with the others, glancing in Holly's direction, but avoided looking at Big Gregg as he joined the queue for his free drink.

Little Belton swarmed around the campervan like bees to free mead. They cheered and drank and then cheered some more.

Holly and Big Gregg were left alone on the green, both of them having followed a star destined to crash to earth while Mr MacFarlene shrank in the crowd.

Chapter Twenty-Six

"Thanks for coming with me," Holly said, crouched behind a crumbling drystone wall. "Big Gregg can't lose his best customer. Do you think the Masterlys have got to Mr MacFarlene?"

"That's what we're here to find out," Callum said.

"If the Masterlys divide the community," Holly said, "we've lost this fight before it's even begun."

"We need to stick together," Callum said, jamming a loose stone back into the wall. "I'll be reminding Mr MacFarlene of that when he shows up."

The sun was setting over the grasslands of the estate. Grey cows moved in slow waves, cresting at one side of their field before turning and flowing in the opposite direction. Holly and Callum, together with the cows, were on the border between the estate and Mr McFarlane's farm. His house was nestled in a crown of trees at the end of the track Holly was waiting on.

"I lost him at the Masterlys' stupid media hub thing," she said, "but he won't get past me again."

Callum selected another rock and stacked it on the wall.

"Can you stop doing that please?" Holly asked.

"I might as well do something while we're waiting," Callum said. "Mr MacFarlene's cows could walk right through this gap."

Holly rolled her eyes. "I don't know why you're bothering. If he doesn't care about his livestock, then why should you?"

Callum continued rebuilding the wall, his muscles bulging as he forced the rocks into formation. "This used to be one heck of a farm before Mr MacFarlene lost his wife. He wasn't always a drunk, you know? It just sort of happened, but even he wouldn't want his cows straying into that."

Holly followed Callum's pointed finger to a watery bog filled with sedge grass and buzzing flies.

"It's called Myrtle's Water," he said. "It's dangerous. The bog the final resting place of Myrtle Hainsworth. She was tricked by a shapeshifting goblin posing as a horse. After a tiring day, Myrtle accepted a ride from the goblin before she was bucked into the water never to be seen again."

Holly tried not to laugh at the sincere expression on Callum's face.

"You're right about the cows," she said, holding up her hands in surrender. "You're doing a great service, but the most dangerous thing about that marsh is the foot rot you're likely to get if you go in without any shoes."

Callum jammed the last stone in place and stepped back to admire his work.

Holly had to admit, it was a good looking wall, capable of withstanding the most wayward of cow. She hoped Mr MacFarlene would be grateful.

The buzz of the marsh flies grew louder.

A frown flickered across Callum's face.

As Holly stared into the cloudy water, wondering what was animating the insects, she realised the noise was coming from behind her.

Callum rushed to her side.

A mud-splattered tractor wove toward them. It straddled the path and the ditch beside it. Smoke belched from the exhaust, its fumes reminding Holly of the defective merry-go-round at the Spring Fair.

The tractor gained speed, like a boulder thundering down a slope. Callum ran along the track, waving his arms above his head.

"You're going to crash," he shouted.

Holly placed a protective hand on the new wall, unsure how that might help.

The tractor engine growled, careening left and right.

"Stop," Holly shouted.

Callum leapt behind a hillock as it hurtled by.

Holly's mouth dropped open. The tractor was steering toward her. Before she realised it, she had leapt over the wall and was wading through the marsh. The mud sucked at her feet. Each step was like something out of an anxiety dream. Her legs wouldn't respond as quickly as she wanted.

Glancing behind her, she saw the tractor burst through the drystone wall, scattering Callum's carefully arranged rocks. They flew over Holly's head, splashing down around her.

The tractor trundled on for a few more metres, pitching into the bog, sending a wave of dirty water over a cowering Holly.

Mr MacFarlene's ghostly face peered at her through the windscreen. The tractor spat and hissed as it sank.

"Are you okay?" Callum asked Holly from the side of the marsh.

Dripping wet, Holly swatted at the flies circling her head. "No, I'm bloody not. Get that idiot out of his tractor."

Callum jumped onto the rear wheel, using the treads as rungs on a ladder. He reached the cabin and wrenched the door open. Mr MacFarlene rolled in his seat, a trickle of blood rolling down his face.

"He's been drinking," Callum said.

Holly waded to the shore, alarmed to find she had lost a shoe to Myrtle Hainsworth. "There's a surprise."

"What happened?" Mr MacFarlene asked.

Callum hurriedly undid his seatbelt, catching the farmer as he slumped forward. Holding him under the armpits, Callum dragged Mr MacFarlene out of the door.

The bog belched and the tractor slipped further into the water, its large tyres submerging quickly. Callum steadied himself.

"Wake up, you old soak," he shouted, but there was no response from the farmer.

Mr MacFarlene belched too.

There didn't seem to be a vindictive bone in Callum's body, thought Holly. There were plenty in Holly's, though, especially after her bath in the marsh. They could have been killed and yet Callum was risking his life further by helping the farmer.

Burying her frustrations, Holly waded back into the marsh as Callum lowered Mr MacFarlene into her waiting arms.

Holly wrinkled her nose. "I'm getting drunk off the whisky fumes. He smells worse than the bog."

Mr MacFarlene tried to steady himself before collapsing and landing with a splash.

Callum jumped from the tractor and lugged him to firmer ground. "How much have you had?"

Mr MacFarlene flopped onto his back, one hand searching for a soaked sporran. With a yank, he produced his hip flask to have it snatched from him by Holly.

"You almost killed us," she said, pouring the contents of the flask into the bog, "and you've destroyed Callum's wall."

The cows in the field were drawn to the commotion, stepping through the gap made by the tractor. One of them lowered its head at the spot where Holly had disposed of the whisky. It gave the alcoholic water an experimental lap of its tongue and moo-ed its appreciation.

"You can tell these cows belong to you," Callum said.

Mr MacFarlene wobbled to his feet. "What happened?" he asked again.

Holly pitched the hip flask into the marsh. This was familiar territory for her. There was no point arguing with a drunk. She'd earned that from late night fights with Derek.

"Nothing," she said with a hiss. "Let's get you back home."

The Defender was only fifty meters away, but it felt like a thousand. Mr MacFarlene stumbled over every step. Holly and Callum guided him with arms around his shoulder, picking him up whenever he fell.

The farmer muttered to himself, holding a conversation they weren't invited to. Holly picked out the odd phrase. 'Media hub' and 'recreational whats-its-name,' but none of it made sense.

They folded Mr MacFarlene into the back of the Defender and took their seats in the front, cracking open their windows to release the combined stench of bog water and whisky.

Driving past the broken wall, Callum sighed at every fallen stone. Steam spewed from the tractor as the bog inched up the tyres, slowly consuming them as a snake devours its prey. Holly didn't believe Callum's tale about Myrtle's Water, but for a second, she thought she saw the watery face of a woman gnashing her teeth at the unexpected visitor.

The track grew dim and Callum switched on his headlights illuminating the farmhouse ahead. It had two storeys and was painted white with black frames around the windows. All the curtains were drawn. It was set among storage buildings made from corrugated iron. Piles of animal feed were buried underneath plastic sheeting weighted down with tyres.

Mr MacFarlene stirred at the nearness of his home, blinking at Holly with bleary eyes.

"Thanks for the lift," he said, struggling with the handle to the door. "Did you pick me up from Little Belton? I can't remember."

Holly bit her tongue and remained silent.

The farmhouse garden was gravelled. Pots filled with the wizened branches of dead plants stood neglected in a semi-circle. A nylon washing line was tied between metal poles. Two sleeping bags were pegged out to dry and Holly wondered who they belonged to.

"We'll be alright, won't we?" Mr MacFarlene asked, finding the handle's catch and falling out of the door. He landed with the luck of the drunk, sustaining no further injuries.

He pulled himself up and held onto the roof of the Defender for support. "I don't know what I'm going to do. I don't know."

"Sleep it off," Holly said. "You'll be alright in the morning."

"It's okay for you lot," Mr MacFarlene said. "You'll get your fancy park. You'll get all the swings and rides promised to you by the Masterlys. What about me? My wee farm is right next door. I read a pamphlet in that bloody media hub. Read it with one hand while they refilled my glass in the other. You know what I get? Some sort of haunted house contraption next door to my lambing shed."

He waved his hand as if swatting an invisible fly. "Barbara will be spinning in her grave."

The mention of his deceased wife stabbed at Holly's heart. Despite her anger, she wanted to offer a reassurance, but she felt the same fear as Mr MacFarlene. It choked her line of thought, like the water swallowing the farmer's tractor.

"Go to bed," Holly said, "and take your washing in. It'll get damp through the night."

Rolling his head toward home, Mr MacFarlene gave Holly and Callum a thumbs-up and tottered through his garden, swiping at the sleeping bags.

Mr McFarlane's garden was a wreck, Holly thought. The boundaries of his farm were disappearing and his livestock were growing drunk on their freedom. Who knew how the farmer lived behind closed doors? Or what state his home was in? If he chose to use a sleeping bag because he had no clean blankets, then it wasn't any concern of Holly's.

CHAPTER TWENTY-SIX

"He's no good to us drunk," she said.

Callum reversed into a layby and pointed the Defender in the direction of home.

"It's funny, though, isn't it?" Callum asked.

Holly picked a clump of sedge grass out of her hair. "There's nothing funny about wasting our time."

"No, I meant Mr MacFarlene," Callum said, driving them through a darkening sky.

Holly stared out of the window, waiting for the punchline.

Callum scratched his chin, a frown troubling his brow. "He lives alone, right? So why would he be washing two sleeping bags, not one?"

Chapter Twenty-Seven

Holly hadn't slept well. Thoughts of Mr MacFarlene haunted her dreams. Holly had misjudged him. Yes, he was a danger to himself and everyone around him, but he wasn't a turncoat. Mr MacFarlene was burdened by a grief he couldn't shake. Not only had he lost his wife, he was facing the prospect of losing his farm. Who would decline a free drink under those circumstances?

Finally abandoning any hope of sleep, Holly took a long shower and dressed in the light of the morning sun.

She called Wansbeck Hospital for any updates on Regina's condition. According to the nurse in charge, Regina had woken briefly to argue about the lumpiness of her bed before falling back asleep. Comforted by the idea of Regina returning to normal, Holly left a snoring Derek on the couch and travelled into Little Belton.

Old Jack's house was at the end of Stationers Lane with views of the estate's moorland. They sat in the back garden on plastic chairs watching Nancy's goat straining on its new chain. It had full reign of the garden, but clearly had itchy hooves. In the short time it had been there, the goat had nibbled most of Old Jack's shrubs down to stubs.

He wore a tatty cardigan with tweed patches on his elbows.

Old Jack inspected the crumpled packet of anti-depressants in Holly's hand.

"I found them on your desk," she said. "I wasn't snooping. I just want to know you're alright."

"Not snooping, eh?" Old Jack asked. "That's what I pay you for."

He produced a bubble strip of pills and slipped them inside the packet Holly had given him.

"How long have you been taking them?" Holly asked.

"Ever since...well, you know," he said, pulling a weed from his lawn and tossing it toward the goat. "Funny, but me and Nancy barely spoke after her disappearance. I thought about her, though."

"Wasn't there anyone else for you?"

"I don't think it's as easy as that, pet. I don't think it's a choice."

"People do it all the time," Holly said.

"Not around here, they don't," Old Jack said. "Maybe if I'd moved away like you, I might have found someone else, but there's no point in wishing down an empty well. My chance is gone. What's done is done."

"I'll find Nancy for you," Holly said, taking Old Jack's hand. "You'll still have your chance."

Old Jack squeezed her hand with a smile. "You know who got lucky? Found true love? Your parents."

"They knew how to make a marriage work," Holly said. "I always thought I'd be able to do the same, but it's not as easy as it looks."

"You hear about these big city types with all the money and the cars and such-like, but none of them look happy. They seem tired and aggravated. Little Belton might not have much, but live here long enough, you'll find that one person you can love no matter what."

Holly thought of Callum and shook her head as if to physically shake him from her mind.

"You make Little Belton seem like a fairy tale kingdom," Holly said.

"Your Mam and Dad thought so," Old Jack said. "They loved it here, especially your Dad, even after he got ill."

"I tried to see him as often as I could, but it was difficult with the business."

"He understood."

"Dad should have received compensation. All that coal dust in his lungs, but he wouldn't have it. He said, the pit had put a roof over his family's head and food on the table. That was good enough for him."

Holly looked away, her eyes glistening. She and her father had never argued, but they'd come close on that occasion. She'd never understood the gratitude he'd shown to the Wentworths and their mine.

Old Jack freed his hand and reached into his cardigan. "Young people never carry handkerchiefs," he said, offering it to Holly.

She dabbed her eyes. "I'm not that young anymore. I've wasted my life. I've ended up right where I started."

"Bringing with you all that you've learned, pet," Old Jack said. "Your Dad was very proud of you. Never shut up about you down the pub, which annoyed the hell out of us all. He had that bleedin' oxygen mask on. It was two puffs for every word. Each story was an hour long. No-one else got a word in."

Holly laughed.

"He always thought you'd come back," Old Jack said.

"I bet he didn't think it would be because of bankruptcy."

"He said you were smart and one day, you'd realise people don't need to travel for miles and miles to find out who they are."

"I felt like I needed to find a new perspective." Holly watched Nancy's goat spin in a circle before dropping to the lawn to sleep. Its breaths came in long, slow draughts.

"You were good friends with my Dad?" she asked. "Is that why you've been so good to me?"

Pulling his cardigan close, Old Jack looked to the sky, the deep blue of it reflected in his eyes. "I've been good to you because I wanted you to stay where you belong. It's as simple as that."

He made to stand, but Holly placed a steadying hand on his arm.

"I have something to ask you," she said.

Old Jack had seemed composed when she arrived, jovial even. Perhaps acting out his role as her protector and carer had brought him strength.

"What is it, pet?" he asked, his voice faint.

She hated to do it. After everything Old Jack had done for her, it was a betrayal of his kindness, but Holly was there for a reason. Even as she hesitated, she knew she would confront him. Holly needed to find the truth.

"When Nancy first went missing," Holly said, "you told me she and her sister had been lost in a blizzard. That when they were found, they'd locked themselves away because they could no longer stand the cold, but that wasn't true, was it?"

Expecting an answer, Holly waited for Old Jack to speak, but he stayed silent so she continued.

"It was Regina who was caught in a storm. She fell ill and stayed at Black Rock Manor for three months to recuperate. Nancy visited her every day. When her sister returned home, Nancy kept visiting."

Old Jack closed his eyes like the sleeping goat on his lawn. Holly imagined he was returning to that time, replaying the story in his mind. He frowned and brought his fingertips to his mouth.

Holly swallowed down her guilt and pressed on. "Nancy didn't shut herself away," she said. "She walked to the manor. In all weathers. She wasn't afraid of the cold. Nancy didn't hide from it, but I think she hid away from you and it hurt you. Deeply. So, you came up with a story to make you feel better."

Old Jack kept his eyes closed, but reached into his pocket for his pills. He slipped one in his mouth and rolled it around his gums.

"I'm a journalist," Old Jack finally said. "I'm supposed to tell people the truth, but the biggest story I ever told was the one I fed to myself over those two sisters. A total fabrication. After that, I lost interest in telling people what they needed to know. The truth seemed too painful."

Holly shifted in her seat, a sick feeling in her stomach. "But it's our job."

"I didn't see Nancy for a week," Old Jack said, opening his blue eyes, "and when I did, she told me about the storm. Told me things had to change. I tried to see her, but she never answered the door after that. Nancy wandered the estate because she didn't love me the way I loved her."

"Oh, Jack, I'm sorry," Holly said.

"I'd heard rumours of her on the moors, but I chose not to believe them."

"I thought..." but Holly couldn't finish her sentence. She couldn't work it past the lump in her throat. Nancy had hurt Old Jack and Holly had joined her in twisting the knife.

This wasn't about being a bad journalist anymore. This was about being a bad person.

Holly returned Old Jack's handkerchief. "I'm resigning from the Herald. You don't need to see me anymore."

Old Jack blew into his handkerchief loud enough to wake the goat. Startled, it clambered to its feet, searching for the threat.

"Don't leave, pet," Old Jack said. "Look how far you've come."

"I'm acting like a mad woman here," Holly said, pulling on her hair. "I've accused you of creating a cover story. I've probably started some sort of war with the Masterlys and I'm still no further forward in finding Nancy."

The goat settled again, curling up into a ball, but keeping one eye on Old Jack, its nostrils flaring with suspicion.

"I'm with you when it comes to the Masterlys," Old Jack said. "We both know something is going on there and it's our job to expose it, just like you've exposed the lie I told myself."

"You were involved, Jack. It was too emotional for you."

"You're involved, too. I can see it. That's what makes you good. Your Dad was right. You're smart and your time away has given you a perspective us bumpkins don't have. We both know I'm not a journalist anymore. I don't have it in me to stir up trouble like you do. Little Belton deserves someone who will protect it from itself."

Holly kissed Old Jack on the cheek, but shook her head. "I can't keep hurling my suspicions at people who don't deserve it. I'm sorry, but it's over."

Walking along Stationers Lane, Holly kept her eyes fixed on her feet as clouds gathered in the sky.

Chapter Twenty-Eight

In the light of dawn, the lake was alive with the chattering calls of unseen animals. As the sun rose, the lake hushed as if taking a breath before embarking on another day of survival.

Grabbing her blanket, Holly had sat outside to await the sunrise over Knock Lake.

At times, her skin prickled and she imagined there were unknown eyes upon her. Whether they were animal or human, she didn't know. She searched the shoreline of the lake, examining tangled brambles and fallen trees for signs of life. There was too much of it to discern a single pair of eyes.

Until a large stag emerged from the bracken, leading his doe to the water. The herd cautiously lowered their heads to drink while the stag locked eyes with Holly. It was the same animal she had seen by the side of the road and if Holly recognised him, it felt like the stag also recognised her. She pressed into her seat, uncomfortable with their strange connection.

Satiated, the rest of the herd melted back into the landscape, leaving the stag to watch Holly return indoors.

She dressed quickly and left her home in silence, pleased to see the stag was no longer there. She drove to Bellcraig Stack. Passing the telephone greenhouse, Holly noticed the tomatoes were ripe and ready for picking.

Callum was waiting by the garden gate, his hands jammed into his pockets.

"Thanks for meeting me," Holly said, climbing from her car.

"I don't want to be here," Callum said.

Holly linked her arm through his, leading him through the garden. It was beginning to look dishevelled. Rhubarb that had been ready to pick when Holly first visited, was now limp, its leaves hanging like torn clothing. The gooseberry bushes were riddled with sawfly and the sunshine faces of dandelions were turning to feathery seeds.

"This feels like unfinished business for me," Holly said. "I never got to pay my respects properly. I was arguing with Derek when we visited the hospital."

Callum's body hardened under her hold.

"How is he? Your husband?" he asked.

"He'll be fine," Holly said.

A lock of Callum's hair fell over his face and Holly brushed it aside.

"I never met Regina," Callum said. "I met Nancy twice, though. I was a young kid the first time around. Dad was picking up supplies from the village. She looked like a laundry basket come to life. While he was loading the Defender, this woman swaddled in clothes watched me, not saying a word."

"I bet you were cute when you were a toddler," Holly said.

"The second time was when Dad died." Callum pressed into Holly, his body quivering. "She came to the cottage with a currant cake she'd baked herself. I remember because it was in a tin for Murray's Malt Crackers. I couldn't get my head around why a cake was in a cracker tin."

"Did she say anything?" Holly asked.

"Yeah. She was talking about my father, heaping praise on him, but I kept staring at the tin. Not listening. On the outside, it was one thing. On the inside, it was another."

Callum's nose twitched and he stared at the line of conifers along the track to Bellcraig Stack.

"You never can tell with some people," Holly said. "It was good of her to bring you something."

"The whole village came when they heard about Dad, but she was the first."

A dampness soaked through Holly's walking boots. Not only did they rub painfully, she realised, but they also let in water. "Did Nancy know your Dad?"

"He never mentioned her. Never spoke of anyone, but the Wentworths."

A call came from the conifer forest, a creature in fear or distress.

"I wanted to come here and say goodbye properly," Holly said.

"Goodbye?"

"This is the end. I can't keep doing what I'm doing."

Callum gazed at her. "I don't understand. Was it something I said?"

"More like something I said."

Returning his eyes to the forest, Callum cracked his knuckles. "You're good at what you do. You'll find Nancy. You will."

"Good at what?" Holly asked. "Making people miserable? I have to stop. Derek is going to leave me."

Callum spun in her direction. His arms wrapped around her and she was pulled into his body, her head pressed into his chest. His heart drummed into her and his heat brought a flush to her cheeks.

"Don't make this any harder than it has to be," she whispered. "I want to make my marriage work."

Holly raised her face and his lips pressed into her ear.

"Arnold Salting," he said. "He's watching us from the trees."

Holly struggled in Callum's grasp, but he held tight.

"He's been here since I turned up," he said. "I don't want to spook him."

Holly's view was blocked by Callum's shoulder. She eased to one side and saw the murk of the forest. Was that a figure in the distance? It was hard to tell. The longer she stared, the more figures she saw. Some appeared in clothing that looked centuries old, as if they'd been lost in the forest and had never returned home.

"I won't let him get away this time," Callum said.

They remained locked in an embrace, cheek to cheek, with neither willing to let go.

"What are we going to do?" she asked.

"He left Black Rock Manor when we discovered his little camp," Callum said.

"Not to mention Regina's body."

"Maybe he moved into Bellcraig Stack afterwards," Callum said. "He knew Nancy was missing. He hurt Regina so he had somewhere else to stay."

"Which doesn't answer my question," Holly said. "What are we going to do now?"

The green of Callum's eyes took on a darker hue. "When you're stalking your quarry, you move soft and you move light."

Taking Holly's hand, he led her through the rhubarb, keeping to the shadow of the house. A woodshed had been built by the kitchen door. Its warped walls were dotted with yellow lichen. It was surrounded by the same flowers Holly had noticed on her first visit.

She stroked her hand through the spires to have it snatched away by Callum.

"Foxgloves," Callum said. "Like the sisters of the same name, they can be a little bit poisonous."

He dragged her into the woodshed and crouched low.

"We need to flush him out," Callum said.

Holly peeked through the slats, seeing nothing. "Are you expecting me to rugby tackle him? Do I look like a scrum-half?"

153

"No, but you have the same cauliflower ears." Picking up a dried log, Callum offered it to Holly. "Use this if things turn nasty."

Holly weighed it in her hand, rolling it around her palm.

"Ow," she said, dropping it to the ground. "Splinter."

"This is going to be chasing Nancy's goat all over again," Callum said, spying through a gap in the shed. "I think he's gone. Wait here."

Callum crept around her, keeping low. Holly watched him go, grinding her teeth. She remembered falling at the manor when she'd failed to heed Callum's words, but her feet started moving anyway, copying Callum's movements.

She found him crouching behind a gooseberry bush.

Callum jumped as she sidled in beside him.

"Do you ever do what you're told?" he asked.

"This guy is dangerous," Holly said. "He's unstable."

"Which is why I don't want him wandering around my estate."

"It's not your estate anymore. It belongs to the Masterlys."

Reaching in the bush, unmindful of the thorns, Callum jerked a gooseberry free. It was over-ripe with a coating of powdery mildew. He crushed it between his thumb and forefinger, watching the pulpy juice run down his hand.

"I'm going hunting," Callum said, "and this time, Holly? Stay here."

Callum broke cover, hurrying along the garden, his eyes trained on the forest. He leapt over the garden fence, landing deftly on the other side.

Holly peeked over the fence in time to see him disappear into the darkness. She waited, scanning the forest. It was silent. Even the wildlife held its breath. The ghosts, if that's what they were, had faded.

Holly dropped back down and studied her nails.

If there was any kind of struggle between Callum and Arnold Salting, she assumed she'd hear it. But then what? Would she rush to Callum's aid? Holly was likely to get in the way, but sitting on the side lines wasn't her style.

The Defender, she thought. If Callum got hurt or more likely Arnold, then they'd want to be on their way to the hospital as soon as possible. With a second glance at the forest, Holly stole toward the jeep. There was a rustling, branches were snapped, but she didn't turn to look. Her eyes were drawn to the Defender's windscreen.

"He's gone," Callum said, jogging to her side. "I don't know where."

"I do," Holly said, reading the words written in the dirt of the glass. "He was here."

It was another clue, though not as cryptic as the one pinned to the Herald's door.

Cursing, Callum spun on the spot. "How the chuff did he get by me?"

It didn't matter, Holly thought, rubbing the raised goosepimples on her arm. Arnold had got past Callum to within yards of where Holly was waiting and she didn't like it. Neither did she like the words on Callum's windscreen.

They read, 'You Stole From Me,' and for the first time since arriving, Holly wanted to return to London.

Chapter Twenty-Nine

"How can we be sure he'll turn up?" Holly asked.

They lay under camouflage netting high on Caitloon Hill. The sun threw a spotlight on an intersection of roads. They came from the north, south, east and west of the estate. It wasn't dead centre, but it was close. The ruins of a farmhouse stood nearby, a place for animals to shelter through the night.

Callum lay on his front, propped up on his elbows with Holly lying behind him. He lowered his binoculars, but continued to stare at the salmon tins he'd left by the road.

"It's a feeling," he said.

"So Mr Winnow was transporting the plant bulbs for Arnold Salting?"

"Think about it," Callum said. "Mr Winnow was told to take the bulbs to Black Rock Manor where Arnold was staying. Only I got in the way and now he wants them back."

"This is a feeling then?" Holly asked. "That's why I'm up here lying on rocks?"

"Arnold isn't deranged. His brother lied." Callum twisted the binocular straps around his knuckles. "It's easier to dismiss someone when they're labelled that way. Dad said that. Call them mad and you rob them of their voice."

"He attacked Mr Winnow. He stole Nancy's file. As far as we know, he may have killed her," Holly said, jabbing her own binoculars at him.

"He definitely left Regina for dead."

"I'm not saying he isn't dangerous," Callum said, "but he's been roaming this estate without me catching hide nor hair of him. That's not easy. Not to mention, he devised a pretty smart way of smuggling those bulbs onto the estate."

"That doesn't explain why you think he'll fall for your trap."

"He wants those bulbs," Callum said. "Anyone who goes to those kinds of lengths won't give up. Arnold must have been so angry when he realised his delivery wasn't going to arrive. While he was trying to figure out what went wrong, I'd already taken them."

Wriggling into a more comfortable position, Holly gasped as yet another rock jabbed into her body. "So we wait until he turns up?"

"I'm surprised you're here at all. I thought you were giving up."

"That's not fair," she said.

"You don't give up just because things are getting difficult."

"I suppose your Dad said that as well, did he? What a fountain of knowledge."

Callum looked at her over his shoulder. "And you deliver a goodbye like I should simply accept it."

He turned away, leaving Holly to stare at the back of his head. With a sigh, she shuffled forward, dragging the camouflage netting with her, exposing them both to the eyes of the estate. Callum reached around her and pulled it taut.

"Coming home was supposed to be a fresh start," Holly said. "It was going to make things better."

"It has."

"For who?" Holly asked, lying on another rock. "If Derek doesn't get a job soon, we'll have to leave regardless. I'll probably have to sell the cottage."

Callum was motionless, only his breath and the movement of his chest gave him away. He was like the hill they lay upon; part of a larger landscape that didn't need to shift and jump to prove it was there.

"Your parents left you that cottage for a reason," he said.

"Maybe they knew I needed a safety net."

"What happened to them?"

In the distance, Holly thought she could see the deer. Like Callum, they were part of the estate. Like her parents had been.

"Dad died of CWP. Coal workers' pneumoconiosis." Holly picked up a stone and rolled it around her hand. "Mam died two days later. She wound down like a broken clock. I wasn't there for either of them."

"You were making a life for yourself," Callum said. "Like they expected you to."

"What kind of daughter only visits her parents after they die?"

Callum took the stone from her hand and placed it on top of a carpet of moss. "You're here now. Part of the place as much as anyone else. They'd be proud of you."

"Proud?" Holly asked with a snort. "What difference am I making to Little Belton?"

"You made a difference to Old Jack because he's relying on you," Callum said. "Nancy, too. The Winnows and Big Gregg. They all have a new friend because you're here. This isn't about one person. It's about everyone as a whole, working and living together."

Holly gazed at the contours of the land, around trees that were beginning to bud and onto streams gathering fragments of sunlight in their ripples. Her eyes went to the horizon where she saw the rooftops of Little Belton. They were undefined, like a stubborn smudge on the lens of her binoculars, but no matter how many times she had attempted to wipe it away, it remained.

Holly and Callum were the only two people for miles around. They were in an estate so vast, they could disappear without anyone ever finding them, but under the netting, snuggled shoulder to shoulder, Holly's world shrank to a pair of green eyes refusing to look at her.

"I'm sorry I made you think I was going to leave you," she whispered. Callum pressed his head gently against hers, his lips an inch from hers.

"Then you'll stay?" he asked.

"I thought you'd set this trap for someone else," Holly said with a smile. "Were you trying to get me up here on my own?"

Callum poked out his tongue. "I had nothing but honourable intentions. We're here because of a feeling."

"And what are you feeling now?" Holly asked.

"Right now, I'm feeling like Arnold has been following you."

Holly sat up abruptly, the netting draping over her face, like the veil of a dark bride. She yanked it free and threw it to one side. Callum tried to cover them again, but Holly batted his attempts away.

"He's been following me?" she asked.

Callum swallowed. "It's the only explanation. The best way to avoid detection is to stay close to your quarry. It's every predator's first instinct. They stay close and wait."

"Wait for what?"

"An opportunity. Everybody knows you're investigating Nancy's disappearance. When his bulbs got shipwrecked, it wouldn't have taken him long to figure out you're involved in that disappearance, too."

"That was you," Holly said. "Not me."

"It was both of us," Callum said.

Holly glanced around her, searching the shadows, but there were too many. If Arnold Salting was following her, he could be anywhere.

"And how long have you known this?" she asked, recalling her suspicions as she sat by Knock Lake.

"I told you," Callum said, his face strained. "It's just a feeling. How else would he know we had the bulbs? And I reckon he's trailed us to this hill and he's figuring out how to get those bulbs without us getting to him first. Which is why I've left them out in the open for the world to see."

Undoing her jacket, Holly tried to get more comfortable. It seemed like a long shot. And a long wait if Callum was wrong, but if he was right, it meant Arnold had been following her.

Holly didn't know which option she preferred. "Does that mean you're using me as bait?"

Callum pointed down the ridge to a shape weaving along a track from the north. "Look. I was right."

As the shape grew closer, they saw it was a car, the sound of the engine confirming it needed a tune-up. It approached carefully, slowing around bends, pausing on crests, as if searching for something.

Callum and Holly watched it through their binoculars.

"He knows we're out here," Callum said. "As soon as he stops, we rush him."

"We?" Holly asked.

"Okay, me, but we have to get within striking distance."

Holly adjusted the sights on her binoculars, focusing on the car. It was a hatchback with dinted wings. A crucifix swung like a pendulum from the rearview mirror.

"This doesn't feel right," she said. "How did Arnold get his hands on a car?"

Jamming the netting into a rucksack, Callum threw it over his shoulder.

The driver was hidden behind the glare of the windscreen, but Holly saw him unfold a paper map, consulting it as he crawled along.

"If this guy has been watching me," Holly said, "you'd expect him to know where he's going."

The car stopped ten feet from the salmon tins. They were in full sight, stacked neatly and looking at odds with the wilderness they inhabited.

Callum scratched his chin, making no move to descend from the ridge.

The driver got from the car and gazed around. He was a portly man in his sixties with ruddy cheeks and a perplexed look on his face. His beard was twisted into a ponytail and he played with it nervously. He walked to the tinned salmon and propped his hands onto his hips.

"I don't believe it," Callum said. "It's Reverend Applecroft."

Chapter Thirty

The vicarage was reached through a rainbow garden of the Reverend's design. Swathes of purple crocuses nestled under the boughs of blossoming magnolia, their flowers like cups catching the morning dew. Green leaves unfurled and the first of the spring insects took succour from the nectar.

The building itself nestled in the church grounds. It was stern looking with a red brick face, but the inside was at odds with first appearances. Holly and Callum sat on the edge of a tweed sofa, afraid to disturb the array of cushions behind them. Some were embroidered with flowers. Others with verses from the New Testament.

The Reverend's partner Bryan had introduced himself when they arrived. He gave a handshake to Callum and a hug to Holly. He was younger than the Reverend, but sported the same ruddy cheeks. He had a gap between his front teeth when he smiled, which was often and without discernible reason.

Bryan served tea on a tray, placing it on a wooden coffee table embossed with an image of the Turin Shroud. "Sugar or lemon?" he asked.

In the corner of the room was a gilded cage housing a black bird with golden patches around its eyes. It hopped along its perch, ruffling its feathers and barking like a dog.

"Give it a bleedin' rest." Bryan grimaced at Holly and Callum.

"Casandra is a Mynah bird."

"Are those the ones that talk?" Callum asked.

Bryan worked fingers into his temples. "Supposedly, yeah. We adopted her from a parishioner who couldn't look after her anymore. What we didn't know was that the parishioner also had two Jack Russells. Instead of talking, Cassandra learned to yap like a dog." He got from his seat and draped a cover over the cage. "Still, she's good for deterring burglars."

"Where is the Reverend?" Holly asked.

"I think you rattled the old bugger," he said, dropping sugar cubes into china cups. "He's drawing himself together in the bathroom. Won't be long."

Holly sipped her tea, enjoying the warmth. "We didn't mean to startle him."

Bryan waved her concerns aside. "He's harder than he looks. Worked the mines when he was a boy, but he knew it wasn't for him. Taking up the Bible was harder than taking up a pickaxe in those days. You might say he saw God's light at the end of the coal tunnel." He wheezed, his laugh whistling through the gap in his teeth. "Battenberg cake?"

On the tray was a teapot with steam curling from its spout. There were four cups, bowls of sugar and slices of lemon, together with wedges of cake, a selection of cheese scones and a tower of sausage rolls threatening to spill onto the carpet.

"Sorry about that," the Reverend said, entering the room. He had changed into a tracksuit, though his round stomach said it was more for comfort than exercise.

"Did you have any Battenberg?" he asked.

"Not yet," Callum said. "We'd prefer to ask you some questions first, if you don't mind?"

The Reverend walked around a room crammed with battered furniture and chipped vases. The walls groaned under the weight of paintings and framed photographs. A fire raged in the hearth, keeping the occupants warm.

He tugged on his ponytail beard as he joined them around the Jesus table. "I'll do what I can."

"Who told you to find those tins?" Holly asked, a chewed Biro pen in her hand.

The Reverend frowned. "You did."

The notebook slipped from Holly's grasp and her fingers struggled to pick it back up. When she straightened, the Reverend was peering at her over the rim of his glasses.

"Of course, I realise now that I was duped," he said.

"Someone pretending to be me asked you to the intersection?" Holly asked.

Bryan poured a cup of tea, dropping in a lemon slice and gave it to the Reverend. "His heart is bigger than his head, sometimes, but he can never ignore a person in need."

"What did they say?" Holly asked.

"It was a phone call. I was in the vestry and the line there isn't very good."

"They ought to fix it," Bryan said, nibbling on a scone. "Hardly our fault."

"The cows use the telephone poles as scratching posts," the Reverend said. "Can't hear a thing. All because some bovine has an itchy bum."

Callum held up a hand. "If you don't mind, you were talking about a phone call?"

The Reverend nodded. "Sorry," he said. "I'm a little shaken up since you ambushed me."

Seeing the Reverend loading the tinned salmon into his car, Callum and Holly had rushed down the hillside. Callum was leagues ahead while Holly struggled to stay upright, swearing she could hear a rattle in her lungs. The Reverend turned in fright at their arrival. Callum had snatched the tins away, loading them into the hessian sack.

Holly did her best to offer an explanation between gasps, but together with her red face and shaking limbs, they thought it best to retire to the vicarage for tea and cake.

"We should have handled that better," Holly said, rubbing her aching legs, "but if you could tell me what they said, I'd appreciate it."

With a slurp of hot tea, the Reverend continued. "She introduced herself as you and said you'd had a car accident. She said you were fine, but you'd spilled your shopping all over the road. It was a driving hazard."

"Why contact you?" Holly asked. "Why not my husband?"

"Presumably because I don't know your voice very well. I've only ever heard you shouting at Mr Masterly. I was an easy target."

Bryan placed a hand on the Reverend's knee and gave him a tender look.

"What else did they say?" Holly asked.

"Not much. Your car was out of commission and would I mind retrieving your shopping. I said, I'd be happy, too."

"I know this might seem weird," Callum said, "but are you sure it was a woman?"

Holly's face flushed, but she bit her tongue. She knew why Callum was asking. It wasn't a woman they were hoping to trap.

A grandfather clock chimed somewhere in the vicarage. Its bell was deep and sonorous, commanding attention. The Reverend let it sound while he considered his answer.

"The line was bad and now I'm not really sure of anything," he said, "but I think so. It could have been."

"So, it could have been a man pretending to be me?" Holly asked.

"I don't know," the Reverend said. He put down his cup, spilling a puddle of grey tea into his saucer. "Why on earth were you buying all that tinned salmon anyway? Mr Winnow does an excellent range of fresh fish."

"Tell me about it," Callum said into his chest.

Holly rubbed her face and got to her feet. She was drawn to the window over-looking the rainbow garden.

"Which one of you is the horticulturist?" she asked.

"That would be Bryan," the Reverend said. "He's the expert. I'm just the lump at the end of a spade."

Bryan brushed scone crumbs from his front and beamed. "I wouldn't say expert, but I have an interest."

Holly turned back into the room. "That wasn't my shopping and those tins don't contain salmon."

She nodded at Callum, who produced the tin he'd shown to Mr Winnow. It was already open and he tilted the contents toward Bryan. "Do you recognise this bulb?"

Bryan held it up to the shaft of light coming from the window. He spun it around slowly, his lips pursed in concentration.

"Well, it's not a bulb for starters," he said. "It's a corm. They're smaller than bulbs meaning the flowers are usually smaller, too. Wait here a second."

He bustled out of the room, taking the corm with him.

"You haven't told me what this is all about," the Reverend said.

"We're trying to find Nancy Foxglove," Holly said, retaking her seat, together with a sausage roll for good measure.

"And these corms have something to do with that?" the Reverend asked.

Holly shrugged. "Do you know much about the two sisters?" she asked, churning pastry around her mouth.

The Reverend handed Holly a serviette to wipe her chin of crumbs.

"Not much at all. They weren't very sociable," he said. "Not church-goers. I once asked them to buy a raffle ticket for the tombola. They gave me such a stare, I couldn't sleep for a week."

"Someone must know something," Holly said.

"I've heard the story from Old Jack," the Reverend said, "same as everyone else. How both the sisters went missing. How they survived the cold. It didn't seem right to me, but then, I didn't know them very well. There's another story I think is true, though."

"What's that?" Holly asked, swallowing the last of the sausage roll.

"They didn't like each other very much."

"Who told you that?"

"It was just gossip. Snippets you pick up." The Reverend clasped his hands over his round stomach. "I'd see them in The Travelling Star now and then. They'd eat their meal in silence. Never spoke to each other."

"That sounds like every couple who've been together too long," Holly said. "Doesn't mean they don't like each other."

Holly had rushed to the Foxglove's defence too quickly and she shifted in her chair. Most of her evenings with Derek were spent that way.

"You're right, but if Nancy didn't like the cold, why did she spend so much time out wandering around the estate away from her sister?" the Reverend asked.

Bryan returned to the room, swinging a large book in his arms like a baby. Pushing the teapot and cups aside, he laid it flat on the table.

"The Flowering Bulb Dictionary," he said.

The book looked well-thumbed with a soil stain on its cover.

"Seems like a favourite of yours," Holly said.

"Books are what we have instead of the internet," Bryan said. "There isn't a flower growing in Northumberland that won't be in here."

"So did you find the name of the corm?"

"Nope, but then books don't come with Google search. It's going to take some time."

Rather than watch Bryan flick through the dictionary's pages, Holly and Callum decided to leave him to it. After her gallop down the hillside, Holly was hungry and took two more sausage rolls. Bryan confirmed he would keep searching for the mysterious corm and Holly and Callum went outside to the Defender.

"There's something odd about the Reverend's story," Holly said.

"Which one?" Callum asked. "The one about Nancy and Regina? Or how he came to find the salmon?"

Holly kicked the tyre of his jeep. "We've both met Regina," she said. "I'd prefer to brave the weather than spend a lifetime with her. Plus we already know the truth behind Old Jack's story. No, I'm talking about the phone call."

"He doesn't know if the person who called was a man or a woman. Do you think he was telling lies?"

"No, I think he was being manipulated," Holly said. "It was his explanation of why they'd called that felt strange. He's right about Derek. He would have known the voice on the phone wasn't me, but there are other people they could have chosen. Old Jack. Big Gregg. The Winnows. Like he said, I've never really spoken to the Reverend. Why choose him?"

"His name starts with an A. Maybe he was just the first person they found in the directory?"

Holly watched a fledgling chaffinch swaying on the tip of a lilac tree. Its feathers stuck out at odd angles, the chirping beak too big for its body. The parent chaffinch fed the fledgling and flew off in search of more unfortunate grubs.

"Did you believe what Bryan said about the Reverend?" Holly asked. "About him looking after his flock so enthusiastically?"

Callum nodded. "He's devoted to this village. Everyone knows that."

"That's my problem," Holly said. "Everyone knows that. I think that's why he was chosen. He'd do anything to help. They knew he would go along with whatever he was told."

"So, what? He's a good guy."

"Do you think Arnold Salting would know a detail like that?"

"He's from Crockfoot. He doesn't know his partridge from his pear tree."

"Exactly, which makes me think it was someone else. Someone who knows Reverend Applecroft, possibly the same person who knows Little Belton has a terrible internet connection and went to Crockfoot to email Mr Winnow."

Callum's face twisted into a sneer. "They're from the village? No way. That's awful."

"I don't want to believe it, but with the Masterlys involved, who knows? People are hurting and money talks."

Opening the jeep door, Callum looked over his shoulder at Holly. "Even if you're right, what did they actually achieve?"

He slipped off his jacket, preparing to throw it on top of the hessian sack. The jacket never left his hand and his mouth dropped open.

"Ah, that's what Arnold was doing," he said, staring at the space where the sack used to be. "He followed us here. He's taken the bloody bulbs."

Chapter Thirty-One

They drove through the centre of Little Belton. A silence hung over them like a cobweb. Holly and Callum were fearful of disturbing it. To do so would start an argument and anxiety levels were already high.

Callum rarely locked the Defender. Little Belton wasn't that kind of place, but Holly clearly remembered her words to him when they discovered the corms. That they were dangerous. That they were valuable. Two important reasons to lock the damn jeep.

They passed the Masterlys' media hub. Residents dropped in and out, going in empty-handed and leaving with a plastic glass of booze. On the other side of the green, Big Gregg hovered by his open door, his damp bar cloth over a broad shoulder.

"The Masterlys are winning," Holly said. "Big Gregg will be bankrupt soon and then they'll target someone else. Maybe the Winnows. Maybe you."

"I've got nothing for them to take," Callum said.

Holly breathed on the passenger window, misting it up. She drew a cross, watching droplets of water roll down the glass like tears.

"The Masterlys enjoy playing with us," she said.

"What do you mean?" Callum asked.

Holly recounted her meeting with Mrs Masterly in the Herald's offices, though she omitted the fact she'd been caught snooping around Old Jack's office. Or the embarrassing comparisons made between Mrs

Masterly's expensive handbag and her own.

"Why else would she be there?" Holly asked. "Other than to watch my face fall when I hear about the appeal process?"

Callum pursed his lips and placed a heavy foot on the accelerator.

Clearing the houses of Little Belton and approaching the estate, Callum lunged down a side track cutting through a green verge of ferns. Their fronds brushed the side of the Defender, wiping dirt from its flanks as they went.

"Where are we going?" Holly asked.

Callum stopped by a beck where clear water bubbled over glassy stones. The water sounded like ringing bells as it headed toward the sea. Climbing from the Defender, Callum cupped his hand under the surface, allowing the water to pour from his fingers.

"The deer come here to drink," he said, pointing to a trail. "Their track marks look like arrows."

Stumbling on the cobbled shore, Holly stared at the ground. It had been whipped into a muddy meringue. If there were hoof marks there, Holly couldn't see them.

"Come on," Callum said, wading through the water and marching ahead. "We need to find them."

Within moments, he was a figure in the distance, weaving in and out of the landscape.

Holly's walking boots weren't waterproof, something she'd learned the hard way. The beck was three feet wide. The only way over was to jump and Holly reared up, preparing to launch. After a whispered countdown, she made a run for it, leaping over the water, clearing it easily.

But the deer's trail wasn't a sturdy landing pad and her feet slipped out from under her. Holly squealed, pitching forward into the mud. It splashed up in a wave, coating her in a brown film smelling of deer droppings.

Dragging herself along, Holly used ferns as a hand-hold. She didn't want Callum to see her prostrate again. It would be further confirmation she wasn't as outdoorsy as the rest of Little Belton. The mud gave way to a patch of grass and she clawed herself upright.

Callum was a speck on the horizon, but she caught up, surprised to find his face and clothes caked in mud.

He gave her an admiring glance. "Well done."

"I'm not as unfit as I look, you know?"

"No, I mean, you used earth to hide your scent from the animals. I didn't think you'd know how to do that."

Holly brushed muddy hair from her face and straightened her clothes. "Well, it's obvious, isn't it? I didn't want to give my position away."

"The deer are on the other side of these conifers," Callum said, placing a finger over his lips.

"Wait," Holly said. "What are we doing here?"

Callum crept under the branches of the forest with Holly holding her breath behind him. The floor was carpeted in brown pine needles. It was springy beneath her feet, but Holly had no intention of falling again. She had got away with it once, but twice would be pushing it. The light died and they trudged in silence until Holly saw flashes of a meadow through gaps in the trees.

"I planted that," Callum whispered.

The grasses were a foot high, flecked with blue flowers, like Christmas baubles hanging on tiny trees. They danced in the breeze, swaying to the inaudible music of the wilderness. Through the blue came ribbons of pink, the petals of the flowers so fine the sun shone straight through them.

Standing in the middle of the meadow, their heads held to the sun, was a herd of deer.

Callum hunkered on his knees, gesturing for Holly to do the same.

"There's too many of them," he said. "They're over-running the estate."

"They're beautiful," Holly said, her fingers covering her mouth.

"They're destructive. They'll devour this meadow and then move to someplace else."

"What will you do?" Holly asked, remembering Callum's rifle and his readiness to use it.

"Nothing without Mr Masterly's say-so. The shooting season is almost done. These deer are safe for now."

"But how can you shoot them?" Holly asked. "They're so majestic."

Callum ran his finger through a pile of pine needles, disturbing a sleeping beetle. He picked it up, allowing it to run over his hand as he studied it. "It's my job and it's not always easy. I do it because I care for them. They'd eat everything in their path if I let them and then they'd starve or become diseased. It's my job to protect them from that."

He lowered his hand and the beetle scurried for cover.

"I never thought about it like that," Holly said.

"It's how this place works," Callum said. "I told you, we all look after each other here, except I'm not holding up my side of the bargain. It's my job to cull them, to control their numbers so they don't damage the estate."

"There's hundreds of them," Holly said.

Callum glanced at the ground. "I can go weeks without seeing another person. Sometimes, these deer are all the company I have."

Holly understood Callum's reluctance to cull them. Although her two jobs were exhausting, she was glad of the people it brought her into contact with.

The herd shifted as one, a few steps, a nervous pause, their tales flicking left to right.

"They must be able to smell us," Callum said.

A large stag forced its way to the front. It was the same height as

Holly, but its body was broad and littered with welts. Its muscles worked like pistons moving under its fur.

"That's who we've come to see," Callum said. "That's Star."

There was something about the stag's august stature that felt familiar to Holly and she remembered her encounter on the journey home the night she knocked over the bird. It was the same deer. Holly was sure of it. She recalled the cross shaped mark on his chest.

Follow the Star, she thought.

Holly looked at Callum, but he was pointing at the stag. "You see that scar on his chest? That's where he gets his name from. He was my first ever shoot. My Dad took me out and it was a perfect hit to the heart. It should have killed him, but he stood back up. I went to try again, but Dad stopped me. He said, an animal that strong should be left to pass on his genes to the rest of the herd. We made sure he was okay, that he wasn't suffering and he's been my friend ever since."

"If that's how you make friends, I'm not surprised you live alone."

Star headed in their direction. He sniffed the air, his head raised like a king about to address his subjects.

"He's never come this close before," Callum said, grinning like an excited schoolboy.

"Maybe that's because you shot him," Holly said.

"He's old and suffering," Callum said. "I should have dealt with him this year."

Holly swallowed. "Dealt with him?"

"It would be kinder, better for the herd if I did my job properly, but he's been in my life longer than anyone else. I can't finish him now. Truth is, I can't kill any of them. I've not had the stomach for it since my Dad died."

"Do you think the person who sent the note knew that?"

Callum scratched at his temple. "Maybe this is the Star we were meant to follow. He wanders every inch of the estate. He could lead us somewhere."

The stag skirted the outside of the trees, casting a shadow darker than the forest. Holly heard him breathing, saw the moisture misting from his nostrils.

Star looked at her. His eyes were dark, almost human, asking silent questions of her.

Was she a friend or foe? An ally or a threat?

Later, when she was home, listening to her husband snoring beside her, she would swear Callum had reacted before the gunshot. In her memory, he was already rising from the ground when the crack split the air. The herd scattered, kicking out their hind legs as they ran. She remembered thinking – who would be stupid enough to release a firework so close to these beautiful animals?

It was the pain in Callum's face that had awoken her to reality. He stood there, his mouth misshapen with panic. He took a few steps forward and seemed to come to his senses, returning to bundle Holly to the ground. The wind was knocked from her lungs and she gasped, but Callum refused to move. Lying on her back, she felt his heart hammer against her own. Holly wriggled free enough to keep watch on the meadow, staring at Star stumbling through the grass. He fell. He got back up. He fell again.

Star's previous wound was masked in fresh blood. Like Holly, he was struggling to breathe. His eyes searched her face. They were wide and frightened. His eyelids flickered closed and his chest rose for the last time.

And Holly swore she heard him cry.

Happy voices of congratulation filled the meadow. A knot tightened in her stomach when Holly recognised one of them. It had an American twang, a Californian drawl. Footsteps grew closer. Mr Masterly appeared with a group of men, his rifle cocked over his arm, the barrel still smoking.

They stood over Star's body. A cigar was offered to a grinning Mr Masterly and Callum was no longer on top of her, no longer protecting her from gunshot.

He was racing toward Mr Masterly.

Chapter Thirty-Two

Holly chased after Callum, adrenaline driving her rubbery legs, but it wasn't enough. He broke through the lining on the trees ahead of her, trampling through the flowers he'd planted.

The smile froze on Mr Masterly's face, his smouldering cigar idling in his hand. The chorus of men behind him were dressed in tweed and wore green wellies to their knees. Each took a step back as Callum bolted toward them, but Mr Masterly stood firm.

"Cal, dude," he said. "Just the man I was looking for."

Holly emerged into the meadow, skidding to a halt at Star's dead body.

There was no hesitation from Callum. He rounded on Mr Masterly, his right fist cutting through the air. Mr Masterly pivoted on his heel. His forearm shot upwards, protecting his head.

Callum's fist connected, but landed no damage. He swung again, but Mr Masterly was ready. He crouched, his leg sweeping through Callum's, his smile widening.

Crumpling, Callum fell onto his back, gasping.

"Stop it," shouted Holly, but Callum jumped to his feet and leapt forward.

Mr Masterly slapped the attack away. He spun in a graceful arc and drove a fist into Callum's stomach.

Once again, the gamekeeper crumpled to the ground. Holly rushed over, throwing defensive arms around him.

"Leave him alone," Holly shouted.

"Jeet Kun Do, dude," Mr Masterly said, tucking his fist into his other hand and bowing. "The way of Bruce Lee."

"What do you think you're doing?" Holly asked.

"Kicking ass," one of the group said in an American accent, instigating a round of whoops from the others.

"I was showing my friends around the estate," Mr Masterly said. "As no one has bothered with culling these deer, we thought we'd better start."

"Shooting season is over," Callum said, wiping his mouth with the back of his hand.

"Almost over," Mr Masterly said, "and it's my right as the landowner to host a shoot."

Callum stood, rubbing dirt off his clothes and went to Star's side. His jaw was set. He blinked, once, twice and turned away.

Holly caught his eye and they looked at one another to the din of the American voices. For the first time since meeting him, Holly saw Callum's true age. He was a young man alone in a life that had known isolation. His father was gone. Star had been taken. His shoulders weren't strong enough to bear a grief so weighty.

"We'll be okay," Holly said, placing an arm around his waist.

"Will we?"

"How are your butchery skills, dude?" Mr Masterly said, shouting over from his friends. "I figure I've done your job by shooting that stag. The least you can do is make sure we have a venison dinner tonight."

"Why are you doing this?" Holly asked Mr Masterly.

He mimed eating, using an invisible knife and fork to cut the air. "Tuck in. There's enough for everyone."

"People like you don't share," Callum said.

"I've been very generous with you," Mr Masterly said, wagging his finger. "You run out of the forest like a mad dude and attack me. I didn't make a thing of it. No one was hurt, after all, but you're crossing a line here."

A shadow passed over Callum's face. "I gave you the benefit of the doubt. I've wanted to be part of something for so long that I turned a blind eye to what you were."

"And what's that?" Mr Masterly asked.

"Not fit to live in Black Rock Manor," Callum said.

"I'm sorry you feel that way, Cal," Mr Masterly said, turning to his friends. "No venison today, guys. Why don't we fly to London for sushi? I own a great place there."

Mr Masterly's friends consented with a round of high-fives. None of them, including Mr Masterly, looked at Holly and Callum again. They marched to the Range Rover, chattering like monkeys.

"I'm not leaving Star to be picked apart by Black Eye Bobby," Callum said. "I want to bury him."

Holly didn't say anything and followed him back through the trees to the Defender. They didn't have any spades, but Callum's cottage was only three miles away.

"I've got stuff at the house," he said, mangling the steering wheel while he drove.

With the sun racing toward the horizon, Holly watched Callum from the corner of her eye. She steeled herself. There was no way she was going to allow the Masterlys to win. Not after witnessing how cold Mr Masterly really was. Holly wasn't going to give up. They'd find Nancy and discover what she knew about the take-over of Little Belton. Together they'd stop the village from turning into a car park for the Masterlys' Adventureland.

"I'm sorry about Star," Holly said as they neared the cottage.

Callum's knuckles whitened.

"I know this isn't the right time, but can I ask you a question?"

179

Callum nodded stiffly.

"Do you think that's what the note meant?" she asked. "The person who wrote it. Do you think they meant follow Star and see what the Masterlys do to him?"

Callum slowed the jeep before pulling into his driveway. He parked and stared at his front door.

"What the hell is that?" he asked.

Over the door, yellow and black tape formed the shape of a cross. The lock had been broken and replaced with a padlock. Nailed to the frame was an envelope protected by plastic.

Callum tore it open, his lips moving as he read. When he finished, he handed it to Holly, who scanned it quickly.

"It's an eviction notice," she said.

"It wasn't there when I left this morning."

"Citing none payment of rent."

"I didn't have anyone to pay it to," Callum said, pacing along the walls of his locked home. "Where am I going to go?"

"You can stay with me until we get this sorted," Holly said.

"Derek would love that, wouldn't he?" Callum asked. "I'll take a room at The Travelling Star. Big Gregg could do with the business."

"You can't do that. You haven't been paid in years."

"I'll work something out," Callum said, kicking at a tuft of grass. "I had a dust-up with Mr Masterly less than half an hour ago. How could he get me evicted so quickly?"

Holly read the notice again. "He didn't," she said. "Look at the date."

She pointed at the corner of the paper and Callum frowned.

"It's today," he said quietly.

"You'd already been evicted by the time we met him in the meadow."

Chapter Thirty-Three

Holly lingered by Derek's newly erected shed, a cup of hot coffee in her hand. The steam rose ghost-like, fading to nothing in the early morning light. Birds flitted between trees, singing as they flew, but turning silent when they landed amidst the growing foliage.

She had never been this close to the shed before, sensing her presence wasn't welcome. It was Derek's shrine to their failing marriage or a folly he'd erected in memory of it. She could no longer claim it was a waste of money. Derek spent more time in it than in the house. The door was bolted shut and she listened to him shuffling around inside.

"What are you doing here?"

She jumped at the voice. Derek stood behind her, tightening the belt around his dressing robe. His skin was the colour of clay, his face baked hard in the heat of another hangover.

The shed was as silent as the birds in the trees. Holly glanced at it and then at Derek, motioning the coffee cup toward him.

"Thought you could do with some," she said.

Derek took it, looking at it suspiciously. "Thanks."

A mist had settled over Knock Lake, masking the dark waters beneath. A disembodied duck's head cut through it as it made its way to a muddy bank. Gliding to a stop, it dipped through the mist and water with a splash. Holly waited for it to re-emerge, but it was lost in the murk.

"So what are you doing today?" she asked Derek.

"Do you have to?"

Holly's stomach sank. "What do you mean? What are you talking about?"

Derek lowered the coffee from his lips. "I can organise my own day."

"I was only asking."

"Well, don't. I don't need the extra pressure, thanks."

"I won't ask again, okay? Do what you want."

"I will," Derek said, pouring his coffee to the ground. "I suppose you'll be out with the gamekeeper?"

The duck re-appeared, pondweed trailing from its beak. Some things were meant to float, Holly thought. Others destined to sink.

"I told you, there's nothing going on, honey," Holly said.

"Honey?" Derek asked, arching an eyebrow. "Now, I am worried."

"Forget it," Holly said, throwing her hands in the air. "Forget it."

"That's right. Walk away. Like you always do."

Holly jabbed a finger at Derek. "I was going to spend the day here. See if we could talk like adults, but you make it impossible to stay."

Their argument was interrupted by the sound of a groaning engine. Mr Winnow and his olive-green delivery truck trundled into view. Holly saw him through the windscreen. His face was puce and sweaty as if he had run up the hill rather than driven up it.

Holly went to the truck and Mr Winnow wound down his window, sending a sideways glance at Derek.

"Can I have a word, Mrs Fleet?" he asked in a low voice.

"This won't take a minute," Holly said to Derek, expecting him to leave, perhaps disappear into his shed.

But Derek adjusted a gap in his dressing robe and waited.

"What is it?" she asked Mr Winnow.

He picked at the window's rubber seal. "Do you remember our last chat? You didn't tell anyone about it, did you?"

Holly shook her head. "We said we wouldn't. Why do you ask?"

Finished with picking at the window, Mr Winnow began peeling flecks of reindeer paint from his fingers.

"I got another email," he said. "Asking for a delivery."

"Of bulbs?" Holly asked.

Mr Winnow nodded and opened the passenger door. "Might be good if you come with me this time. Make sure I don't get into any trouble."

Holly looked to her husband. "I won't be long. I promise."

Derek forced a smile and sloped into his shed.

A cold wind whipped around her shoulders and Holly climbed into Mr Winnow's truck. "The email? I'm guessing they didn't give a name this time either?"

"It was from Crockfoot again," Mr Winnow said, attempting an eighteen-point turn in the small driveway.

Holly kept watch on the shed's door, picturing Derek's glowering face behind it. It was all his fault anyway, she thought. He'd been abrasive and unpleasant. Who would want to spend time with him?

An unexpected pang in her chest answered her question and Holly's hand went to the door handle, ready to leap out.

Deadbolts on the shed door shimmered in the morning light. They looked new and Holly couldn't remember seeing them before.

There'd been noises in the shed this morning. Holly was sure it had been her husband. Who else could it have been? But Derek had appeared behind her, leaving Holly pondering over the new locks.

Mr Winnow made the last of his wrenching yanks on the steering wheel and they faced downhill to Little Belton.

"Judy's done a new spoken word cassette, if you fancy it?" he asked. "This one's a Stephen King."

Holly shook her head. "Tell me more about the email."

Jamming his foot on the accelerator, Mr Winnow careened along the road. "Well, they said, there was no more point in hiding."

"Who did?" Holly asked.

"A guy called Arnold. Do you know him?"

Chapter Thirty-Four

"Where are we going?" Callum asked.

He was wedged in the passenger seat next to Holly, his knees locked together, his arms folded on top of one another.

"The email said to go to Hamley village," Mr Winnow said.

"Why? What's there?"

They'd decided to collect Callum on the way. He'd been involved in this from the beginning and Holly wanted to take his mind off losing his home. Mr Winnow didn't argue and was probably pleased with the extra help. His face was still puce. He fiddled with the broken radio, pressing the buttons over and over again, receiving nothing but static.

The seatbelt latch bit into Holly's right hip. Callum was too close, pressing in too hard. She gave him a shove, angling for extra room.

"I can barely move here," Callum said, shoving back.

"Stop it," Holly said.

"No, you stop it."

"Both of you stop it," Mr Winnow said, "or I'll turn this van around. Understand?"

Callum and Holly lowered their heads. "Yes, Mr Winnow."

Holly stared out of the windscreen as they traversed the A69 to Hamley village. There was no traffic to distract her. The fields by the road were empty. This was the Northumberland she remembered as a child. Rolling green hills of nothingness, studded with crumbling farmhouses. There was no life to be had, no adventure.

"Why does he want us to go to Hamley village?" Callum asked.

"To pick up a delivery of his bulbs from the pub," Mr Winnow said.

The Vallum pub was the only one in the village. Holly recalled it was named after a nearby Roman earthworks, but couldn't be sure. According to her Dad, the Romans stayed for seventeen years before being driven mad by the woad faced Picts and their superstitions.

The pub was a two-storey building made from local stone. Its slate roof was pitted with green moss and smoke drifted from the chimney.

Mr Winnow parked away from the main entrance and scanned the walls of the pub.

"What are you looking for?" Holly asked.

"CCTV cameras," Mr Winnow said. "I don't want any record of me being here."

Callum wiped condensation from the passenger window for a better view of the car park. "For a poacher, you're pretty nervous about getting into trouble."

"I'm not a poacher," Mr Winnow said. "I'm an entrepreneur."

"An entrepreneur who steals fish from the estate," Callum said.

Holly held up her hands. "Guys, we're all a little nervous. This is a nervous situation. Can we just go over what we're doing here please?"

Mr Winnow reached for the broken radio and Holly slapped his hand away.

"And stop playing with that," she said.

"I was told to come to the Vallum pub car park," Mr Winnow said, rubbing his hand. "I'd be approached by someone I didn't know and be given another package to deliver to Black Rock Manor. This time I have to make sure it arrives."

"Originally, you were supposed to deliver the bulbs to the manor," Holly said, "where Arnold Salting was waiting for them. When you didn't arrive, he went looking, but he couldn't have known they were washed up on a beach."

"And if he did," Callum said, "it was too late because I'd already cleared them away."

Holly tugged on her fringe. "One day, he returns from searching the estate to find Regina there. A fight ensues and he disappears before the police show up."

"But according to them, there's no evidence of Regina being a victim of foul play," Callum said, "so they don't immediately search the manor, giving him plenty of time to collect his things and abscond."

Holly turned to Callum, her heart rate speeding as the pieces of the puzzle came together.

"He asks around the village," she said.

"No one has secrets in Little Belton so it doesn't take long," Callum added.

"He follows me around and finds out we have the bulbs. He spots our trap and calls the Reverend."

Callum drew a church on the window. "The Reverend can't tell if it's a man or a woman on the line. But because he's a good man, he takes the call at face value."

"While we're distracted, Arnold steals the bulbs from the Defender."

"Which I should have locked."

Holly dug her elbow into Callum, but gave him a smile. "That has to be the answer. That has to be it."

Holly and Callum threw their arms around each other, pulling in close and laughing. Holly was shaking, aware that Callum felt the same. She'd done it, despite her faults and insecurities. She'd pieced it together.

"I knew you could do it," Callum whispered in her ear.

Mr Winnow cleared his throat and they broke their embrace.

"Something the matter?" Callum asked.

Mr Winnow picked at his fingernails. "I'm sure you're right."

Holly swallowed, but couldn't force the anxiety down. "Do you have something to say?"

Staring into his steering wheel, Mr Winnow cleared his throat again. "If Arnold has his bulbs already, what are we doing here? Why does he need more?"

"Well...I mean..." Holly said with nothing more to add.

"And you seem to have forgotten about Nancy. Where is she? Has Salting kidnapped her? And what about poor Regina?"

Holly looked at Callum and he shrugged in her direction.

"And why all this cloak and dagger stuff?" Mr Winnow asked. "We've already established the depths to which I'll sink for money. Why keep me in the dark? And why isn't Arnold collecting these bulbs for himself?"

Out of the windscreen, Holly watched a minibus pull up. A hen party poured from its doors, staggering toward the pub on prosecco and high heels. Their dresses carried L-plates and condom balloons. The bride-to-be emerged last, already the worse for wear. Her L-plates were askew and her single balloon was wrinkled, deflating rapidly, like Holly's sense of achievement.

"Did you say that spoken word tape was Stephen King?" Holly asked.

Mr Winnow gave a nod and pulled it from the glove compartment, inserting it into the player. His wife's softly spoken voice recounted the tale of a car possessed by a demon. They watched the car park empty and refill. Visitors didn't stay for long, stopping only to use the bathroom on their journeys elsewhere. The driver of the minibus sat in the stairwell eating limp sandwiches and reading a newspaper.

Callum cranked the window open when the truck grew stuffy. "He's taking his time."

"Maybe he got lost," Mr Winnow said.

Holly listened to the tape and allowed her mind to wander. She thought about the tribe of Picts driving out the regimental Romans using superstition and faces painted in blue. The Picts had been thought of as savages, but their unruly ways confounded and scared an entire army. Arnold was like a Pict, living rough on the estate, but always staying one step ahead. He was using her regimental mind against her, compelling her into situations where he had the upper hand.

Holly sat rigid in her seat. "What if this is a trap?" she asked. "What if Arnold lured us here for an ambush? The same way we tried to lure him with the tinned salmon?"

Callum stretched his legs, accidentally kicking Mr Winnow in the shin. "I doubt it," he said. "Why drag us all the way out of Little Belton?"

Mrs Winnow's storytelling suddenly stopped, but the tape kept playing.

After a moment of static, another voice began speaking.

"By now, you should be sitting in a car park wondering where I am."

Holly shivered with a sudden chill. "It's Arnold," she mouthed to Callum.

Arnold's voice was high-pitched and could easily have been mistaken for a woman's if the line was bad enough.

"No one locks their doors in Little Belton," Arnold said. "I recorded this message for you, Mrs Fleet, guessing Mr Winnow would play it on his journey to Hamley village. I'm also guessing he brought you along for the ride."

Holly wafted her hand in front of her face, feeling nauseous.

Callum straightened and put an arm around Holly's shoulders.

"He won't harm you," he whispered. "I promise."

"You're in no danger from me," Arnold said, "especially with that lump of a gamekeeper around. Why are the pretty ones so dumb, eh? Did he think he could fool me by leaving my bulbs by the side of the road?"

Callum grunted and looked away.

"So I decided to use your idea against you," Arnold said. "I'm not showing up. I won't be in Hamley village. I have more pressing matters to attend to, but I will offer this warning. If things don't go my way, the blood of Little Belton will be on your hands."

With that, the tape stopped and ejected itself from the player, as if possessed by a demon of its own.

Mr Winnow quickly turned it over to play side two, but it was his wife's voice that greeted them, continuing her tale about a Plymouth Fury.

"Time to go home," Holly said.

Mr Winnow fumbled with the ignition, working the key too harshly for it to catch. When the engine fired up, he tore out of the car park.

"I need to check my wife is okay," he said, almost knocking over the drunken bride, who had left the pub for a breath of fresh air. She waved her L-plate angrily as they passed.

"I don't get it," Callum said, testing the security of his seat belt. "Why did he want to waste our time?"

Holly stared out of the window, watching fields of nothing blur by.

Tricked again, she thought. Not of Arnold's design, but of their own. They'd given him the idea of placing the cheese in the trap. Mr Salting had described Arnold as deranged, but Holly saw him as calculating. Whatever Arnold was doing, following her was no longer his priority. It was a relief until she began to wonder why.

Holly barely noticed when they arrived by the kerbside of The Travelling Star.

"I could do with a drink," Callum said. "Anyone else?"

"Not for me," Mr Winnow said. "I'm putting new locks on my doors."

Holly and Callum slipped from the truck, waving goodbye to Mr Winnow as he drove ten feet up the road to his shop.

"To be honest, I don't have the money to get the kind of drunk I want to," Holly said to Callum. "Another time?"

"I'll pay," Callum said, "but let me nip upstairs first. This whole thing makes me want to change my clothes."

Callum climbed the stairs to his rented room while Holly sloped into the Lounge, dropping into a stool by the bar. She hoped to see welcoming faces, but the room was empty.

"What'll you have?" Big Gregg asked, appearing from nowhere. Without waiting for an answer, he pirouetted to the optics and drained gin into a glass. "Feels like a gin day, doesn't it?"

He poured one for himself and added tonic to both of their glasses. As the tonic water drained from the bottle, so did the humour from his face.

"I've got some bad news," he said, gulping down his drink.

"Please, Big Gregg. Not today. I've had my fill of bad news," Holly said.

"We all have." Big Gregg smacked his lips, glancing at the gin optic, but resisting the urge for a second glass. "I had to get rid of my computerised till. Couldn't afford to keep it, but they won't let me out of the contract."

"What do you mean?" Holly asked.

Big Gregg twisted his damp bar cloth in his large hands. "I was stupid. Never read the small print, but with all the new tourists, I thought it was a good investment. I'm paying a fortune for something I no longer have and with that bleedin' hub out there, I'm not making any money."

Holly hung her head, her hair trailing into her G&T. "I know what you're going to say."

"I'm sorry," Big Gregg said. "I can't afford to keep you on."

Footsteps boomed through the ceiling and down the stairs. Callum burst into the Lounge, his face as thunderous as his feet.

"I know why Arnold Salting wanted us at that car park," he said and disappeared back to his room.

Taking Big Gregg's hand in hers, Holly pressed it against her lips.

"We're going to be okay," she said, jumping from her stool.

She followed Callum up wooden stairs that creaked with every footfall.

Callum was waiting outside his room, pointing inside. "I've been burgled."

It was a single accommodation with a single bed. An IKEA wardrobe stood with its doors open, its contents strewn on the floor. Callum's bags had been emptied, tipped out and ransacked. Even his rifle case was open, his rifle discarded, but its inner pockets were inside out.

"What was he looking for?" Holly asked, venturing into the room.

"Nothing's been taken, except for a few hides I'd brought from the cottage."

"Hides?"

"Deer hides and rabbit fur. Just to keep me warm."

Holly's hands turned into fists. "He lured us away so he could go through your room." Hot air jetted from her nostrils. "I'm starting to get really sick of this guy."

"He left us a message," Callum said. "Something to show us it was him."

He tiptoed through the debris of his room and reached for a pair of Y-fronts lying on his pillow.

"These aren't mine, by the way," Callum said.

"Arnold must have known we'd seen them back at the manor when we first discovered him."

"I only hope they're clean," Callum said, stretching the elastic band between his thumbs. "That's the message."

As the Y-fronts expanded, Holly saw writing inked onto the baggy material.

"He can't believe we're going to fall for it again, can he?" she asked.

CHAPTER THIRTY-FOUR

The message read – Meet me at the Faery Ring.

Chapter Thirty-Five

Callum crawled along Holly's driveway, his eyes scanning the windows of her home.

"Are you sure you don't want me to come in with you?" he asked.

Holly patted his knee. "Go back to The Travelling Star. Tidy your room. I'll be fine. It's just a quick visit. I know where the Faery Ring is. I'll meet you there."

"Okay, but you better take this," Callum said, handing her a rucksack. "It might save your life."

"What is it?" Holly unzipped the bag and rummaged through the contents. There was a map, compass, spare socks and something that looked like Kendal Mint Cake. "Seriously? There's enough in here for an exploration of deepest Peru. I don't need all of this."

Callum reached into the rucksack and pulled out a Maglite torch. He slapped it into his hand as if he was about to club someone.

"It's for your protection," he said, dropping it back into the rucksack. "We don't know what we're dealing with"

Holly didn't want to argue. They weren't playing Arnold's game anymore, she thought. It was time to take the fight to him.

Holly leapt from the Defender before Callum had the chance to frighten her anymore. She waited for him to leave and crept toward her house.

The garden was clear. Nothing lurked in the bushes. Derek's shed was locked. For a second, she thought she heard something scratching at the door. Holly paused, but when she heard nothing more, she dismissed it as an overactive imagination.

Outside of the shed, Derek had cemented a wooden cross into the ground.

Arnold's note to meet at the Faery Ring was another diversion. While they chased him around the estate, he'd be free to ransack another home, but not this one.

Dropping the rucksack by the door, Holly slipped into her cottage, stealing down the corridor. Her eyes were fixed on a shape through the glass of the kitchen door. It was bulky, too bulky to be Derek. The figure was hunched over, humming to itself while it worked.

Holly held her breath, gripping the door handle with her right hand, making a fist of her left. She wished Callum hadn't left so readily.

The door banged against the wall as she threw it open. The figure in the kitchen spun around in shock.

"What are you doing here?" she asked.

Two glass tumblers fell from Mr MacFarlene's loose grip and he clutched a hand to his chest. "Bloody hell. I think I passed a stone."

"I asked you a question," Holly said, stepping into the kitchen.

Looking to the half empty bottle of whisky on the counter, Mr MacFarlene turned to the broken fragments of glass on the floor. "Having a wee dram with your husband or I was until you nearly gave me a heart attack."

Holly smelled alcohol. She wasn't sure if it came from the whisky on the floor or if it was seeping through the pores of Mr MacFarlene's skin.

"I hope you're not planning on driving your tractor again," Holly said.

Mr MacFarlene raised his eyebrows. "Again?"

Holly ground her teeth together. It was hard to berate a person for something they didn't remember.

"Well, don't just stand there," she said, straddling the broken glass. "Help me tidy this up."

Holly grabbed a dustpan and brush and thrust them into Mr MacFarlene's hands. He swept up what remained of the tumblers and emptied the dustpan into the kitchen bin while Holly watched over her folded arms.

Placing the cleaning tools on the bench, Mr MacFarlene wasted no time in finding new glasses to fill.

"Would you like one?" he asked. "You look like it might do you some good."

Holly shook her head. "I'm busy, thanks. Where's Derek?"

Mr MacFarlene sipped from his whisky. "He's in the sitting room, drunk as a skunk. I saw him at the hub and thought I better get him home."

"I don't suppose the fact that he had more booze persuaded you any?" Holly asked.

Mr MacFarlene drained his glass and started on the other. "He's in a bad way. I was trying to help."

Leaving the kitchen, Holly opened the door to the sitting room. It was small and dark with a brick fireplace and an unlit fire. A plum coloured sofa was pressed under a window and facing a wooden coffee table. A flat screen TV Holly had inherited from her parents was mounted on the wall.

Derek sat on the edge of the sofa. His hair had a greasy hue. His shirt was tight around a bulging midriff and he swayed over a wedding album gripped tightly in his arms.

"What are you doing?" Holly asked.

Startled, Derek dropped the album, the photographs scattering from their thin sleeves. He looked up, his eyes taking a moment to focus on Holly.

"There you are," Derek said, his words heavy with booze. Trying to stand, he fell back into the sofa, his legs wriggling in the air, like a woodlouse on its back.

Holly rushed forward, dragging Derek into an upright position. When he waved away her assistance, Holly picked up a photograph of herself from the floor. She was younger with fewer lines on her face and more hope in her eyes.

"When are you going to be my husband again?" she asked, unsure if she was asking herself or Derek.

If it was Derek, then he didn't answer, but his face crumpled as if he was going to cry.

"I know things aren't easy for you here," Holly continued, "but this is our home now. We have to accept that."

"It's not my home," Derek said. "It's yours. Your house. Your village. Your friends."

Holly gathered the photographs from the floor, slipping them inside the wedding album and slamming it shut.

"And where is your friend? Your gamekeeper boyfriend?" Derek asked.

Holly's jaw ached from clenching too tightly. Hissing out a breath, she forced herself to relax. "He's busy."

"Too busy to come to your home? I thought he liked it here."

"For your information, I had to make an excuse," Holly said. "He wanted to come inside, but I knew you'd be drunk. I knew you'd be bitter and making a fool of yourself. I lost everything in London too, you know? You have to get on with the rest of your life and you have to decide if I'm going to be a part of that."

Holly turned at the sound of Mr MacFarlene clearing his throat. He stood in the doorway staring at his feet.

"Is there anything I can do to help?" he asked the floor.

Holly returned her gaze to Derek, who was holding his head in his hands.

"We're fine," Holly said, swallowing down the lie. "I'm not here to fight, but I need to know if anyone's been here. Anyone suspicious."

"No-one's been here," Derek said. "Just me and the farmer man."

Mr MacFarlene stepped around Holly and handed Derek a tumbler of whisky.

"Isn't it time you stopped that?" she asked.

Derek raised the glass and downed the liquid in one.

"We've just got started," he said. "It's not like I've got anything else to do. Not like I've got a job."

"You could find one," Holly offered. "I could ask around for you."

"Never used to drink," Derek said. "Not till I got here. People need a purpose in life. Without it, what else is there?"

The sofa creaked as Derek slopped forward, his hand slapping on the wooden table. His fingers crawled over the wedding album, pulling it toward him. Opening it, the photographs dropped into his lap.

"We used to be good together," he said. "It used to work."

He cut a pathetic figure, Holly thought. It was difficult to see him reduced so low, painful to realise the love for her husband wouldn't save him. She was tied to Derek in ways she couldn't explain, but his current trajectory was taking him to a place Holly couldn't go.

She caught Mr MacFarlene's eye. "While you've been here, has there been anyone skulking around?"

"Like who?"

"Like never you mind," she said. "Answer the question."

"No one," Mr MacFarlene said. "No one I could see. Why are you asking?"

"I'm worried someone might try and break into my home." Holly danced on the spot, itching to start her journey to the Faery Ring.

"I need you to stay with Derek," she said to Mr MacFarlene as she moved to the doorway.

The farmer crouched by the sofa, removing Derek's shoes and placing them safely on a newspaper. "What for?"

"In case someone comes calling," Holly said, "and don't be getting drunk and falling asleep. Eyes open."

With a saddened glance at her husband, Holly left them to it, hurrying down the corridor.

"And lock the front door after I'm gone," she shouted back to Mr MacFarlene.

Outside, the air was cooler than when she had arrived. It nipped at her face. Looking over Knock Lake, a herd of deer lingered by the shoreline. They weren't drinking. They were staring at her, jostling to get a better view. The herd seemed lost without Star, looking to Holly for inspiration.

She did up the buttons of her coat and marched in the direction of the Faery Ring. Callum had told her of a shortcut and she hoped he would be there when she arrived.

Chapter Thirty-Six

The Hanging Tree was far behind Holly as she climbed the next hill. Puffing like a steam engine and ankle deep in spring grass, she saw the track that had led her to Callum's cottage. To the right was the cairn where she'd been humiliated by sheep.

The ravens watched her through beady eyes. Like black arrows, they circled overhead, never resting or silent.

She turned to the south where the broken branches of a forest scratched the sky. Holly remembered Mr Winnow mentioning the Faery Ring, but with her life spiralling out of control, she hadn't had time to visit it. Some part of her was pleased to have the opportunity. The other part was scared.

Adjusting the straps on Callum's rucksack, its weight rubbed against her shoulders. Holly struggled over a drystone wall. The forest loomed above her as she approached. According to Callum, the ring was on the other side, but it was best to walk around the circumference. Too many tangled roots, too many watery bogs, he'd said.

Holly liked how Callum worried about her, but it could be cloying. Her city days had wiped clean any residual understanding of country ways, but she wasn't completely useless, she thought. She could still walk through a forest without getting lost.

Stepping into the shadows, Holly waded through the trees. The ground was slippery and wet with last year's leaves. Yellow mushrooms twisted from the ground. Holly felt eyes upon her, hoping they belonged to the ravens.

The trees were thirsty for light, yearning for the sky in a jumble of branches. The trek seemed endless and Holly attempted to ignore the panic gnawing at the back of her skull. With each step, her feet grew increasingly damp and her legs grew leaden. Her mind turned to ghosts and a tale she'd heard from her mother. Legend held that the forest was also the home of a land hydra, a multi-headed dragon living in the forest trees. When one head was removed, two more grew in its place.

Little Belton was mired in local legends and gossip. The estate inspired tales of magical creatures and while gossip might hold a grain of truth, Holly was certain the legends were false. But her surety did little to calm her racing thoughts as she imagined the many eyes of the hydra watching her from the canopy.

Holly was tired and almost prepared to admit she was lost. Exhaustion and fear fed the supernatural, she warned herself. Not science or discovery.

The cracking of a branch jerked her to a stop. It had come from her right, but the forest was too gloomy to make anything out. She ferreted through the rucksack, producing the Maglite torch Callum had given her. Casting the beam through the trees, she caught sight of a long, white face floating in the dark.

Holly pressed her hand to her mouth. It wasn't a hydra or a ghoul. It was a single buck deer rubbing its velvet horns against a tree. Pausing in a ray of light, the deer snorted at her. He butted the tree, shaking his head in the leaves fluttering around his haunches. He trotted through the forest before looking at Holly over his shoulder.

With a decreasing number of options, Holly decided to follow. The deer skipped ahead, pausing now and again for her to catch up. He never allowed her too close, but neither did he lose sight of her. Was this the reincarnation of Star, she wondered? Had he returned to guide her home?

The deer bolted, leaping over a sunken bog. Holly raced after him, lancing the torch through the dark, but the deer had disappeared. She listened to the silence, hoping to track him somehow.

The forest was denser here with rotten trees fringed with wet fungi. Holly heard nothing but the call of Black Eye Bobby.

The buck was gone and she was more lost than ever.

"What an idiot," she shouted, throwing Callum's rucksack at a tree. There was a crack and the tree shifted, splintering as its rotten stump broke free of the ground. With a groan, it collapsed into the arms of other trees and they fell like dominoes, clearing a path for Holly.

Through the gap was the stony outcrop known as the Faery Ring.

Holly made hesitant steps toward it. Whether it was land dragons, faeries or the karmic reincarnation of a stag, she was simply glad to be out of the forest. She made a cursory search for Callum's rucksack, knowing full well it was buried under a ton of wood and mushrooms.

Holly walked out of the treeline, turning her face to the sunlight. Despite the cool air, it felt good on her skin. She sat on a tuft of grass at the base of the outcrop. She'd arrived. She was at the Faery Ring, but there were no faeries. No ring. Instead, Holly was surrounded by rocks whose faces were twisted into gargoyle grins.

The buck, which was not a ghost, waited for her with his herd by a meandering stream.

The outcrop towered over ten feet, ending in triangular rocks jutting into the sky. Lichen carpeted the stone, painting it a mottled yellow. To Holly, the Faery Ring resembled a crown until she noticed beetles and millipedes scuttling over its surface.

A rock tumbled from above, missing Holly by an inch. The noise startled the deer and they scattered. Holly jumped to her feet and looked to the top of the crown.

At the height of the outcrop was a figure silhouetted by the sun. Forcing her heart to stop hammering, Holly took a stand.

"I'm here, Arnold," she said. "What do you want?"

The figure was difficult to make out, but it seemed to retreat from view, melting into the sunlight.

Holly heard rocks falling as if something was scaling down the outcrop. She held tightly onto Callum's Maglite, gripping it with her right hand, slapping it into her left. If Arnold got too close, Holly would protect herself.

The figure appeared from behind a boulder. It wasn't Arnold Salting. It was the last person Holly expected to see.

The Maglite slipped from her hand. It bounced over the rocks and cartwheeled into the muddy boots of a woman, who picked up the torch and held it like a weapon, pointing it at Holly.

Chapter Thirty-Seven

"Nancy?" Holly asked, clutching a hand to her chest. "I can't believe it. We found you."

In the distance came the distressed calls of the herd, calling each other together.

"I think I found you, dear," Nancy said. She lobbed the Maglite to Holly, who fumbled the catch. The torch hit the jagged edge of a rock and ejected its batteries.

"We've been so worried about you," Holly said. "Are you coming home?"

Nancy was dressed in woollen cardigans and dresses. They were layered like the pages of a book swollen with damp. They made her look rounder than Holly remembered, but her face was thin and raw from the weather.

"You got our message?" Nancy asked.

"Message? On the Y-fronts?" Holly gasped. "You're working with Arnold Salting?"

"For what it's worth, he's sorry for what happened with Mr Winnow. He shouldn't have lost his temper."

"And for rifling through Callum's belongings?" Holly asked.

"Actually, that was me." Nancy retrieved a handkerchief from the folds of her dress. "Young people don't carry these anymore, do they?" she asked, looking pointedly at Holly's grimy hands.

Holly took the handkerchief and wiped her palms clean, remembering how Old Jack had said the same.

"Arnold had to make sure you went to Hamley village," Nancy said. "He was watching you while I took the opportunity to search Callum's room."

"But why?" Holly asked, casting the handkerchief aside.

"I'm afraid, we need more bulbs."

"Arnold stole all that we had," Holly said. "You must have them."

Nancy ground her heel into the floor. "We're running out of time, dear. Arcadia Leisure is more dangerous than you know."

"You're wrong," Holly said. "I read your notes. I know what happened in Eureka. I know what they've got planned for our village."

"Then you know what's at stake."

"You didn't go missing, did you?" Holly asked. "You went on the run."

"It doesn't matter anymore," Nancy said. She bit into the knuckle of her forefinger, her false teeth glinting under a ray of sun. "The bulbs we have are rotten. Turned bad with salt water. They'll never grow, thanks to that crackerjack Mr Winnow. Without them, we'll never stop Arcadia taking over the estate."

"If you tell me what's happening, maybe we can find more," Holly said.

Nancy dismissed her with a snort.

"You sent the emails to Mr Winnow, didn't you?" Holly asked. "You knew his greed would over-rule his common sense. When Callum left the bulbs by the side of the road, you spoke to the Reverend knowing he would do anything to help. It *was* someone from the village. You were behind it all."

"I'm doing what I think is best."

"And what about your sister?" Holly asked. "Are you behind that too?"

There was a shine to Nancy's eyes that spoke of madness. It reminded Holly of Arnold and his drive for...His drive for what, Holly asked herself? Whatever it was, Nancy presented the same signs and Holly needed to proceed with caution.

"Regina is in the hospital," she said. "Your sister was attacked."

"Not by me." Nancy tugged at seeds from a tuft of yellow grass and scattered them into the wind.

"I know. It was Arnold," Holly said. "Are you sure he won't do the same to you?"

"We all have our crosses to bear and I've grown strong over the years." Nancy smiled, but it was like the flicker of a flame. Caught by an unseen wind, it was there for a moment and then gone. "After what happened when Regina and I were children, I thought living with her was a kindness, but Regina got possessive. She wouldn't suffer fools gladly. I wanted a dog as an excuse to leave the house, but my sister wouldn't allow one indoors. A dog couldn't live outside through our winters so do you know what I did?"

"You got a goat."

"I got several over the years. You see, I could keep that outside, but Regina knew if it stayed in the garden, it would eat the vegetables. I had to take it out for walks."

"It was the perfect excuse to roam the estate," Holly said, "but why take it to the manor?"

The lines on Nancy's face were etched deep from the outdoors, but they appeared to lighten at the thought of her victory over Regina. They became less like battle scars and more like a map of her life.

Holly took another step closer. "Old Jack is looking after your goat. He misses you."

"Does he?" Nancy asked.

"He told me how he felt about you," Holly said.

"That seems so long ago, dear."

CHAPTER THIRTY-SEVEN

"What happened at the manor? What changed?"

"Everything," Nancy said, backing away.

Holly held out her hands. "Don't go. Come with me. We'll visit Old Jack. He's falling apart with worry."

Behind Holly came the crashing of feet. She turned to see Callum burst from the forest, twigs protruding from his hair, dirt smeared on his face. He grabbed her and pulled her in for a hug.

"Are you okay?" Callum asked. "Is he here?"

His laboured breath warmed her neck.

"You're crushing me," Holly said, wriggling from his hold.

"What is it? What's wrong?" Callum asked.

Holly searched for Nancy through the jagged rocks, but she had disappeared, like the young buck who had led Holly to the Faery Ring.

Nancy had provided answers and Holly now knew the bulbs were part of a bigger plan to save the village. She didn't know what part or why. Typically, like cutting off the head of a hydra, a single answer spawned more questions and Holly didn't know what to do next.

And then she did.

"Are you hungry?" she asked.

Callum rubbed his stomach. "Always. Why?"

"Because we have to visit the Reverend again," she said.

Chapter Thirty-Eight

Reverend Applecroft knelt in a patch of marigolds. Their yellow petals reflected the sun into his bare chest, painting him in gold. He wore faded dungarees and green wellies. An electrical lead looped out of an open window trailing to a CD player playing thrash metal at a low volume. The Reverend bobbed his head to something that was more of a series of grunts than a song.

Holly coughed politely and he looked up from his flowers.

"Bryan told me to dig out the dandelions," he said, scratching his head, "but I can't tell one flower from another."

Holly pointed at the plant swinging from his muddy grip. "I'd suggest putting that one back."

"Oh Lord," the Reverend said, quickly digging a hole and shoving the marigold into place. "I don't know why he makes me do this."

Brushing himself free of soil, he got to his feet. "Is there anything I can help you with?"

"It's Bryan we've come to see," Callum said.

"He's just nipped out to the shops, but he won't be long," the Reverend said. "Do you want to wait inside? We have more scones."

Callum grinned. "We hoped you might."

Holly opened a squeaking garden gate, alerting Cassandra the Myna bird to an intrusion. She barked repeatedly, alternating between a yap and the theme tune to *The Archers*.

"We can wait outside," Holly said. "It's fine."

The Reverend gestured to a bench and they took a seat, watching over the garden.

"How's the investigation going?" the Reverend asked. "Have you found Nancy yet?"

Holly filled him in on the details, omitting her recent discovery. Little Belton was awash with rumours regarding Nancy's disappearance. Holly was sure the residents would be relieved to know she was safe, but there was still so much to learn. Was Nancy safe? What was she up to? Where had she been? They were questions shrouded in mystery and Holly didn't want the rumour mill providing answers that would cloud the truth.

"We're getting there," Holly said, "and I called the hospital again. Regina is still in there, but apparently, she is spending more time awake than asleep."

"That's good news, but I feel for any doctor who comes into contact with her sharp tongue," the Reverend said. "What about the Masterlys? Are you any closer to stopping their dastardly plans?"

Holly opened her palms to the heavens. "I don't know, to be honest. There's a lot going on. All I know is we have to look after each other. Mr MacFarlene is at my house keeping Derek company."

"Really?" Callum asked. "I thought Derek didn't like Mr MacFarlene."

As Holly was about to answer, a string of men in heavy boots and hi-vis jackets marched down Little Belton's high street. Some carried chainsaws, others balanced pickaxes on their broad shoulders. The white helmets they wore hid their faces. Behind them came mini-diggers and fork-lift trucks, their wheels churning up tarmac and spitting it out in their wake.

It was a parade, a show of force. As the machinery passed, the Masterlys' Range Rover followed. A black window in the rear rolled down and Holly saw Mrs Masterly smiling at her.

"The appeal process is over," Holly said, wringing her hands. "They're getting ready to tear everything up."

"They can't be," Callum said.

Holly patted his knee. "We knew it was coming."

"But there's time to stop them yet."

"We will," Holly said. "Don't worry."

The procession marched on. The drum of footsteps and the rumble of machines shook the flowers of the Reverend's garden. Cassandra barked incessantly from her cage.

"Charles Wentworth would turn in his grave," Callum said.

The Reverend ran a hand through his knotted beard and Holly noticed a twitch in his fingers.

"Did you ever meet Sir Charles?" Holly asked him. "You worked in his mine."

A hair had worked loose from his chin and the Reverend held it between a thumb and forefinger, watching it pirouette in the air.

"Only once," he said. "He called for me when he found out why I was serving my notice."

"What happened?" Holly asked.

The Reverend released the hair and watched it float away on a breeze. "I left to join the ministry. When Wentworth heard, he wanted to congratulate me on my choice of career."

"He would have done," Callum said. "He was a God-fearing man himself."

The Reverend shifted on the garden bench and continued. "I was invited to the manor, but I was early, keen to meet him. I'd spent half the morning polishing my shoes, getting ready. I didn't know there was any kind of etiquette involved when meeting a man like Wentworth."

Callum nodded sagely. "Dad worked at the manor," he said. "Told me all about them etiquettes."

"So, I accidentally barged into his office without warning," the Reverend said. "Sir Charles Wentworth knew his Bible front to back, but I doubt he ever read it. I caught him with one of the maids. She was undressing and he was getting close. There was a hullabaloo, as you could imagine. Wentworth claimed it was Bible study, but I've hosted a few of those in my time and we generally keep our trousers on."

Callum left the garden bench. He stood next to a laurel bush, pushing his thumbnail through the leaves. "I'm sorry, but I don't believe you."

"I never told a soul," the Reverend said, his eyes on Callum's back. "People around here hold Wentworth in such high esteem and rightfully so. He did a lot for this village. I didn't want to undo that."

"Did he ever confront you over what you saw?" Holly asked.

The Reverend shook his head, the beads in his beard rattling together. "I don't think either one of us wanted to revisit it, but from what I heard later, it wasn't an isolated event."

Holly shuffled to the edge of the bench. "Why would you say that?"

"I'm pretty sure this part is untrue," the Reverend said, "but they say, Black Rock Manor has a secret entrance."

"What?" Callum asked, turning away from the laurel bush.

The Reverend flinched under his stare. "Nonsense, really. A way to ferry his women in and out without Mrs Wentworth knowing. I don't buy it."

Holly and Callum shared a look.

"Then again," the Reverend said. "For all the rumours around here, I never heard another one about Wentworth and his women so maybe he did keep it all a secret."

Holly felt Callum's eyes upon her. They were both thinking the same thing. Nancy had known about the secret entrance to the manor. And if she'd known, then there was a possibility she was one of Wentworth's women. She'd been young at the time, a teenager, the perfect age to be hypnotised by an important man like Wentworth. As her sister

211

recovered, Nancy had seemingly fallen under his spell.

It explained her sudden indifference to Old Jack. It also explained her devotion to the estate. Hadn't Regina said Nancy wanted the estate to remain in Wentworth hands? When Nancy had learned of the Masterlys' plans, she had decided to put a stop to them. Not as a committed conservationist, but as a bereft lover.

The Reverend sat up in his seat, a smile splitting his face. "There's Bryan coming back," he said. "I'll go put the kettle on."

He peeled off his garden gloves and disappeared into the vicarage where Cassandra barked at him on his way to the kitchen.

"Hello again," Bryan said, entering the garden. "I've been out for custard creams. Would you like one?"

Holly's head was spinning from what the Reverend had told her. She screwed her eyes closed, opening them quickly to focus her mind.

"Are you okay?" Bryan asked, placing a light touch on her arm.

"Long day," Holly said. "We were hoping you might have some information about our bulbs."

Bryan's face fell and Holly feared the worst.

"There's nothing," he said. "I went through every book I had. I even went to the library in Amble. They're quite distinctive, but they don't appear to exist."

"You didn't need to go to all that trouble," Holly said.

"I needed a haircut anyway."

"You and the Reverend are well suited," Holly said with a smile. "Working for the community the way you do."

"I'm only sorry I couldn't help more."

"Ever since I clapped eyes on those bulbs, I suspected they were different," Holly said. "Why else would you hide them in a tin? What I wanted to know is – where would you get something like that?"

Bryan eyed the wilting marigold the Reverend had hastily returned to the soil. "Well, I suppose specialist species come from specialist growers."

"And they'd be expensive, right?"

"Absolutely," Bryan said. "Did you know some snowdrops sell for over seven hundred pounds per bulb?"

Callum whistled over his half-eaten Custard Cream. "That's a lot of money for a plant."

"Pass on our apologies to the Reverend," Holly said, making for the garden gate, "but we better get going."

"Where to?" Bryan asked.

"The hunt continues," Callum said, through a mouthful of food.

Holly rubbed her eyes. There was a lot to mull over. The threads kept slipping from her grasp. As soon as she thought they were making progress, the landscape changed and Holly was lost again. Old Jack, lovelorn and lonely, had pressed Holly to find Nancy. She'd done that and discovered there was a whole lot more to the story.

Identifying the bulbs would unlock the whole mystery, Holly thought and she'd hoped Bryan might have taken that burden from her. What he'd done was raise another question.

As she watched Callum devour the last of his food, Holly's appetite deserted her.

Judging by Nancy's home and clothes, she didn't appear to be rich. Ditto for the jobless Arnold Salting, but somehow they'd come into possession of dozens of expensive plants.

So the question became, how did they afford them or who had they stolen them from?

Chapter Thirty-Nine

The Defender coughed exhaust fumes as it climbed the road to Holly's cottage. She glanced at its driver. Callum took his time, seemingly content to trundle through the bends without any sense of urgency. However, his frown told another story.

Holly yawned, making a show of stretching her arms. "Can't wait to get home," she said. "I need some time to think."

Callum chewed the tip of his thumb. "Do you believe what the Reverend said?"

"About Wentworth's wandering hands?" Holly asked. "He wouldn't be the first man to abuse his position of power."

"Dad never mentioned anything," Callum muttered.

"Would he have? It's not the sort of thing a father talks about on a family evening. He was protecting you."

Callum wiped a wet thumb on his shirt.

"It makes sense, though, doesn't it?" Holly asked. "You were thinking the same thing as me. I saw it."

"Nancy being seduced? The secret entrance?" Callum asked. "Yeah, I was thinking the same thing, but what do we do about it?"

His tepid pace finally brought them to Holly's home. A mist had descended down the valley walls, smothering Knock Lake in silver.

"I can't trust that man to do anything," Holly said, casting her seatbelt aside.

"What are you talking about?"

"Derek," she said. "He's left the door open. I told him to keep it shut."

She struggled to get out of the Defender, her frustration with her husband transferring itself to the jeep's stubborn handle. "Bloody, stupid thing."

Callum reached over her, releasing the handle from its jam. "I'll come with you this time."

"There's a strong chance I'm about to murder my husband," Holly said. "I'd prefer it if there weren't any witnesses."

But Callum wasn't listening. He had slipped out of the driver's seat and was already joining her on the other side of the Defender.

"What if Derek did close the door and Arnold opened it up again?" he asked.

Holly's stomach dropped and they crept toward the cottage together, hovering by the door.

"The lock seems fine," Holly said. "I don't think anyone has broken in."

"Me first," Callum said.

Holly barred him with an arm. "Wait."

"Okay, okay." Callum yanked off his boots, leaving them on the doorstep. "Better?"

"No, I meant, I'll go first. It's my house," Holly said, pointing at the ham-handed stitches in his sock "I see you've been busy with your sewing needle."

They entered quietly to be greeted by the sound of snoring. Following the rumble to the sitting room, they found Derek slumped on the sofa, bellowing into the crook of his arm.

"Mr MacFarlene seems to have left," Holly said.

"Shhh," Callum hissed. "You'll wake up Derek."

Holly rolled her eyes. "You could play Mrs Winnow's *Lord of the Rings* full volume and he wouldn't wake until they got to Mordor."

Derek's shoes were side by side, Holly noticed. Not kicked off and abandoned in far flung corners of the room. There were pillows under his head and a glass of water on the table. Holly turned full circle through the room. Her paintings weren't hung. They leaned against the wall where she'd left them. The box of books by her empty shelf was unopened and her vases remained stuffed with newspaper.

"False alarm," Holly said. "Nothing has been touched."

"Are you sure?"

"Remember your room at The Travelling Star?" Holly asked. "It was like a bulldozer went through it, but this place is tidier than when I left it."

"What about the door?"

"Mr MacFarlene probably left it open by mistake."

"We better check around to be sure," Callum said.

Holly stretched her arms above her head, feeling the satisfying crack of her shoulders as they settled into position.

"It's fine and I'm really tired," she said, rubbing her eyes. "I need a break."

Callum scanned the room, searching for any kind of threat and then seemed to relax.

"As long as you're okay," he said. "Get some rest and I'll be back in the morning."

Callum stopped at the base of the stairs, staring at the landing above. "Does Derek usually sleep it off on the sofa?"

"Most nights," Holly said, her face flushing red and she followed his gaze up the stairs."

"Derek's shoes are in the sitting room," Callum said, scratching his chin. "So why are there dirty footprints going upstairs?"

Holly took the steps two at a time, fighting the urge to be sick. The dirty prints continued along the floor to her bedroom. Holding onto her stomach, Holly burst through the door and clasped a hand around her mouth.

The search wasn't as destructive as it had been in Callum's room, but that wasn't the point. The drawers to her dresser were open. Clothes had been removed from her wardrobe.

Holly's privacy had been violated while her stupid husband was asleep downstairs.

"I feel ill," she said.

Callum dropped to his knees, running his hand over the indents in the carpet and examining the dirt on his fingers. "Has anything been taken?"

"I don't know. I don't think so." Holly wrapped her arms around herself, but was far from comforted. "After everything we've done, Arnold still managed to get inside my house."

"It wasn't Arnold," Callum said, getting to his feet.

"How can you be sure?" Holly asked, fighting back a tear.

Callum showed Holly his hand. It was covered in a dusting of mud, but it meant nothing to her.

"What are you trying to say?" she asked.

"This isn't mud," Callum offered as an explanation. "It's dried manure, something you get a lot of in a farmyard. By the looks of it, Mr MacFarlene took off Derek's shoes, but kept his on. Derek was probably too drunk to notice."

"I didn't notice either," Holly said, her throat constricting in shock. "Mr MacFarlene was in my bedroom? Why? Why would he do this? He's a drunk, but he's not a bad man."

Callum shook his head in silence, cleaning his hand on his trousers.

Holly allowed herself a tear and then swiped it away. The sickness in her stomach disappeared. The doubting voices in her head were gone. All the insecurities she'd carried since returning to Little Belton were gone.

Looking at Callum, her face hardened.

"Why don't we find out then?" she asked.

***

Dusk was setting. The dead branches of Mr MacFarlene's garden cast long shadows, coating his house in black tiger stripes against the orange of a dying sun.

Holly wrapped her knuckles on the front door, its paint cracking under her persistent fist.

"I told you, he's not in," Callum said.

"I want answers." Holly tried the handle and found it locked. "Let's try around the back."

Holly took a cobbled path down the side of the house. The rear garden was twice as big as the front, but just as overgrown. Tall grass had collapsed in a matted tangle. Three mature apple trees waited to come into leaf. Their branches were locked like hands in prayer. They blocked Holly's view, but she heard sheep bleating from the field beyond.

"Farmers make the worst gardeners," Callum said, swiping his booted foot through the grass. His foot connected with something hard and he reached down to find the weathered statue of a garden gnome fighting to stay above the vegetation.

"They don't make great friends, either." Holly pulled at the collar around her throat. It felt tight, suffocating. The image of her desecrated bedroom came to mind and she forced her eyes shut to block it out. "I trusted him."

"We should wait for him to come home and explain himself," Callum said.

"He didn't wait for me," Holly said. "MacFarlene ransacked my home. The least I can do is return the favour."

Callum rubbed his forehead. "Look, we'll not find anything. If his garden is anything to go by, his house will be a tip."

But Holly didn't care. Deep down, she knew this wasn't about finding answers. It was payback and it was petty. The kitchen door was made of nine panes of glass. Her hand lingered on the handle. What would it say about Holly if she tried it?

Callum came to her side. "You know this is wrong, right?"

She didn't need the gamekeeper's moral compass swinging in the right direction and she braced herself to commit a crime.

He gently pulled her grip from the handle. "You don't want to do this," he said and tried the handle for himself. It was locked and Callum grabbed the gnome by the head, forcing it through a glass pane. Jagged shards fell like rain and he reached inside to undo the lock.

"He'll know we've been here now," Holly said.

Callum wiped a smear of blood from his knuckles. "Good."

The kitchen was not what either of them expected. The surfaces were clean. The sink was empty of dirty dishes. There was a taint of bleach in the air as if the stone floor had recently been cleaned. A shelf sported a selection of well-thumbed cookery books. Next to *Tapas for Beginners* was a copy of *The History of Northumberland*.

"We haven't broken into the wrong house, have we?" Callum asked.

The cast iron of the Aga pinged with expanding heat, making Holly jump.

"He's not who we thought he was, that's for sure," she said.

"We should go," Callum said, glancing at the shattered glass.

"Let's have a quick look around," Holly said. "We're here now."

Leaving the kitchen through another door, Holly walked into a sitting room. The smell of bleach was replaced with something floral. On a central table was a vase of freshly cut wildflowers. The sofa was covered with a tartan throw and faced a fireplace free of ash. There were paintings of cows and sheep on the wall, but Holly was drawn to a framed black and white photograph on the mantlepiece. It showed a bright-eyed Mr MacFarlene with his beautiful wife. They looked happy, thought Holly.

"Okay, I think we can go now," she said.

"Not yet," Callum said, twisting his fingers through his hair. "Look at these."

Behind the sofa were two sleeping bags, tucked into rolls.

"These are the same bags Mr MacFarlene was drying on the washing line," Callum said.

Next to them were two rucksacks plump with clothing. Two sets of boots rested on newspaper.

"What's that?" Holly asked, lifting one of the bags to one side. Underneath was an opened envelope.

"The postmark," Callum said. "It was sent from South Tyneside. The Port of Tyne is in South Tyneside. That's where Mr Winnow was sent to collect the bulbs."

"It was posted over six weeks ago." Ignoring her guilt, Holly teased out the letter. She also ignored the look on Callum's face. The letter was printed on a blank piece of paper with no identifying signatures or marks and yet its contents were familiar.

It read - Follow The Star.

Voices came from outside.

Holly and Callum froze, their mouths open.

"Run," Callum hissed.

They bolted from the room into the kitchen. Fighting to be the first one out of the door, Holly knocked the shelf, spilling cookery books onto the floor. They both stopped.

"Go, go, go," Holly hissed.

"No, wait." Callum turned his ear to the rear of the house. "They're coming in the back way."

Holly and Callum returned to the sitting room.

"Through here," Callum said.

They took another door as they heard the kitchen door opening. The voices were louder, speaking in clipped tones. They paused and Holly heard the tinkle of broken glass before Mr MacFarlene raised his voice.

"I've been burgled," he shouted.

Boots were stamped and voices were raised.

Urging her panic to be still, Holly saw the front door ahead of them. She tried the handle, knowing it was locked. "We need the key."

Callum's head swivelled left to right, scanning the hallway. Pictures. Table. Boot rack. Vase.

"There," he said, pointing.

The vase was glass. Inside was a set of keys. Holly tipped them out, dropping them on the floor.

"What was that?" she heard a voice say from the kitchen.

"Hurry," Callum said.

Holly's heart drummed in her chest. She tried one key. Nothing. Another. Nothing.

Callum danced on the spot, his eyes trained in the direction they'd come from.

Holly inserted another key and twisted. It worked. The door opened. She returned the keys to the vase and they slipped outside, closing the door quietly. They kept their heads low, ducking behind a hedgerow opposite the house.

"Can we go now?" Callum asked. His face was grey and he seemed to have developed worry lines overnight.

"I want to see who is with Mr MacFarlene," Holly said.

"What difference does it make? They're probably calling the police by now."

Holly wriggled her arm through the hedgerow, clearing away branches blocking her view.

Someone in the house switched on a light.

"Because those sleeping bags belong to someone," Holly said. "Someone who got the same note I did."

The first person to appear by the window was the farmer. He was carrying a whisky bottle in one hand and a telephone in the other.

Callum pushed in beside Holly, his reservations giving way to curiosity.

Then two people came to the window at once. They looked tired and weather-worn, probably from tramping through the estate all day and night. When Arnold's camp had been disturbed at the manor, he'd found sanctuary elsewhere. He stood in profile, talking animatedly to Mr MacFarlene, who lowered the phone from his ear. Holly wasn't surprised to see Nancy Foxglove next to him.

"So that's where they disappeared to," Callum said. "I knew they couldn't be on the estate. I would have found them."

Holly slithered back from the hedge. "Mr MacFarlene isn't an eco-warrior. Why would he help Nancy and Arnold?"

"We're worried about the village being run into the ground by the Masterlys. He's worried about his farm. It's all he's got."

"He has his drinking problem."

Callum stroked his throat with his finger. "I think one thing bleeds into another."

Holly was angry with Mr MacFarlene, but she had to admit it was waning. His house was immaculate, which was a miracle considering how drunk he constantly was. The pride missing in most winos was found in the farmer's home; the home he once shared with a wife he loved.

It didn't excuse how he'd acted at Holly's home, but it raised a larger question mark over Mr MacFarlene's head.

"There's no point in waiting here," Callum said. "We should confront them."

Holly held onto him. "You can't. It's too much of a coincidence. They'll know it was us who broke in."

"Mr MacFarlene isn't calling the police," Callum said. "For some reason, Arnold seems to have talked him out of it."

"Because the pair of them have been doing exactly the same thing. They obviously don't want to attract any further attention."

"What are we going to do?" Callum asked.

Holly crawled away from the hedge, lying in a dip in the field. With dusk deepening to nightfall, starlight pricked into existence. Little Belton settled down to sleep and planets a billion miles away were waking up.

We need another plan, she thought.

Chapter Forty

Over the next few days, Callum trailed the trio from Mr MacFarlene's farmhouse. Holly left him to it. Her skills as a tracker were as well-honed as her skills as a barmaid. When she'd stated the same to Callum, she had hoped he might disagree. After five minutes of him talking about the weather, Holly realised it wasn't going to happen.

She didn't mind. She had bigger farmers to fry.

Little Belton's high street was deserted. There was no moving traffic and few pedestrians. Up ahead, a young mother pushed a buggy over the divots of the village green. She glanced at Holly and down to her sleeping baby

Holly tried to smile, but it was met with a hard stare. The young mother pushed harder, picking up her pace until she disappeared around a corner.

A handful of people milled around the Masterlys' media hub. They held tattered leaflets in their hands. They'd been read before. In their other hand was free alcohol and the chance to forget.

Opposite the hub, Big Gregg rested in the doorway of The Travelling Star, his arms folded. A Sold sign hung above his head.

"How are you, love?" he asked as Holly approached.

The sign read 'Building a Better Future Today.' It belonged to the Salting Brothers.

"What happened?" Holly's mouth was dry, the shadow of the sign falling across her face.

"Got an offer on the pub. A good one."

"You can't take it," Holly said.

"What else am I going to do?" Big Gregg asked.

"You can fight. You can fight back."

Big Gregg rapped his knuckles on his prosthetic leg. It emitted a hollow sound. "I've done my share of fighting. Doesn't do much good in the end."

"It's only been a couple of weeks," Holly said. "You can't be bankrupt."

"I'm not, but I will be. That new till is an anchor around my neck and without any customers, it's only a matter of time before I'm out on my ear."

"What about Callum? He's paying for room and board," Holly said.

"Paying over the odds, too, but it's not enough."

Big Gregg's body was strong enough to carry beer barrels around like they were children's toys. Looking at him now, Holly thought, he was barely able to raise a smile. He was a giant. Reduced to nothing.

Holly rushed into his arms, pressing her cheek against his chest. "Who made the offer on the pub?"

"I think you know. The Masterlys ground me to dust and swept up the pieces. I was an idiot to believe they were here for our benefit. It felt like I was back in the Forces. We were called The Iron Fist Brigade and we never questioned those above us. We went all over the world to fight, but I mainly saw desert."

Big Gregg stepped out of the hug, leaving Holly holding onto an empty space.

"What happened?" she asked.

"You fight because you're trained to. They expect it of you, but when you can't – when you're no longer capable – they don't need you anymore."

Holly stared at Big Gregg's artificial leg, her lips trembling. "What was it? An IED?"

Big Gregg brushed his ginger locks from his face and laughed. "Didn't anyone tell you?" he asked, slapping his leg. "I was knocked down by a herd of cows."

His laughter was infectious and Holly managed a confused chuckle. "A what?"

"I was on leave. I came home to Little Belton and had one too many in here," he said, touching the brickwork of The Travelling Star. "I went wandering into a field and spooked the cows. They get jumpy at calving time. By the time they got through with me, the surgeons couldn't do a thing."

Holly scratched her cheek. "You fought all over the world and you lost your leg in Little Belton?"

"I would have been safer in Iraq," Big Gregg said. "They really did look after us out there, but I guess it's different times now. I don't matter enough anymore."

"You matter to me," Holly said.

"This village is my home," Big Gregg said. "If a rampaging herd of cows can't scare me away, the Masterlys won't either, but I'm tired of fighting. Sometimes, retreat is the better option so why don't we go inside and have a couple of gins?"

Holly's smile slipped when she saw the man she was waiting for.

Mr MacFarlene shuffled along the high street, heading toward the media hub. Gone were the days when he propped up Big Gregg's bar, not when he could get drunk for free. She didn't even blame him. At least not for that. The media hub was the perfect honey trap, distracting the residents while their homes were demolished around them.

"Another time," Holly said to Big Gregg. "I promise."

She hurried after Mr MacFarlene, catching him before he made it to the hub.

He spun to face her, his face draining to white. "I'm so sorry. I'm so sorry for what I did."

"You were my husband's guest."

"I know, but it wasn't like that."

Holly stamped her foot, unheeding of his words. "Derek thought you were his friend," she said. "I thought so, too."

"I can explain." Mr MacFarlene said.

"Why did you do it?" Holly asked. "What were you looking for?"

Mr MacFarlene searched the buildings, searched the people. His eyes only stopped roaming when they looked over Holly's shoulder.

"Come to my house tonight. I'll explain everything," he said, stepping away. Breaking into a run, Mr MacFarlene fled down the street.

Holly turned around to see what had frightened him.

Mrs Masterly smiled back at her.

"Causing trouble?" she asked, her flawless teeth gleaming.

As if on cue, there was a distant rumble of thunder. It reverberated around the village green, drawing gasps from those at the hub. The rumble continued, building into a high pitched keen.

"Chainsaws," Mrs Masterly said. "The clearance is going at quite the pace."

"You can't do that."

"My husband always gets what he wants. How is yours, by the way?"

The frustration in Holly's throat threatened to choke her. "Fine. Thank you."

"I'm surprised to hear that," Mrs Masterly said. "We saw him here the other day. Asked my husband for a job. Again."

"Why don't you leave Derek alone?" Holly asked.

"We told him to come back when he was a little less inebriated."

The thought of a drunken Derek begging for a job mixed with the cries of the chainsaws. It clouded Holly's vision and flipped her stomach with shame.

"Why are you here?" Holly asked. "Surely, you have some liposuction that needs doing."

Mrs Masterly's porcelain skin coloured around the edges, but showed no signs of cracking.

"I'm supervising the removal of our media hub," she said.

"Is the dissemination of your propaganda over?"

Mrs Masterly looked to the Sold sign on The Travelling Star pub. "I think we both know that was never its purpose."

"Didn't we just. So who's next on your list? Me? The paper? The Winnows?"

"Don't get paranoid, Mrs Fleet. We're here to help."

"I'll tell everyone what you're doing," Holly said. "I can see what you're doing from a mile away. Nothing gets past me."

Holly leapt out of the way as a silver truck almost reversed into her. A driver hopped out and began shackling the media hub to the tow bar.

"Go ahead and tell them," Mrs Masterly said, reaching into her handbag for a vial of perfume. She dabbed it on her wrists, rubbing them together, like a stick insect cleaning its legs. "The paper will die without a village and from what I hear, the Winnows are their own worst enemies. Shouldn't take much to deal with them."

The perfume's scent nauseated Holly. It smelled of flowers and burnt wood. Mrs Masterly had a protective aura stemming from privilege. It was like her perfume, toxic and impenetrable. No one was allowed too close, not that Holly wanted to be.

Unless she got the chance to slap the Botox out of her face.

Holly swallowed hard, wafting the smell from her nose. "There are people trying to stop you. They're getting close."

Dropping the perfume into her bag, Mrs Masterly inhaled deeply. "The missing lady Nancy Foxglove. The madman Arnold Salting. Yes, I know. I'm also told they are residing with the farmer Mr MacFarlene.

The man you were chatting with earlier."

"I don't know who you mean."

"Mr MacFarlene is more troubled than you think. What did he say?"

Holly frowned, fully aware of the wrinkles now grouped around her own eyes. "We were talking about starting a band together. It's going to be called 'None of Your Business.'"

"And you'd be right," Mrs Masterly said, her painted eyebrows rising, "but he's a gossip with nothing to say. I wouldn't trust him, if I were you."

The black Rover appeared by the kerb and Mrs Masterly slid inside.

The media hub was secured to the silver truck and they pulled away in tandem.

Holly watched Mrs Masterly's car cruise along the high street. It paused by the Winnows' new souvenir shop before continuing out of sight.

Without their free alcohol, the residents saw no reason to stay. They offered garbled goodbyes and staggered to their homes to sleep it off.

Holly was left alone with the stink of Mrs Masterly's perfume in her nostrils and the whine of chainsaws in her ears. Big Gregg was inside his lonely bar, probably packing his memories away in makeshift boxes.

Holly hoped Callum was having a better time of it. She'd guessed Mr MacFarlene would break away from Nancy and Arnold to indulge in his favourite pastime. She hadn't expected him to bolt at the sight of Mrs Masterly, though Holly understood why he might.

She'd meet Mr MacFarlene tonight and perhaps more pieces of the puzzle would be revealed. Holly allowed herself a moment of optimism until she noticed Black Eye Bobby watching her from a distant rooftop. The raven cawed, its voice sounding like a deep-throated laugh.

Chapter Forty-One

Holly arrived at Mr MacFarlene's farmhouse to the sight of flashing blue lights. It was dark and they lit up the sky like beacons. Two police cars were parked nose to nose as if they'd come from opposite directions in a pincer movement. Officers mooched around the front garden, kicking up gravel. The lights shone from inside the house, making their high-vis jackets glow as if they were angels.

Holly killed her headlights and reversed into a lay-by. She left her car and crept along the hedgerow to get a better view. Being a diligent journalist, Holly cursed when she realised she'd forgotten her camera.

A figure crawled out of the hedge. "What are you doing here?" it asked.

"For the love of God, Callum. I need to put a bell around your neck," Holly said above the decibels of her heartbeat.

Callum brushed leaves from his clothes and dragged her down into a squat.

"What's going on?" Holly asked.

"They came from nowhere. Screeched to a halt and went inside."

"Are Nancy and Arnold in there?"

Callum shook his head and a twig fell out. "No. They were on their way back, but they saw the lights and scarpered. It's just Mr MacFarlene."

"What have the pair of them been doing?"

"Nothing. All day long," Callum said. "They've been walking around the estate for days."

Poking her head above the hedgerow, Holly watched the police as they stiffened to attention.

The black Rover emerged from the night, its powerful headlights robbing the officers of their glow. They rushed to the vehicle's window and a white face appeared.

Holly could almost smell her rotten perfume. Mrs Masterly spoke a few whispered words and the police bustled into the farmer's house. Slender legs appeared and Mrs Masterly climbed from the Rover, facing the hedgerow.

Holly ducked behind the hedge, her breath caught in her throat. There was no way she could be seen, no way Mrs Masterly knew Holly was there, but she wasn't going to take the risk.

Mrs Masterly had an unerring ability to be one step ahead.

"What's going on?" Callum whispered.

"Something bad."

Holly waited until the sound of a car engine told her Mrs Masterly was leaving. She parted the shrubbery and saw brake lights floating like UFO's in the distance. The tension drained from Holly's shoulders to return when she looked at the farmhouse.

Mr MacFarlene stood in his doorway, grim-faced officers on either side of him. His cheeks were cherry red, the result of years of whisky abuse, but the rest of his face was a shock of white. He was dragged along the garden path, his arms locked behind him.

Holly staggered out of the hedgerow, stepping into the light of Mr MacFarlene's home.

He saw her and raised his head high. "The farm is all I have left of my wife," he shouted. "I'd do anything to protect it. Anything."

The officers hurried him to a waiting car and Mr MacFarlene was manhandled inside. The door was clanged shut, waking dormant wildlife, who emerged with a howl.

Callum pulled Holly behind the hedge before she was spotted by the police.

"I overheard two of the officers talking before you got here," Callum said. He moved position, but didn't look comfortable. "It's serious."

"How serious? He's just a farmer."

Callum picked a stray twig from the ground and snapped it in his hand. "Mr MacFarlene. He was the one who hurt Regina."

Chapter Forty-Two

Old Jack stood in the garden and threw a tennis ball in the air. It landed, rolling into the hooves of Nancy's goat, who eyed it imperiously.

"I swear to you," he said, "yesterday, that goat caught the ball and brought it back to me."

Holly watched him from the patio, her hands resting on the back of a plastic chair. The air was filled with rain waiting to fall. Judging by the angry faces of the clouds, when it arrived, it would be heavy and persistent; the kind of rain that forced people indoors to wince as it washed down their homes.

With a grin, Old Jack retrieved the tennis ball and tried again. It bounced awkwardly, spinning to the edge of the lawn. The goat followed, nudging it with its nose until the ball was pushed under the fence into the neighbour's garden.

"There goes another one," Old Jack said.

"You seem better," Holly said.

Old Jack gave her a wink. "The pills are finally kicking in, pet. Plus I've had time to think things through."

"That's good," Holly said, rubbing the nape of her neck. This wasn't going to be easy, she thought. "Shall we have some tea?"

They went inside, settling in the kitchen away from the burgeoning rain. Old Jack busied himself making tea while Holly sat at a table, playing with her wonky fringe.

"I'm not out of the woods yet, of course," Old Jack said. "One day at a time. Isn't that what they say? But I'm glad to see you're still working on our little problem."

Holly had told him what she'd witnessed at Mr MacFarlene's farm. Old Jack had pursed his lips in sympathy before finding a fresh tennis ball for the goat.

"I'm not sure how far I'm getting," Holly said.

Old Jack set two mugs on the table, steam spiralling over the hot liquid.

Holly stared into the mug. "Are you sure you're okay?"

"Don't worry about me, pet," Old Jack said. "It was a funny turn, that's all."

"Jack?"

"What is it? Come on, drink up afore it gets cold."

Holly shifted in her seat. "You forgot to put the tea bags in."

Old Jack craned over the mugs, his confusion reflected in the clear water. He looked over his shoulder at the kitchen counter. "But I got them out. They're on the counter. I can see them."

Glancing at the unopened box of teabags, Holly cradled her mug in her hands. "Don't worry about it."

"I guess I must have..."

"Why don't you sit down?" Holly asked. "I've got some good news."

Old Jack fell into the seat opposite her. His chin trembled and he shrank inside his woollen cardigan. "It's hard to concentrate sometimes. I forget things."

"I'm not that thirsty," Holly said, her mouth dry. "Do you want to hear my good news?"

Old Jack's blue eyes blazed razor sharp, like a drowning man finally finding a lifeboat on the horizon. They burned for a second and then dimmed as he pulled at a thread on his clothes.

"We've found Nancy," Holly said. "She's fine."

"Is she here?"

"No, she's not here, but she was asking after you."

Old Jack smiled, some of the colour returning to his face.

But Nancy hadn't asked after Old Jack. She'd been dismissive of him. Contemptuous, even. What was it about Old Jack that had stoked Nancy's ire?

"What is it?" he asked.

Holly stood from her seat, taking their mugs to the sink. "I better go. Things to do."

"I might not be able to make a cup of tea," Old Jack said, "but I still know when someone is hiding a secret."

"You say things like that and I believe you," Holly said, pouring hot water down the drain, "but it never makes it into the Herald. You know everything and everyone in the village. You could help people with what you know."

"I do help people," Old Jack said. "People like you."

"And I appreciate it, but are we really journalists? Are you?"

The last of the water circled the drain. Holly turned from the sink and held Old Jack's gaze. "Nancy isn't okay. She's mixed up in something I don't understand. I'm trying to help, but I'm worried she's going to get hurt."

Without meaning to, Holly told Old Jack everything. The bulbs, the Wentworths and the Masterlys' slow strangulation of the village. It slewed out of her and with each word passing her lips, she felt lighter and Holly knew why. She was placing her burden onto the frail shoulders of Old Jack.

Lost in a sea of insurmountable questions, it was the reason she was visiting her boss. And in knowing that, Holly realised something else. She saw her deceased father in the diminished figure before her. They were both men whose strength had been rinsed from them, like laundry washed clean of its colour. She should be more protective,

Holly thought and she should have been there for her father's demise.

Old Jack stared through the kitchen window to the village he'd grown up in. His gaunt face was reflected in the glass until he returned his attention to Holly.

"Nancy never did what people expected," Old Jack said, tracing his finger along the grooves of the table. "Even her sister failed to control her, failed to keep her indoors. I wish I could have helped them more."

"What am I going to do?" Holly asked.

"The important thing is the village," Old Jack said. "Us doddery old has-beens will be gone soon enough. It's the young blood, people like you who need to protect it."

Holly slapped her hand against the sink, accidentally turning on one of the taps. Water gushed out, hitting the mugs and covering her in cold liquid. She switched it off and searched the kitchen for a towel.

On a shelf above a rattling old freezer was a pile of unopened post.

"Mrs Masterly believes the Herald will need new owners soon," Holly said. "I think she'll make you an offer."

Old Jack cupped his chin in his hand. "Good for her."

"Could she have mailed something to you?" Holly picked up the envelopes, her fingertips skipping through them until she found one with the Salting stamp.

"I think this is it," she said. "This might be the offer."

"I'd sooner see the place burned to the ground," Old Jack said, his eyes flashing an icy blue. "It's not for sale. At any price."

If Holly was going to protect the village, it meant protecting its residents first. It was too late for Big Gregg. He was the hero who had seen too many fights. He was resigned to whatever fate had in store for him, but it wasn't too late for the others.

She placed the envelope in Old Jack's gnarled hand.

"Think about it," she said. "We don't all have to lose."

Holly made Old Jack another tea, remembering to include a bag this time. Saying her farewells with a promise to return, she walked toward the Winnows' shop. Callum had lost his home. Big Gregg had lost his pub. There was a hope that Old Jack might take the money and run, but the Masterlys' hit list was long and cruel.

And the Winnows could be next.

Chapter Forty-Three

They stood behind the counter, their shoulders rubbing and causing static. Hot sparks shot from their eyes.

"I told you to order more," Mrs Winnow said, throwing her arms above her head.

"No, you said the order needs doing," Mr Winnow answered, furiously polishing the counter. "Not that I needed to do it."

"Oh, so you assumed I was going to do it? Typical."

Mr Winnow took the rag in his hands and strangled it. "I didn't assume anything."

"Why don't you just do what you say you're going to do?"

"Who's saying anything?" Mr Winnow said, a vein threatening to burst in his forehead.

The hiss of their heated conversation forced a mushrooming headache onto Holly. She pressed soothing fingers into her forehead and waited to be noticed. She'd learned a long time ago never to interrupt a couple in the middle of an argument.

"Well, I'm saying it now," Mrs Winnow shouted.

It sounded like the old 'I said, you said' classic; the argument all married couples were doomed to have from time to time. Derek and Holly had had a few zingers like that.

"Thanks for that," Mr Winnow said, interrupting Holly's train of thought. She looked up to find him on his own, leaning on the counter with his head in his hands.

"Thanks for what?" she asked.

"I told her about...you know." Mr Winnow looked left and right. "Everything, and now she's on my case. She won't let me out her sight."

"And that's my fault, how?"

"It's not, I suppose," he said, straightening, "but life was a lot easier when I had my secrets."

"Where is your wife now?" Holly asked and Mr Winnow pointed to the ceiling.

"Upstairs. Writing out an order for more books and thinking of more ways to make me miserable." Mr Winnow hung his head. "I don't really know anymore."

The bookcase was well stocked with walking maps, tourist guides and wildlife books. There was a gap in the middle with one book lying on its own.

Holly picked it up. "The History of Northumberland," she said. "I keep seeing this around."

"It's a big seller," Mr Winnow said, stepping away from his counter. "I think with all the new changes around here, people want to reminisce."

Flicking through the pages, Holly saw chunks of dense text and photographs of castles and beaches.

"It's the last one," Mr Winnow prompted.

Holly couldn't see the appeal, but tucked it under her arm anyway. "Are you doing okay?" she asked.

"Apart from starting World War Three every time I open my mouth, you mean? Things are fine."

"The Masterlys haven't been interfering?" Holly asked. "Nothing strange going on?"

Mr Winnow picked at skin around his fingernails. "Do I need to be worried about something?"

Holly wanted to say yes. Not to frighten him, but to put him on his guard.

"Not at all," she said. "Just being nosey."

Despite being involved in activities that skirted close to criminality, Mr Winnow was a nervous man and Holly didn't want to worry him unnecessarily. Perhaps the Masterlys would leave him alone.

"Good," said Mr Winnow, wiping his brow. "What with Judy on the warpath and the tax man on my back, I don't need any more trouble. I have little enough hair as it is."

"The tax man?" Holly asked.

"It's nothing. Her Majesty's best are doing an audit on our business accounts. It's routine. All part of a bigger picture, they say."

"But they've never looked at your books before?"

Mr Winnow shook his head and gave her a grin. "They'll not find anything. My books are as tight as a gnat's chuff. Speaking of which, are you buying that book or shoplifting?" He pressed in close and whispered into her ear. "If you pay cash, I don't have to put it through the till."

It was too much of a coincidence, wasn't it? Little Belton businesses were being picked off one by one and suddenly HMRC was interested in the Winnows. The reach of the Masterlys was long and wide-ranging. Holly suspected the worst. The Winnows were going to need help.

Checking the price tag, Holly fished for money in her purse. She found her emergency fiver and looked apologetically at Mr Winnow.

"Don't worry," he said. "You can pay me the rest when you have it."

But Holly was worried. She was worried about everyone.

Chapter Forty-Four

She'd returned the last of her clothes to the wardrobe. They'd stayed there for a painful five minutes before Holly removed them again. Filling her arms, she carried load after load to the washing machine downstairs. Deep clean cycle. Hottest possible setting. While her clothes were boiled, she cleaned her bedroom furniture. First with a light bleach solution and then with disinfectant. The air smelled like a swimming pool.

Holly's arms ached and her feet were swollen. She longed for a shower to rinse away the feeling of an intruder in her house, but her body wouldn't move. She slumped on the edge of her bed and stared at a wall.

A floorboard creaked in the hallway. Holly saw Derek in the doorway. He was dressed, which was something new, and his hair was combed.

Holly picked up *The History of Northumberland* and pretended to read.

She heard Derek huff from the doorway.

"I know you're not talking to me," he said, "and I don't blame you. If I'd known Mr MacFarlene was going to go through our house, I would never have allowed him inside."

Holly turned a page, slapping it into place.

"Did he take anything?" Derek asked.

"We have nothing worth taking."

"I suppose what we had, we lost a long time ago."

The truth of his remark stung and the words on the page blurred. Holly blinked back a tear, turning to a new chapter. She didn't want it to be true.

"I'm sorry," Derek said. "For everything."

"Why didn't you try harder, Derek? This could have worked." Holly's voice sounded small in her head, not really belonging to her anymore. "I could have done the same."

The floorboard creaked again as Derek altered the weight in his stance. "We're not all like you. Not everyone adapts so readily."

"What are you saying?" Holly asked, her eyes narrowing. If her voice was unfamiliar before, she was finding it now.

"All your new friends. Disappearing for days at a time. This silly obsession you have with Callum."

"Leave him out of this," Holly said. "He has nothing to do with what you've done."

"You're twice his age," Derek shouted.

Holly snorted hot air from her nostrils, her breathing coming in short blasts as she tried to control her anger. Cruel words formed in her mind, things she knew she'd never be able to take back. She wanted to say them. She wanted to scream them inches from Derek's face until he withered under her disappointment, but she didn't.

Derek was telling the truth. She had moved on quicker than he had. She'd had to, but the more time she'd spent in the village, the more she enjoyed it and the more she dreaded coming home.

And Callum was a part of that.

She returned to the book, forcing herself to read and calm down. It was only when she noted a particular word that her interest was piqued.

Star.

Derek sighed. "I didn't come up here to argue with you."

Holly studied a picture of a flower. It had five white petals with a faint green vein down the centre.

"I called my brother this morning," Derek continued. "He's starting his own business."

The flower was unusual because it opened at night when it was pollinated by nocturnal insects. It had grown wild in the Northumberland hills, becoming part of local lore. It was said the flower was used by devil worshippers as a sleeping draught from which the recipient never woke.

"He wants me to be his partner," Derek continued. "It means moving to Chiswick, but I said, yes."

Holly's stomach flipped and she held the book tightly to her chest.

"There's no point in delaying the inevitable. I'm driving down today," Derek said.

This was it, Holly thought. This was what they were after. Follow The Star. It seemed so obvious.

Holly jumped to her feet, spiralling in a circle, unsure where to start, but she knew she had to find Callum.

"Are you even listening to me?" Derek asked. "I've just said, I'm leaving you."

Holly's steps faltered on her way to the door. Derek was waiting for a response. His eyes bored into her. He looked angry. No, not angry. Exasperated. Alone. Her heart lurched. What had she done to him to make him look that way?

Even as the thought bubbled up in her mind, she knew she was about to do it again.

"Don't leave," she said.

"You don't want me here. I'm getting in your way."

"You're not," Holly said, squeezing past him through the door. "I want you to stay."

Derek's face lightened. "Really? But why?"

Holly swapped the heavy book from arm to arm. Callum needed to see it.

A hesitant smile appeared on Derek's face, but Holly edged away.

By the front door, there was a bowl on the table where they kept their car keys.

They had one vehicle and Holly couldn't let Derek take it.

Oh God, she thought. You deserve to be divorced.

"Just stay," she said and hurtled down the stairs before Derek could stop her.

Holly snatched the keys. "I can save the village and I can save our marriage. Just give me time."

"I need that car," Derek shouted after her. "I'm going to Chiswick."

She bolted from the house, jumping into their grumbly car and throwing the book on the passenger seat.

Holly fled toward Little Belton.

Don't look back. Don't look back. Don't look back. But she did and found Derek watching her from the driveway, his figure shrinking the faster she went.

Holly parked as close to The Travelling Star as she could, but it wasn't close enough. She ran along the high street and burst through its doors.

"Where's Callum?" she asked in between gasps for air.

Big Gregg looked up from polishing a glass with his rag. "He's in his room. What's that you've got there?"

Holly lifted up *The History of Northumberland* so Big Gregg could see it.

"Not you as well," he said. "Every bugger and their dog has a copy of that."

"It's not a book," Holly said, grinning. "It's our answer."

She charged up the stairs to the hotel above. Coming to Callum's room, she thought briefly of knocking before barging straight in.

Had she knocked, she realised later, she might not have been so shocked.

Chapter Forty-Five

Callum was by the window, his hands clasped behind his back. He had tidied his room after the break-in, returning it to normal. What remained of his animal pelts were folded neatly and toiletries stood like soldiers on a chipped mirrored cabinet. With everything in place, the room looked larger or it would have done if it wasn't for the two people perched on the side of Callum's bed.

Nancy and Arnold sat up on Holly's entry. They stared at her and she stared back.

"They turned up five minutes ago," Callum said.

"How did you get here?" Holly asked them.

Arnold tried to stand, but Nancy yanked him back.

"We followed Callum here," Nancy said. "We had nowhere else to go, dear."

Holly was fully aware that Callum was supposed to be following them, not the other way around, but now wasn't the time to bring it up. She closed the door and looked for a seat. Holly desperately needed to sit down.

"What do you want?" she asked.

"Bulbs," Arnold said. "We need more bulbs."

Nancy shot him a withering glance and he fell silent again.

Although Holly knew what the bulbs were, she didn't understand their significance. She held tightly to her book, not yet ready to divulge her findings.

"I think we're all on the same side," Holly said. "We're all trying to stop the Masterlys from destroying the village. Perhaps it's time we joined forces."

Nancy gave a curt nod. "When we talked on the estate, I thought the same, but I had to be sure. There's too much at stake."

"Either that or you just need a new place to stay," Callum said. "Now that Mr MacFarlene is banged up in jail."

"He's not in jail, dear," Nancy said. "He's being questioned and he'll be out soon enough."

"How do you know that?"

Arnold's hands flexing into fists. "He was set up."

"We saw Mrs Masterly there," Holly conceded. "She seemed to be directing operations."

Nancy adjusted her many skirts, a frown etching deep into her brow. "We were working in the manor after Arnold stole the keys, but when we had to leave – "

"Thanks to you two," Arnold said, interrupting.

"Mr MacFarlene found us on his land. He was sympathetic. He stands to lose as much as anyone if the estate is developed so he gave us somewhere to stay."

Holly recalled her encounter with Mrs Masterly outside of the hub. She'd been suspicious of Mr MacFarlene and the farmer had certainly been afraid of her.

"We swore him to secrecy," Arnold said. "He was very committed to saving his farm."

"He broke into my house," Holly said, her temper flaring.

Nancy cast her eyes to the floor. "We do need more bulbs. We'd hoped you might have stashed some away. Either in this room or in yours, dear."

"Why didn't you talk to us?" Callum asked.

"Too dangerous," Arnold said.

"We'd already brought Mr MacFarlene into the fold," Nancy said. "We couldn't risk widening our circle any further. There are enough rumours flying about this village as it is."

"Will someone explain to me why these bleeding bulbs are so important please?" Callum asked, scratching his head.

Holly handed him the book. "Page 146," she said, turning her attention back to Nancy. "You can't buy these bulbs anywhere else, can you?"

Nancy and Arnold shuffled their feet, mud from their boots peppering the floor.

"Because you're not supposed to have them," Holly continued. "That's why they were made to look like tinned salmon."

Callum finished reading *The History of Northumberland* and slammed it shut with one hand. "No wonder Bryan couldn't find those bulbs. The flower has been extinct for over two hundred years."

"It's not extinct," Arnold said. "It's endangered."

"How would you know?" Callum asked. "You're a headcase."

Arnold bristled, but remained seated. "It's my job to know. I do land surveys. Before any building work or redevelopment can take place, the authorities have to be sure specialised habitats aren't about to be destroyed."

"So, what happened?" Holly asked.

"The Masterlys put pressure on my brother to rush the process through. We fought about it, but my brother was always too greedy. Have you seen all those ugly, stuffed animals in his office? He didn't think it was important and the ecology survey was never done."

"Nancy had been pestering you for months about the proposal," Holly said.

"I found an ally in her," Arnold said. "We knew how far the Masterlys would go to secure their damned theme park so we decided to stop them."

Holly picked at her fingernails. "Nancy decided to go missing to help you search for something, anything to block their plans."

"A body called Natural England decides if a developer has their building plans approved," Arnold said. "They have enforcement powers. They'd close the Masterlys down if they discovered due compensations hadn't been carried."

"The fact that a survey hadn't been completed wasn't enough," Nancy said, placing a hand on Arnold's knee. "If we'd based our objection on that, the Masterlys would simply produce one out of thin air. We had to find something special, something endangered, but the deer had grazed the land. What they didn't eat, they trampled. Ecology is all about balance. When one species grows too dominant, it makes it difficult for all the rest."

"Just like Arcadia Leisure," Holly said to herself.

"When we lost the bulbs, we were desperate," Arnold said.

"But you didn't leave it there, did you? You bought sticklebacks from the Winnows," Holly said, "hoping they might be a rare variety."

Arnold nodded.

"You stole my furs in case they were from endangered mammals," Callum said. "As if I'd do anything like that."

"But there was nothing special about me," Holly said. "Why follow me?"

"They were hedging their bets," Callum said, waving the book. "Maybe hoping you kept snow leopards in your back garden."

"When we found out you were looking for me," Nancy said, "we thought it best to keep you on our radar."

Arnold worried at his stubbled chin. "And you had our bulbs, of course."

"They came from some sort of specialist collector," Holly said. "Somewhere like Kew Gardens, but more open to bribery."

Nancy and Arnold slid closer together and said nothing.

"You plant them in the estate," Holly said, "and quicker than you can say protected heritage site of interest, the building work grinds to a halt."

"We're trying to save the village, dear," Nancy said.

"By doing something illegal?" Holly asked.

She let the question hang in the air. Nancy and Arnold clearly thought of themselves as eco-warriors, defenders of the rural ways, but they were acting like criminals. Their hearts were in the right place, but it didn't excuse them from breaking the law.

"You must have known what you were doing was a deception," Holly said.

"What about the Masterlys?" Arnold said, his voice raised. "After everything they've done?"

"What have they done that was so bad?" Holly asked.

The atmosphere in the room cooled to freezing. Callum, Nancy and Arnold looked at her aghast.

"They've been underhand, manipulative and sly," Holly said, "but they haven't broken the law."

Callum ran a hand through his hair. "What about Mr MacFarlene?"

"If what Arnold said is right, he's been set up. Probably to stop him from doing something stupid. More stupid, I should say," Holly said, remembering her wreckage of a bedroom. "All that took was a phone call from a concerned citizen. Nothing illegal in that."

"But he's a good man," Arnold said.

Holly stared pointedly at Nancy. "What is illegal, though is tricking Mr Winnow into transporting bulbs for you."

"I didn't do that," Nancy said.

"The Masterlys bankrupted Big Gregg," Callum said, "and I've been evicted."

Holly paced the floor. The room was too small and she only managed two steps in one direction before being forced to turn around. "I'm sorry, but all they did was what big business has been doing to the little people from day one. Manipulating the system and cashing the cheques."

They fell silent, listening to the distant sound of chainsaws tearing the estate apart.

"I never knew it was called the Star of Northumberland," Callum said quietly. "The flower. We got your note and we thought Follow the Star meant following a particular deer."

"What note?" Nancy asked.

Callum paused, closing his eyes briefly before continuing. "It never made any sense. By the time we caught up with the herd, whatever endangered species they'd eaten would already be falling from their back end."

Holly winced, trying to scrub the image from her mind. "We thought it had something to do with this pub, but that didn't make sense, either."

"On some level, Nancy, you must have known you were heading down the wrong path. That's why you left the note on the Herald's door. It was for Old Jack. You knew he'd move mountains for you. He was supposed to find the flower before you did anything silly, but I got the note. Not him."

Hanging her head, Nancy gulped back a sob. "I can't believe we've failed to save the estate."

Arnold's face grew ashen. "They're going to win, after all."

Holly sat next to them, keeping quiet. Whatever they'd done, they'd done it for the good of others. That should have meant something, but Holly knew that it didn't. Good intentions paved the road to hell.

And in this case, they'd pave over Little Belton to make way for a car park.

The chainsaws died and Callum began whistling. He bent over to tighten his bootlaces and stood up with a grin.

"Callum?" Holly asked. "Are you alright?"

"Champion, thanks," he said, putting on his wax jacket.

"Maybe this isn't an appropriate time for whistling show tunes," Holly said.

"I said, I didn't know they were called the Star of Northumberland. Not that I didn't know what they were." Callum went to the door and opened it. "Are you coming?"

"What are you talking about?" Holly asked, beginning to get frustrated.

"I know every inch of this estate," Callum said. "Better than anyone and I know where to find the flowers."

Chapter Forty-Six

"My Dad showed me strange flowers when I was a kid," Callum said from behind the wheel of the Defender. Bouncing along a cobbled path, the occupants held onto one another for support as they raced against a setting sun. Mountain shadows stretched like creeping fingers across the estate, closing it down for another night.

"You're going too fast," Arnold said, slamming into Nancy in the back seat.

Callum pressed harder on the accelerator. "They only open when it's dark, he'd said, but we have to get there soon."

Holly held onto her seatbelt with both hands. "Why?"

"Because they're in a dell," Callum said.

"What dell?" Arnold asked. "We never found anything like that."

The Defender plunged down a road cutting through Crannock Hills like a scar. Sheep stood by the wayside, watching them with dumb curiosity. The sound of the engine drew the animals into their path and Callum swore under his breath.

"It's called the Devil's Bathtub," he said, swerving in and out of wool. "Dad said it was where Lucifer bathed before going out to cause his mischief."

"But why are you rushing to get there?" Arnold asked.

"The dell is twenty feet deep. It's too dangerous to descend at night."

The road took them to the northern fringe of the estate. The grassland was pitted with boulders. Trees lay on their sides, blown over by winter gales. There were no birds or game. Not even the sheep dared to stray this far north.

It was easy to see why the devil would choose this area for bath night, thought Holly.

"How much further?" she asked.

"Over this next hill," Callum said, cresting the slope.

He slammed on the brakes and the Defender skidded, its back wheels skirting to the left. He corrected its trajectory, hissing through his teeth.

Traffic cones were stacked in the road like plastic stalagmites.

Callum slipped from the jeep and stalked closer for a better look.

The road dipped to a wasteland devoid of trees. They hadn't fallen. They'd been felled, their branches stripped and their trunks lying naked in a pile. Brown portacabins and muddy white caravans were arranged in rows. There was a communal area where men and women in orange vests sat on barrels or patio furniture. It was the end of the day and their work was done. The workers laughed and joked with one another or sat back on deckchairs with a beer.

"Who are they?" Holly asked.

Callum crouched by a hillock.

"Contractors," he said. "They live here until the area is cleared and then move to another site."

"They're more like a plague of locusts," Nancy said.

Someone from the camp turned on a radio and people started dancing, raising their drinks in the air.

"It makes me sick," Arnold said, crawling forward. "Look at them. Don't they understand the damage they're doing?"

"They're just happy to be working again," Holly said, watching them sing and dance. She wasn't surprised to recognise a few faces from the village. Mrs Threadle, the nettle-wine drinking teacher, stumbled from a portacabin. She wore an orange vest like the others and carried a bottle in each hand. Winding through the group, she poured out refreshments, each drop accompanied by a drunken giggle.

Arnold jumped to his feet. "Scab. Scab. Scab."

Callum grabbed him by the neck and threw him to the ground. "This isn't the miner's strike, Arnold and you won't use that word around me. Understand?"

Arnold lay where he fell, ruffling his clothing like they were the feathers of a deposed cockerel.

"Where is the dell?" Holly asked Callum.

Wrenching his eyes from Arnold, Callum looked to the other side of the encampment. "Over there. We're going to have to go around. The contractors won't take kindly to us strolling through their sing-song."

They gathered what they needed from the Defender and set out on foot. Callum led the way, scrambling from foothold to foothold as he made his way down a slope. Nancy and Arnold followed, sure-footed and moving like a breeze. Holly brought up the rear, shuffling downward on her bottom.

Reaching the valley floor, she rubbed the soreness from her cheeks and attempted to catch up with the others. It was hard going. Night was fast approaching and Callum was setting a blistering pace. She saw him have a word with Nancy and Arnold, pointing in a certain direction. They moved on, but Callum waited.

"We need to be faster," he said as Holly collapsed to her knees in front of him.

"I'm too old for this," Holly said, wiping her brow.

"Don't say things like that," Callum said, picking her up. "I might have to shoot you."

They fell into step with one another. Callum hiked quickly, head bowed, but Holly could tell he was holding back. Grateful for that small mercy, she worked harder than she would have liked.

"You were pretty hard on Arnold back there," she said.

"I don't like him."

"Seemed like more than that," Holly said.

Callum waded through a patch of sedge grass, guiding Holly through by her hand. "Dad told me about the strike. Friends, families, fathers and sons. They turned on each other. Even after the strike, those that broke the picket line were always known as the S-word."

"But he was a gamekeeper," Holly said. "He wouldn't have been involved."

"He worked for the Wentworths and people thought he should have come out in solidarity." Callum stopped by a rotten tree stump and kicked it until his boots were covered in shards of wood. "He kept working. He was loyal to a fault."

"Like you," Holly said.

"It cost him his reputation. That's why no one came to his funeral. It's why I don't go to theirs."

"They were scared and bitter and hopeless," Holly said. "You can't blame them for that."

"I know," Callum said. "My Dad never did, either."

"And here you are," Holly said, "saving a village that turned their back on you. Your father would be proud."

Callum shook his boots free of splinters. "I'm doing this for you, not them."

A high-pitched whistle cut through the air. Holly and Callum saw the others waving frantically.

"Let's go," Callum said.

A quick march led them to a brook where water bounced over rounded rocks.

"Which way now?" Nancy asked.

Callum pointed in the direction of the flow and they followed the trickling water for half a mile. Nancy stumbled in the fading light, but

Callum caught her before she fell.

"We're not going to make it," he said.

"We have to," Arnold said, increasing his speed, leaving the others behind.

"Don't go too far," Callum shouted after him.

Arnold stomped onward, his form blurring in the dark.

Nancy watched him go. "He's lived under the shadow of his brother for so long. He wants his share of the light."

"Hang back," Callum shouted at Arnold. "You're almost there."

They listened to his footsteps receding.

There was a yell and clacking noises, like rocks hitting each other. For a brief moment, there was silence followed by a thump.

Callum rushed along the brook, his arms pumping at his sides. The water gushed over the edge of the dell. It tumbled into a circular pool, sending foam and spray into the air. Lying next to it was Arnold. His leg was twisted at an awkward angle.

By his head was a circle of white flowers opening in the dusk.

Chapter Forty-Seven

"We can't leave him like that," Nancy said.

Dropping to her knees, she searched for a place to descend, her hands scratching at the ground near the edge. She moved fast, too fast, dislodging a rock. It plummeted into the pool, inches from Arnold's head. Water splashed over his face, stirring him from his stupor.

"Help me," he said weakly.

"We have to leave him," Callum said. "We try to rescue him and we could all end up down there."

Nancy twisted her skirts in an iron grip. "It's too cold to leave him."

"It's his own fault," Callum shouted at Arnold's writhing form.

"What are we going to do?" Holly asked.

The horizon was crowned with a red corona as the sun continued its course around the globe. It was replaced by the artificial light of the encampment and the faint ring of laughter.

"I'll go back," Callum said. "I'll get the Defender and then try to persuade some of the contractors to help."

"We don't need the likes of those people. It's their fault he's down there," Nancy said.

"Arnold fell because he wouldn't listen to Callum," Holly said. "Don't make the same mistake."

Callum shrugged off his jacket, handing it to Nancy. "Throw this into the dell," he said, "and make sure he covers himself."

He took Holly by the elbow, leading her to one side. "The Defender doesn't have a winch so I'm going to need rope and a few people to haul him out."

"I'm coming with you," Holly said.

Even in the dying light, she saw the disapproval in Callum's face and she held up her hand in defiance.

"And before you say I'm too slow," she said, "it will save time. You go to the Defender and I'll go to the encampment."

Callum folded his arms. "The ground is treacherous at night."

"I'll be careful."

"I can't slow down for you."

"You're doing an awful lot for someone you don't like." Holly cupped her hand to his cheek, drawing a thumb across his bristled jaw. "And I'm not asking for your permission."

"You're wasting time," Nancy shouted.

Holly waited for a response from Callum. His face was lost in shadow, but his green eyes shone like a cat's.

He let go of a long breath. "Do what I say when I say it, okay?"

Tightening her boot laces, Holly ran alongside Callum, matching him stride for stride. Her legs were already aching, but they operated independently of her, spurred on by desperation. She was careful, but swift, skipping over divots, spotting rocks before they had a chance to trip her.

Callum took the lead, checking over his shoulder from time to time. Holly ignored him, concentrating on her own path through the darkness.

The noise of the encampment grew louder and they stopped by a tower of bin bags filled with rotting rubbish.

"I'll get the Defender. You get the rope and extra hands," Callum said before disappearing into the night.

Holly wiped sweaty hair from her brow and rubbed her swollen calves.

Now that Callum was out of sight, she allowed her gait to return to normal. Holly lumbered into the encampment, holding on to a chest flexing like an accordion.

The crowd of contractors had thinned, most of them having retired for a few hours of precious sleep.

Holly walked into the light of a bonfire. Yellow flames shimmied through wooden pallets. Branches of fallen trees lay on top, their outer twigs shrivelling with heat, looking like a hand curling into a fist. Hissing in the embers were several aerosol cans used to mark trees before they were pulled down.

Tired men and women reclined in their chairs, enjoying the warmth, their eyelids drooping.

"There's been an accident," Holly said, waving her arms. "I need your help."

The contractors turned in their seats, their faces crinkling into scowls.

"Can someone help me?" she asked.

"What's the problem?" A woman around Holly's age, but wider and greyer, picked something from her teeth. "You lost or something?"

"A man has fallen down a dell," Holly said.

"A well?" someone else asked.

"No, a dell. We need to get him out. We need rope and some people to pull him out."

The grey-haired woman got to her feet. "I know you, don't I?"

"No," Holly said. "No, I don't think so."

"Yeah, I do." The woman made a show of placing her finger on her chin. "You were that mouthy bird on the village green."

An aerosol can exploded in the fire. It flew into the air, showering the contractors in sparks.

The grey-haired woman watched Holly cower from the explosion.

"You told the boss to get stuffed," she said. "You told him where to go."

"I didn't," Holly said. "I was just concerned – "

"Yeah, you did," the woman said. She plucked a lager can from a bucket of water and directed the opening spray at Holly. "You'd prefer it if we didn't have jobs."

The woman belched at the same time as another aerosol can detonated. It sailed over their heads, landing at Holly's feet, who danced out of its way.

"Someone is hurt," Holly said.

"We're hurting," the woman said, "but the Masterlys are coming to save us."

The contractors murmured to themselves, no longer looking at Holly.

What was wrong with these people, Holly thought? Someone's life was hanging in the balance. Why weren't they more concerned?

Mrs Threadle emerged from the darkness, steering Holly away from the fire.

They walked to the edge of the encampment where a halogen lamp lit up a car park of municipal vehicles.

"I remember you," Mrs Threadle said. "From school. Always asking questions. Question after question, it was."

Holly looked back to the fire. Most of the contractors had forgotten about her, content to watch the flames and wait for the next explosion.

But the grey-haired woman remained on her feet, her eyes trained in her direction.

"Why are they acting like that?" Holly asked.

Mrs Threadle was an attractive woman. She was curvy with brown hair and a Cupid's bow mouth. Nettle wine had done little to diminish her outer beauty, though Holly wondered how it had affected her in other ways.

"They need to keep their jobs," Mrs Threadle said.

Holly glanced at the grey-haired woman. "At the expense of another human being?"

"They aren't cruel, but you aren't the only one who needs help." Mrs Threadle twirled her hair through pudgy fingers. "Take some nettle wine and get to know them. You'll find they're just like you and me."

If Holly could return to Little Belton, there were people who would help. Big Gregg. The Winnows. Old Jack. But how long would that take her? How long did Arnold have?

Shaking her head, Holly's eyes found a row of vehicles lit with a tempting glow.

"Who keeps the keys for that Ford Ranger?" she asked.

The vehicle had a broad, chrome face and as many dints as a dropped fruit. More importantly, Holly saw it had a winch.

Mrs Threadle checked her pockets and found them empty. "I keep a register of all the vehicles. Part of my administration details."

"Do you think I could borrow the keys for the Ranger?"

"Oh, I don't have them on me," Mrs Threadle said. "We leave them in the ignition. It's not like they'd get stolen all the way out here, is it?"

Holly bit her lip and nodded. "Could you maybe ask your supervisor for permission? It's an emergency."

The light in Mrs Threadle's eyes dimmed as she looked to the portacabin behind her. "He doesn't like to be disturbed this late at night."

Holly pressed her hands together in prayer. "Please?"

"You always were a star pupil," Mrs Threadle said, a smile fluttering on her lips. "I'll do my best."

She shuffled to the portacabin while Holly swallowed her guilt. The moment Mrs Threadle's back was turned, Holly sidled toward the Ranger.

Callum would be arriving soon, drawing further unwanted attention. Holly would have to be quick. She crept to the Ranger, finding the keys inside. Turning on the engine, Holly ground the gears and sped off into the unknown. The encampment faded in her rearview mirror, but she could see the confused faces of the contractors around the fire. They stood and pointed in her direction.

Even though the Ranger was an all-terrain vehicle, the going was tough. Holly bounced and swerved her way around obstacles lit by her headlamps. There was no clear path to the encampment and there wasn't one going back.

Two headlights appeared behind her. Holly's heart fluttered, sending fear through every nerve ending. Someone was giving chase.

She pressed on, careening into the brook and sending a cascade of water over her windscreen. Holly checked the direction of the flow and followed it to the dell. She slowed, not wishing to repeat Arnold's mistake and plummet over the edge. She parked close enough to use the winch, suddenly realising she had never used one before.

The other vehicle closed in, coming to a stop beside her.

Callum leapt from the Defender.

"Thank God," Holly said. "I thought I was getting arrested."

"You're stealing cars now?" Callum asked.

"I'm not as popular as I thought," Holly said. "It was this or nothing."

Callum narrowed his eyes into the night. "Where's Nancy?"

They stared around the dell, but she wasn't there.

"Nancy?" Holly shouted.

"She hasn't, has she?" Callum asked.

Dropping to their stomachs, they wriggled as close to the edge as they dared. The combined light of the two vehicles lanced over their heads, failing to illuminate the depths below.

"Wait here," Callum said, backing away.

"Nancy?" Holly shouted into the hole. There was no response, except for the echo of her voice. "Arnold? Are you there?"

Callum returned, a torch in his hand. He shone it into the dell. The light glittered on the white flowers. They looked like the stars they were named after, but Arnold was gone and Nancy was nowhere to be seen.

"It's impossible," Callum said.

"Did she rescue Arnold by herself?" Holly asked.

"She'd be more likely to break her neck."

Holly inspected the sheer sides of the dell. "Is there another way down?"

"Not that I know of." Callum stood, shining his torch around them. "Look at this."

Callum found his wax jacket. It had been retrieved from the dell and folded neatly on a nearby rock.

"They obviously don't like your taste in fashion," Holly said.

Over the horizon came pinpricks of light. They appeared and disappeared as they negotiated the rolling landscape.

"It's the contractors," Callum said.

"I guess they want their car back."

"Time to go," Callum said, grabbing his jacket. He swung it over his head, wafting Holly with air.

"Wait," she said.

"We have to leave," Callum said. "Now."

Holly sniffed loudly. "Can you smell that?"

Frowning, Callum pushed his nose into his jacket. "Someone's been wearing this. It stinks," he said, removing it quickly. "What is it?"

"Perfume," Holly said, climbing into the Defender.

Not just any perfume, either. It was distinctive and memorable, belonging to someone who was hard to forget, no matter how hard Holly had tried.

Chapter Forty-Eight

Black Rock Manor was bathed in an eerie glow as if candlelight had been diffused through a fog. Its touch spread over a tow truck parked in the driveway. A chain swung lazily from its rusting crane. The driver's side door was open, but the driver was gone.

An ambulance bounced along the rutted track, its blue siren turning the landscape into snapshots of silver. It headed away from the manor, joining the road and leaving Holly and Callum behind.

"Busy night," Callum said.

"Park out of the way," Holly said, directing him toward an overgrown bush.

They sat and watched the house, listening to the calls of invisible owls in the trees.

"Are we going to knock then?" Callum asked.

"We can't just turn up like the Avon lady," Holly said. "How can we tell what's going on in there?"

Callum stretched his legs. "By knocking."

He had a point, she supposed.

So why was she hesitating?

"I think the Masterlys are in there," Holly said.

"What difference does that make?"

"You know what they're like. Mrs Masterly in particular." Holly toyed with her fringe, hoping to make it presentable. "She winds me up. I can't seem to think straight around her."

Callum opened the jeep door and got out, peering back inside the Defender. "Just because they're rich doesn't make them better than you."

Holly groaned, but managed a nod. She slumped from the Defender and walked to the manor, seizing a breath with every step.

"You do the honours," Callum said.

Holly braced herself before banging her fist on the door. They heard movement and she straightened her clothing.

"Mrs Masterly won't answer. Too posh," Holly said. "Probably get one of her lackeys to do it."

The door opened, scraping along the tiled floor.

Mr MacFarlene stood on the other side. "We thought you'd come."

He turned into the manor, leaving Holly and Callum staring at each other.

The Reception room was as empty and musty as Holly remembered. The Masterlys might have owned Black Rock Manor, but they were never going to make it a home. Soon it would be reduced to rubble and its history would be forgotten.

To their right was a door framed in light. As they approached, they heard hushed whispers and the stamping of feet.

Holly checked Callum was close and entered with a forced smile.

The room was lit by electric lamps, their white wires trailing to multi-plug extensions. Dust sheets were curled into a single ball by the corner, but there were no chairs, no furniture of any sort. A large fireplace dominated the room. It hadn't seen a fire in years. Replacing the flames was a vase of wilting orange flowers.

Nancy and Mr MacFarlene stood on one side of the fireplace. Mrs Masterly stood on the other, her tiny, expensive handbag in the crook of her arm.

"I would offer you a drink," Mrs Masterly said, twisting a wedding ring around her finger, "but this has been a little rushed. Not quite what I had in mind."

How did Nancy get here?

What about Mr MacFarlene?

Where was Mr Masterly?

"Where is that idiot Arnold?" Callum asked before Holly could.

Mrs Masterly pointed to the ceiling. "Upstairs. Resting. The paramedics insisted. We have twenty bedrooms, but only one bed and for some reason, it smells of goat, but he doesn't seem to mind."

"Is he okay?" Holly asked.

"Twisted knee and a shock to the system," Mrs Masterly said. "Nothing serious. He fully intends to be ready for tomorrow."

"What's happening tomorrow?" Callum asked.

Holly shook her head. "I don't understand," she said. "I don't understand what everyone is doing here."

She heard the clack of high heels on the tiled floor and looked up. Mrs Masterly towered over her. The cloying perfume she wore moved over Holly like a winter chill and yet Mrs Masterly's face was warm, sympathetic even. She undid the clasp of her handbag, retrieving a phone so big, it must have been the only thing in there.

"What's that?" Holly asked.

Mrs Masterly waggled it in front of her. "Satellite phone. It was the only way we could keep in contact."

Looking over Mrs Masterly's shoulder, Holly saw Nancy rummaging through her clothing. She produced a phone identical to Mrs Masterly's.

"You've been working together?" Holly asked.

"I told you over and over again that my husband always gets what he wants," Mrs Masterly said. "You never asked me what I wanted. No one ever does."

Nancy stepped away from the fireplace. "When I found out about

266

Arcadia's plans, I wrote them letters telling them they were making a mistake. One of them got through to Mrs Masterly. She's a conservationist. Like us, dear."

"But that can't be true," Holly said. "You've been working hand in glove with your husband."

Mrs Masterly lowered her head. "I tried to persuade my husband to forget his theme park. To leave the estate alone as a site of natural beauty." She moved to the window and stared into the dark grounds. "He didn't listen and I didn't think he would. I pretended to be a part of his plans until I could come up with another way to protect the area."

"It was Arnold's idea," Nancy said. "When he couldn't find an endangered species, we decided to plant them ourselves. Mrs Masterly used her contacts and money to buy the bulbs."

Holly pointed at Mrs Masterly. "Which you denied when I confronted you at the Herald."

"Of course, I did," Mrs Masterly said, turning from the window. "I couldn't risk my husband finding out I was undermining him. I had a role to play."

"Did that include humiliating Holly?" Callum asked.

Mrs Masterly nodded. "When I heard you haranguing my husband after he descended from his ridiculous microlight, I knew you'd be trouble. Always asking questions. Of others and yourself. I thought you too high-minded to be part of this so I had to keep you off the scent. If a word of this made it into the Herald, we'd be done for."

Callum snorted. "You've done nothing but undermine us."

"Really?" Mrs Masterly asked, her eyes like laser beams. "When I saw Holly hiding in that bush, moments after she broke into the manor, did I tell my husband you were there?"

The blood drained from Callum's face.

"Forget about eviction, my husband would have called the police." Mrs Masterly turned to Holly, waving her handbag at her. "And I spotted her again skulking in the hedgerow while Mr MacFarlene was being detained. If I didn't believe in the pair of you and how you might help us, I could have ended your campaign before it had started."

"You wrote the note, didn't you?" Holly asked. "'Follow the Star?'"

"I went to the Herald's office to leave it on your desk," Mrs Masterly said. "I wasn't expecting to see you so I pretended I'd found it on the door. I'm not who you think I am."

"You used me," Holly said.

"I knew you wouldn't be able to resist something so cryptic and while I couldn't have you working with us, there was no reason you couldn't work on your own."

The blood in Holly's veins fizzed. Callum seemed to sense it, stepping aside, protecting himself from an eruption.

"It was you who sent the email to Mr Winnow," Holly said. "Did you know his marriage is in tatters because of it?"

"Well, between you, me and Mr Winnow," Mrs Masterly said, "I'd say none of us is a great advert for marriage, are we?"

Holly rolled her shoulders, relishing the cracks of her neck as the tension popped in tiny explosions.

"You expect us to believe you did all this for the good of the village?" she asked in a voice that was more like a growl. "Why now? After all the other villages you've destroyed?"

"She has helped us, dear," Nancy said. "She rescued Arnold from his fall in the dell. I called her on the fancy phone and she arranged for Mr MacFarlene to haul Arnold to safety."

"The same man," Holly said, turning to the farmer, "who broke into my home and was questioned by the police for assault."

Mr MacFarlene twitched and clasped his hands. "I thought I was helping," he said. "Going through your house. I thought you might have more bulbs, but I was wrong and I'm sorry."

"How did you get to the dell so quickly?"

"I was there when Mrs Masterly got the call," Mr MacFarlene said. "She was dropping me off at home."

Mrs Masterly smoothed down the lining of her dress. "I'm sure Mr MacFarlene will be the first to admit he can be quite vocal after a drink or five. My husband believed his objections to the development might cause a problem."

"You were there when he was arrested," Holly said. "You decided to remove him from the picture."

Mr MacFarlene stepped forward. "That was her husband. He pretended to be a witness to a crime I didn't commit. He thought it would scare me into silence, but no one can keep me quiet."

"Or sober," Callum muttered.

"When I realised what my husband was doing," Mrs Masterly said, "I tried to stop him, but I was too late. I went to the station instead. Called in a few favours, you might say."

"I already had the tow truck," Mr MacFarlene said. "Needed it to pull my tractor out of Myrtle's Water. Lord knows what it was doing in there, I might add, but after Nancy called us, we used it to winch Arnold to safety."

"Why now?" Holly asked. "Why save this village? What was so special about us?"

"None of this has been perfect," Mrs Masterly said. "Arcadia Leisure is a monster with every kind of resource at its disposal. I love my husband, but I couldn't stand idly by while another village was swallowed by his ambition. We crossed a line in Eureka. If I was going to save Little Belton, I knew we'd have to fight dirty."

The cold of the manor sank into Holly's bones. It was time to leave because this was guerrilla warfare. Livelihoods had been sacrificed. Compromises made. Looking at the sorrowful face of Mr MacFarlene, she saw how his grief had been used as a weapon.

Holly wasn't sure about the rights and wrongs of it. Did the ends justify the means? All war makers had to ask themselves that and for Holly's part, she wasn't sure.

But she knew she could leave the fight. Holly could return to an empty home and to an uncertain job at a newspaper owned by a man who had paid as much as any other.

"I hope the estate is worth the price you paid," Holly said.

She took Callum's arm and they made to leave, but their passage was blocked by Arnold.

"It's not over yet," he said propped up on crutches, "and now I'm incapacitated, we can't save Little Belton without you."

Chapter Forty-Nine

The night had been a restless one. Holly and Callum had found a bedroom in the manor and had locked the door when they had decided to stay. They pulled two armchairs together, facing a cold fireplace where their imagination might keep them warm. Wrapped in dust sheets, they closed their eyes and pretended to sleep.

Thoughts of Holly's husband kept her awake. He was obstinate and had lost his way, but she loved him. Or had done once. Holly had left Derek before he could leave her, isolating him in a home they no longer shared together. It was a long walk to Little Belton, especially when dragging his marriage behind him in a suitcase. She assumed he would wait for Holly to return in order to leave as soon as she arrived, but maybe his desperation would spur him on.

Her thoughts turned to the Masterlys and the battle between them as man and wife. Mrs Masterly claimed to love her husband while waging a secret war against him. Was Holly guilty of the same thing? She hoped not and tried not to think about it.

Leaving Callum purring like a cat in his armchair, Holly went outside to watch the sunrise. The house was quiet as she crept down the staircase. The other occupants were asleep or similarly curled up with their thoughts.

The grounds outside were blanketed in a morning dew. Unseen birds twittered in the trees, preparing for the day ahead. Holly shivered with the cold, pulling her coat closer. There was so much life on the estate, so much left to discover and she wondered how long it would remain.

Holly smelled coffee and followed her nose around a corner. A picnic blanket was spread on the ground and a large open umbrella lay on its side. Nancy's goat stood over a gas fire, the blue flames heating a pan of dark liquid. It regarded her quietly while chewing on a clump of dock leaves.

"Would you like a cup, dear?" Nancy said.

"You're up early."

"Don't sleep much these days." Nancy poured coffee into a cup and handed it to Holly.

The coffee was hot and Holly took a seat. Despite the blanket, the ground was cold. Holly tried to get comfortable, tucking her coat underneath her while she sat cross-legged under the umbrella.

"Does Old Jack know you've taken back your goat?" she asked.

"No one is awake at this hour, dear," Nancy said. "Old Jack was sound asleep."

"What's your goat called?" Holly asked.

"He doesn't have a name," Nancy said. "He's an excuse to get outside."

The goat, as if understanding he was the subject of conversation, trotted toward Holly, pressing his face close to hers. His breath smelled of wet hay. Lowering his head into the folds of the blanket, he picked up a hidden tennis ball and dropped it into Holly's lap.

Holly threw the ball and the goat chased after it, retrieving it from the long grass. She half-expected the goat to return it, groaning inwardly at the game she had unwittingly started. Instead, the goat stared into the distance, rolling the ball around its mouth, slowly reducing it to mush.

"Old Jack has been teaching him new tricks," Nancy said as the goat swallowed the last of the ball.

"You're going to have to see him at some point," Holly said. "Old Jack is pining for you. More than your goat ever did."

Nancy poured out coffee dregs from her cup and refilled it.

"Did he hurt you in some way?" Holly asked, her own coffee cooling in her hands.

Gazing at the blue flames of the fire, Nancy chewed the inside of her cheek, like her goat had chewed the tennis ball.

"What was the first article you wrote for the Herald?" she asked.

It seemed like years ago, but the memory was burned into her brain.

"It was a feature about oddly shaped vegetables," Holly said.

"And the last?"

"Something about the cattle mart."

"You haven't written anything else?" Nancy asked.

"I wrote something about Arcadia Leisure, but it was never used."

Nancy switched off the gas fire, listening to the tings of the cannister cooling. It sounded like distant gunfire.

"Old Jack and I are different," she said. "That's all. He's not interested in the bigger world. Little Belton is enough for him, but he's blind to its problems. When the mine closed, when people began to leave, he was writing articles about church fetes and potholes."

Holly rubbed some warmth back into her legs. "It doesn't make him a bad person."

"No, it doesn't," Nancy said, "but I wanted to get out and explore. I was trapped by my sister, I couldn't risk being trapped by a man."

"What happened at the manor?" Holly asked. "What changed?"

The sun rose higher in the sky, lancing through the trees to bathe Nancy's face in a golden hue. "Everything changed. I fell in love."

The wheels in Holly's mind started spinning. A young woman. Looking for adventure. Through no fault of her own, she was brought into the orbit of a wealthy landowner. A noted philanderer. Seduced by his power, she fell hopelessly in love.

273

Nancy was a beautiful woman. Her age couldn't mask that. When she was younger, Holly could only imagine the effect she had on men.

"You fell in love with Charles Wentworth," Holly said.

Nancy slapped the ground, laughing. "Dear me, no. He was an awful man. No, it was my sister who fell in love with Mr Wentworth."

Holly's eyes widened and her mouth fell open.

"Regina was always the romantic one," Nancy continued with a grin, "and while she was under Mr Wentworth's roof, she couldn't resist him. As Regina got better, it was clear the old rascal was only after one thing and the spell was broken. So was Regina's heart. She became a hermit, never leaving the fireside, fearing the cold might land her back into Mr Wentworth's clutches."

"You gave up your dreams to keep her company," Holly said.

"She was never the same so I did what I could, using the odd walk around the estate to keep me sane. It was all I had so when Arcadia Leisure threatened to take that away, I knew I couldn't stay any longer."

Nancy smiled and stared at the thin skin puckering around her knuckles. Her blue veins snaked through liver spots and wrinkles. The smile turned sour and Nancy closed her hand into a fist.

"This is my last big adventure," she said.

"I don't understand," Holly said, realising the phrase was fast becoming her motto. "You came back to the manor over and over. Something was pulling you back. If you didn't fall in love with Charles Wentworth, who was it?"

"Like all good stories," Nancy said. "It was the butler who did it in the end."

The goat bolted into the shrubbery and Holly and Nancy turned to see Callum walking toward them.

"Is that coffee?" he asked.

Nancy produced a clean cup and filled it with warm coffee from the stove. "There you are, dear."

Callum gulped down a mouthful. "Nothing like coffee brewed outside," he said, smacking his lips.

"That's what your father always used to say," Nancy said, "but you look more like your mother."

The cup dropped from Callum's face. "Did you know her?"

Nancy shook her head. "Not very well. Saw her around the village once or twice."

"What was she like?"

"There weren't many cars back then, but she was the kind of woman who could stop traffic, dear. We were all very jealous. Only someone as beautiful as your mother could turn your father's head."

"What do you mean?" Holly asked, leaning forward.

"He was devoted to his job," Nancy said. "Lived and breathed it, but it was a young maid who finally stole his heart. She came in like the Spring winds and was gone just as fast. Nature can be cruel that way."

Callum's face was ghostly white, working a tongue around his mouth before speaking.

"She died in childbirth," he said to Holly. "With me."

Nancy laid a gentle hand on Callum's arm. "Your father looked after me while my sister was sick."

"You must have known him when he was Wentworth's butler," Callum said.

"I did, dear. Your father kept me out of harm's way. Took me for walks through the estate. He taught me about plants and animals. His world seemed so big to me back then."

Holly gently placed her coffee on the ground before she spilled it.

"Despite the Wentworth's dwindling fortunes," Nancy said, "and Mr Wentworth's diminished reputation, Callum's father was fiercely loyal. Wouldn't hear a word against them. That was just the way it was for him and I thought there was no room in his heart for anything else."

"Except for my mother," Callum said, quietly.

Nancy stood, stretching the early morning from her bones. She gathered up her stove and collapsed the umbrella.

Holly and Callum handed back their coffee cups and Nancy squirrelled them away inside her clothing.

"Do you know anything else about my Mam?" Callum asked.

"Not really," Nancy said, leaving Holly and Callum sitting on her blanket. "But she was a very lucky woman. Like I say, we were all very jealous."

Holly watched Nancy disappear, wearing an age-old heartache like a cloak around her weary shoulders.

"Do you believe her?" Callum asked, twisting his shirt collar in his fingers. "About how much my Dad loved my Mam?"

Holly slapped his hand away and adjusted the collar back into place.

"Do you?" he asked again.

She hung her arm through his. "I do," she said, thinking of the sadness and regret in Nancy's eyes when she spoke of Callum's father. "There was no room in his heart for anyone else."

Not even Nancy, Holly thought.

Chapter Fifty

The rest of the morning was spent in preparation. Maps were consulted, details poured over. Holly was uneasy and the rest of them knew it.

When Mrs Masterly appeared, she was wearing designer Tweeds and knee-high, fur lined boots. There were no provisions at the manor and no running water, but judging from her appearance, Mrs Masterly had spent the previous night in a health spa.

Holly patted down the hair sticking up at the back of her head. "Do we need to do this?"

"This one isn't my decision," Mrs Masterly said. Although dressed for a trek across the rough terrain of the estate, her handbag remained in the crook of her arm. She prized the clasp apart and pulled out a sheaf of moisturising wipes, offering them to Holly.

"If you would like?" she asked.

"Thank you," Holly said, using them to clean her hands and face. When she finished, she felt clean, ready for whatever was needed.

Mrs Masterly delved into her handbag again, producing a hairbrush and vanity case.

"Whose handbag is that?" Holly asked. "Mary Poppins?"

Mrs Masterly looked at the handbag as if it was the first time she'd seen it.

"Christian Dior's," she said.

"It's almost noon," Arnold shouted. "Time to get going."

Holly and Mrs Masterly joined everyone around the tow truck. Mr MacFarlene was already behind the wheel, avoiding eye contact with Holly. Nancy was beside him, her wrinkled face pressed into readiness.

Arnold hobbled about on his crutches. His knee was heavily bandaged, but it didn't stop him from strutting like a general.

"Nancy and Mr MacFarlene will go on ahead," he said. "We'll use the truck to lower ourselves into the dell. From there, I'll instruct everyone where to dig. I can't be of more help, thanks to my knee and the flowers won't be open, but I've spent enough time down there to know where they are."

Callum raised his hand to speak, but was ignored.

"There aren't enough tools to go around," Arnold said, "and not enough time to find more, so we'll have to improvise."

Callum stretched his arm higher, wriggling his fingertips.

"What is it?" Arnold asked, swinging a crutch at Callum.

"What if we're stopped by the contractors?" he asked. "They won't like us trespassing again."

"Plus, they'll want to know why I stole their car," Holly added.

"Mrs Masterly is going with you to smooth out any issues," Arnold said through gritted teeth. "Anything else?"

Holly coughed loudly. "What exactly are we doing?"

Arnold groaned. "The Star flowers are too localised. Arcadia could simply rope the area off and continue building around them. We need to dig them up and replant them throughout the estate."

Mrs Masterly applied lipstick as she spoke. "Natural England will only stop work if they believe the whole estate is filled with an endangered species."

"Is anyone concerned with the idea of committing fraud?" Holly asked, looking around the group.

Nancy and Mr MacFarlene stared straight ahead. Mrs Masterly gazed at the ground. Callum shifted his stance, burying his hands in his pockets. Only Arnold appeared unrepentant, but it was clearly too late to turn back now. Even Holly could see that. There were no more options other than admitting defeat and there was too much at stake for that.

"Alright, then," she said. "Let's get going."

The tow truck pulled away first. Holly and Callum were in the front of the Defender. Arnold and Mrs Masterly climbed into the back. They set off in silence, each lost in their own thoughts.

The vehicles traversed a single lane bouncing the occupants from their seats.

Holly faced Arnold.

"Are you okay?" she asked.

His hands were wrapped around his injured knee, his mouth a thin slash. "Fine," he said, hissing through his teeth. He took a breath, moistening his lips with his tongue. "Listen, I'm sorry about everything I've done to get this far."

"Are you?" Callum asked over his shoulder.

Arnold pressed into his seat, attempting to find purchase. "We shouldn't have ransacked your belongings and I shouldn't have persuaded Mr MacFarlene to go through yours, Holly."

"Are you sure you're doing the right thing?" Holly asked. "A lot of people will lose their jobs if you go through with this."

"If *we* go through with this, you mean," Arnold corrected, "and I know how they'll feel. I've lost my job, too."

The tow truck ahead broke to a stop and Callum pulled up beside it.

There was no need to ask why. The dell was two hundred yards away, surrounded by traffic cones and orange tape. Cars and jeeps swarmed around like bees.

Contractors emptied the contents of their vehicles, hurling metal shards, old timber and bags of rubbish into the dell.

Arnold was first out of the Defender, seemingly faster on crutches than he was on foot. His pain was forgotten and he charged at the contractors.

"There he goes again," Callum said, wrestling with his seatbelt and chasing after him.

Holly followed, without any hope of catching them in time.

By the time she got there, Callum and Arnold were surrounded by men wearing hard hats and stern faces.

"What the hell do you think you're doing?" Arnold yelled.

"It's nothing to do with you, Long John Silver," a contractor said. He was tall with shoulders as straight as an ironing board. A red beard hung in tangles from his chin.

Arnold tried to manoeuvre around Red Beard, but was blocked by his sheer size.

"You have to stop," Arnold said.

Red Beard placed a hand on his chest, shoving him back a step.

"There's no need for that," Callum said.

"Leave him alone," Holly added, having finally caught her breath.

Red Beard looked down his nose at her. "You're the thief who stole my car."

Callum stepped in front of Holly, drawing himself up to full height. "I took the Ranger, mate. Take it up with me."

Holly felt a hand on her arm. She turned to see a cowering Mrs Threadle in a hard hat one size too big for her.

"What's going on?" Holly asked.

Mrs Threadle pushed the hat to the back of her head. Her eyes darted around the many faces staring at her. "They've been looking for a landfill site. Rubbish at the camp has been building up. Too expensive to have it collected."

Holly remembered the stench of the bin bags. "They're going to dump it here? Why?"

"We won't have to dig," Mrs Threadle said. "It's perfect."

More vehicles trundled to the dell with grim-faced drivers behind their wheels. A grey, blunt-faced truck, like a lumbering elephant, forced its way through the congestion. Mottled tarpaulin covered the contents on its back as it reversed to the edge.

Callum and Red Beard argued through a series of growls. Arnold used the distraction to press through the orange tape. It didn't snap, but stretched white with tension, as if he had run a race, but was unable to cross the finishing line. He scuttled to the edge of the dell, peering over the side.

"It's okay," he said. "It's just debris. We can still dig through to reach the bulbs."

Holly's shoulders sank with relief.

"Why now?" Holly asked. "Why here?"

"Because of you," Red Beard shouted over Callum's head. "After your joyride in our stolen car, you left it here. I wanted to have you nicked until we realised this place was ideal for dumping rubbish. You got off lightly, I'd say."

Most of the contractors had drifted away. The show was over and they had work to do, but Holly sensed the accusing eyes of Arnold upon her. She saw the disappointment in Callum. Her skin crawled hot and she yanked on her jumper.

"That doesn't mean you can use it as landfill," Holly said, her voice weakened.

"Private property," Red Beard said, "and we have the permits. When are you hippies going to learn?"

He barked out a laugh, his tangled beard swaying like seaweed before he joined his companions to share a joke at Holly's expense.

Callum placed a hand on the small of Holly's back. "Don't worry. Arnold said it was fine. We'll dig through."

The grey truck reached its final destination, the lip of its rear end hanging over the depths. The tarpaulin skin was whipped away to reveal barrels pockmarked with rust.

Arnold's eyes widened at the sight.

The platform on the truck rose and the barrels skidded toward the dell. One by one, they dropped through the air. The first one landed, puncturing its side on a metal shard. Black liquid gushed out, spraying the walls in glossy globules. The second landed with a clang. Its lid ruptured and a wave of unctuous cooking fat soaked the ground in grease.

Arnold raised his crutches aloft. "Stop what you're doing."

But it was too late. The gradient was too steep and the barrels kept tumbling.

Holly covered her ears against the din, but she couldn't avoid watching. She didn't need Arnold to tell her it was over. Whatever noxious elements were in the barrels were eating their way through the soil, killing the Star flowers under the surface.

Arnold shouted at her, pointing his crutch in an accusatory manner. His mouth was warped into an ugly maw and Holly was glad she couldn't hear his loaded words.

The grey truck finished unloading and with a honk of its horn, returned to the camp. The other contractors continued hurling debris with wild abandon, determined to fill the landfill site Holly had so graciously delivered to them.

She dropped her hands as Arnold's tirade petered out. His eyes were red, wet with tears he fought hard not to spill. His jaw clenched and Holly prepared for the second bout. She stood tall, knowing it was her fault, but refusing to look like a victim.

Arnold shoved his crutches under his arms. "We almost did it, didn't we? We almost saved the village."

He nodded at Holly with a smile that wasn't fixed and hobbled to the Defender.

Holly watched his progress as he passed Mrs Masterly talking into her satellite phone. Her arms gestured frantically, flaying in the air. Ending the call, she pitched the phone into the wilderness. She looked up and noticed Holly gazing at her.

Slowly, Mrs Masterly shook her head.

The contractors left and Holly and Callum stood together at the edge of the dell until the odour forced them backwards. They stayed close to one another, sharing warmth and loss. Clouds gathered on the horizon threatening more rain. Not enough to wash away their regret, but just enough to dampen the last of their strength.

"Come on," Callum said. "I'll take you home."

Chapter Fifty-One

A convoy of vehicles sloped through the tracks of the estate. Out in front was Mr MacFarlene driving Nancy and Arnold back to his farmhouse. When he parked, no one left the tow truck. They sat staring at their hands as Callum's Defender gave a solitary peep of the horn before continuing on.

Mrs Masterly's Rover waited for her at the manor. She climbed from the Defender and smoothed out the wrinkles of her designer clothes.

"I had hoped we might become friends," Mrs Masterly said to Holly.

The blank face of the manor loomed over Mrs Masterly's shoulder. Its windows were empty eyes, the rooms inside were chambers. There wasn't anything there for Mrs Masterly. A friend might have made it tolerable, but it was too late for that.

She delved into her magic handbag and pressed something into Holly's hand.

"A gift," she said before sliding into the belly of her car.

Holly looked at the perfume bottle. "Thanks."

Mrs Masterly smiled, her porcelain skin finally cracking. She issued muffled instructions to the driver and slammed her door shut.

"What are you going to do?" Callum asked, his knuckles white on the steering wheel.

"I don't know," Holly said.

"What about Derek?"

Holly scratched at the mud drying on her trousers. "He might already be gone. The car is still in the village and I have the keys, but who knows? He seemed determined to leave anyway."

The scenery blurred as the Defender took her home. Holly liked watching it roll by, picking out trees or animals to ponder over, but it was too painful now. She concentrated on her stained trousers, not willing to create memories she would later be forced to forget. Little Belton had never been hers. She had grown up there and she had left as soon as she could. Returning had served to remind her of that.

They drove through the village and Holly saw the Winnows in their doorway, searching the barren high streets for customers. The door to The Travelling Star was closed, the windows like mirrors reflecting an open sky. No-one walked the village green, except for rooks and ravens, bickering over scraps. The birds stopped fighting and turned as Holly passed, silently regarding her passage out of Little Belton.

Black Eye Bobby took flight, its long, black feathers trailing behind.

Climbing up the road to her cottage, Holly wanted one last look at Knock Lake. It was still, as always, but she blinked at the deer surrounding its shore. She recognised a buck standing alone from his herd. It was the same creature who had rescued Holly on her way to the Faery Ring. His antlers were full, coming to sharp points, but his face remained downy, betraying his youth.

The buck watched her with careful eyes. The does and younger bucks danced on their hooves, ready to bolt.

But he stood firm.

Holly glanced at Callum. His skin was stretched around his neck, the tendons as taut as a guitar string. His eyes were trained on the road, scanning, watching, but his mind appeared to be elsewhere, perhaps contemplating the goodbye ahead.

He slowed the Defender as they approached the cottage.

"Oh, no," she said.

Derek was by his shed, suitcases gathered at his feet. He wore a long, black coat over a suit that no longer fitted him.

The door to the shed, the place where Derek sulked and sometimes drank, was finally open. Holly sensed it was some dark portent of things to come.

She jumped from the jeep and walked toward him, but Callum lingered on his own.

"Decided to come back, have we?" Derek asked, his face lined with anger. "My brother has been calling non-stop, wondering where I am."

"I'm sorry," Holly said, but she knew how inadequate the words sounded.

Derek held out his hand. It was shaking, but Holly didn't know if it was from unease or alcohol withdrawal.

"There'll be no point asking you where you've been," he said, "so I'll ask for the car keys instead."

Holly handed them over. "Is there anything I can say?"

"Yes," Derek said, "but it should have been said days ago."

"I didn't want this."

"Who would?" Derek asked. Glancing at Callum, he let out a sigh. "I just want you to be happy."

Holly's bones ached. Her head spun. She wanted it to be over. Not the marriage. Looking at Derek now, she was reminded of the man she'd married. He appeared resolute, more contained than he'd been in a long time.

Holly's parents had enjoyed a happy and successful marriage. Couldn't she have the same? She could forgo the money and the status of success. She could endure the humiliating defeat by Arcadia Leisure.

But she needed something to cling to.

Holly and Derek had hit hard times and instead of pulling together, they'd shattered into separate pieces. The marriage hadn't failed. They had failed as people.

She wanted the uncertainty to be gone, the doubts and the worries. If that burden could be released, fall like broken shackles from her feet, maybe their journey together wasn't over yet. Maybe there was more.

Holly knew the decision wasn't hers. It belonged to her husband.

"At least, I'll get your man shed if you go," Holly said, half-smiling.

Derek rolled up the sleeve of his coat, revealing cracked leather padding tied to his forearm.

"Not exactly," he said, extending his arm into the shed. "It actually belongs to someone else."

"What are you doing?" Holly asked.

"Shhh," Derek whispered back. "You'll scare her."

There was a fluttering of feathers followed by a squawk.

"Well, I think she's a she," Derek said.

A bird hopped out of the shadows, launching into the air to alight on Derek's wrist.

It had a regal yellow beak and regal yellow eyes, and its head rotated with disdain. The feathers were a dusty black, except for a tail which spread outwards like a white fan.

Derek's arm strained under the bird's weight and he lowered it to the T-shaped stand by the door.

"Where did you find her?" she asked.

"By the side of the road on the way to the village," Derek said, doing up the buttons of his coat. "Looked like she'd been hit by a car. I've done the best I can, but she'll need to be cared for until she's fully recovered."

Holly remembered all too well the night she'd collided with the bird. The thud and the rattling of the body as it rolled over the roof of her car. She'd had no idea what she'd done and by the morning, her thoughts had turned elsewhere. Holly was ashamed to say, she'd forgotten all about it.

"That's what you were doing in there?" Holly asked. "In the shed?"

Derek untied the leather padding from his arm. "She put up a bit of a fight to begin with. She's quite tame now, but you better use this glove until she gets used to you."

The bird ruffled its feathers and stared down her golden beak at Holly.

"We were quite a team. Me and her," Derek said.

A familiar sense of guilt washed over Holly. Even with two jobs, she'd taken on a missing person case. She'd filled her days running around the estate and interrogating its residents. Holly hadn't meant to, but she'd done it with relish.

Anything to keep herself away from Derek.

It looked like he'd done the same.

"Is that what I think it is?" Callum asked, his jaw slackening.

Derek stiffened at his approach, but managed a shrug. "Don't know what she is. Some sort of kestrel?"

"That's no kestrel," Callum said.

"Whatever. I forgot you were Dr Dolittle," Derek said before turning to Holly. "She'll probably stay a few more days. Her mate is close by. I think they're keen to get back to their nest."

"Her mate?" Callum asked.

Derek bristled, puffing out his chest. "Yes. Her mate. I'm not from around here. You've made that abundantly clear, so I don't recognise all these bloody animals and plants, but I think she has a mate. Okay?"

"What is it, Callum?" Holly asked.

She watched as his slack mouth turned into a grin.

"That is a white-tailed eagle," Callum said. "It's an endangered species."

Holly shuddered from the electricity shooting up her spine.

Callum wiped his brow and laughed. "We better get Arnold. A white-tailed eagle. I can't believe it."

He opened his arms for an embrace, beckoning Holly to join him.

Her heart raced, her fingertips tingled, but Holly took a step toward her husband.

"All this time," she said, wrapping herself around Derek. "You had the answer all this time."

"What are you talking about?" Derek asked, holding on tightly.

"You have to stay," she said.

A shadow fell over Derek and he sagged. "I can't. My brother is waiting for me. I have a job to go to."

Holly released him, tripping over Derek's suitcases as she backed off. She kept her feet, but her face blushed red.

"You saved us all," she said. "You saved the village and our home."

Derek stared at his shoes, his mouth clamped shut.

Holly's days had been spent asking questions, of others and herself. She had reached the end and found what she'd been looking for. As with most things, it had been right under her nose. She'd saved the village, or rather Derek had and only one question remained.

Could Derek fix their marriage too?

Chapter Fifty-Two

Holly's shoes squeaked on the hospital floor. The corridor heaved with trolleys and medical equipment. Nurses in blue scrubs scuttled from room to room. Voices called to one another and somewhere a radio was playing.

"I got a call," Holly said. "Regina woke up yesterday and she stayed that way."

Nancy's dirty boots were silent on the floor. Her woollen clothes hung limply off a body which had spent too many weeks not looking after itself.

"I shouldn't have come," Nancy said, stopping by a vending machine. She fished in her pockets for money only to retrieve a handful of dried leaves.

"Do you want something to eat?" Holly asked.

Running her finger down the glass, Nancy studied the selection. "Not really, no."

Regina was ten paces further along the corridor. The Foxglove sisters had never been apart for so long. They had lived each other's lives. When Nancy disappeared, Regina had withered. This was their chance to be reunited.

"Why don't you want to see your sister?" Holly asked.

"I do want to see her. Of course, I do, but you don't know what it was like." Nancy turned her back on the vending machine and watched the nurses buzzing about their work. "That house was like an oven. There was no air and every night was the same. We'd sit by the fire and watch it die. Wentworth had turned her caustic. I swear Regina could pickle onions just by looking at them."

"You went to The Travelling Star."

"And I practically had to carry her there and back," Nancy said. "By the time our meal arrived, there was a cloud over both of us."

The radio was switched off and Holly became aware of the sounds of the hospital, of the machines that worked to keep people alive.

"What's this really about?" she asked.

Nancy picked soil from her many skirts. "Could you ask her, dear? Could you ask Regina if she wants to see me?"

"Why?" Holly asked.

"Because I feel like I've let her down."

Looking into Nancy's beleaguered eyes, it felt like the least Holly could do. Both sisters had suffered and Holly was in no place to judge a relationship spanning decades.

With a pat to Nancy's shoulder, Holly left her consulting with one of the nurses.

Regina's room was filled with flowers, though the floor was dusted with fallen petals. The blinds had been drawn and Regina was tucked under a bundle of blankets, her head poking out of the top like the Grandma from *Little Red Riding Hood*.

"It's good to see you," Holly said. "How have you been?"

Regina searched the room with watery eyes. "Where is everyone? The nurses told me I had visitors while I was unconscious, but they haven't been back since I woke."

Her flowers were fading with no new bouquets to replace them. Little Belton was in tumult and there was work to be done. An eagle had landed, changing everything. Busy villagers were reconstructing their lives, but Holly suspected that wasn't the only reason they had stopped visiting.

She thought of pickled onions and forced a smile.

"Nancy is here," Holly said. "She's waiting outside."

Regina turned to the window with a snort. "Finished her silly rambling, has she?"

"She'd like to see you."

"Who do you think put me in here?"

The room morphed out of focus and Holly reached for the bed to steady herself. "Nancy hit you?"

Regina drew herself through the blankets, resting her back on the headboard. She rearranged the covers to keep her thin body warm. "Black Rock Manor has brought me nothing but misery. First, it was that awful Charles Wentworth spinning me lies and then it was my own sister. After everything I'd done for her. Keeping her safe. Protecting her from the outside world. You'd think blood counted for something."

With one hand still on the bedframe, Holly wiped the hair from her eyes. "Why would Nancy hurt you?"

"I went looking for her," Regina said, her lip curling. "Oh, I knew where she'd be. Nancy pretended she was walking that goat all over the estate, but when she returned, she'd always talk about the old days, about the fair and the pageants at the manor. I knew she'd been walking down memory lane, leaving me far behind."

"But you've been together for your whole lives."

"I hadn't visited that horrible place in years, but my feet remembered it like it was yesterday. Sure enough, Nancy was there, talking to some fancy man of hers."

"Arnold Salting?" Holly asked.

"He ran off as soon as he saw me and Nancy was furious." Regina tugged on a blanket, holding it to her chest. "We argued. Like we always argued."

"And she hit you?"

292

Regina shook her head. "Nancy ran off and I tried to follow, but I tripped. My legs aren't what they used to be. Apparently, I hit my head and my sister left me there to die. Luckily, an ambulance must have been passing and saw me. The next thing I remember is waking up in an empty room."

Holly finally let go of the bed and stood straight. "An ambulance? Just passing by?"

"How else do you explain it?" Regina asked. "No one could have called for an ambulance out there. You can't get a phone signal, dear."

You can if you have a satellite phone, Holly thought. Nancy may have been furious, but she would never have left her sister to die. She must have seen Regina fall and called for help, perhaps even waiting in the shadows until it arrived.

It was one story Holly didn't want to investigate. Whatever happened was a private affair between two sisters and a lifetime of history.

"I think you should talk to Nancy," Holly said, moving to the door. "There are things you should say to each other."

The sneer slipped from Regina's face and she looked lost among her blankets.

"It's too late," she said.

Holly heard echoes of her relationship with Derek and she didn't want that to happen to the Foxgloves. Holly slipped into the corridor, searching for Nancy, but she had disappeared. She recognised the nurse Nancy had been speaking to. He was a man in his twenties, juggling several clipboards in his arms.

"Excuse me," she said. "You were talking to my friend earlier. An older woman wearing too many clothes. Do you know where she is?"

The nurse grappled with his clipboards, securing them to his body. "Ah, yes. Not sure where she is, but she said she wasn't going home. You're both Little Belters, right?"

Holly nodded. "That's right," she answered, her mouth drying. "Did she say why she wasn't going home?"

"She said, it wasn't too late," the nurse said. "There were more adventures to be had."

Chapter Fifty-Three

A month later, Holly and Callum were back at the manor, surrounded by the clink of glasses and the scent of champagne. Flames danced in the fireplace, sending surges of flickering warmth around the room. Holly was dressed in a shimmering gown she'd borrowed from Mrs Masterly while Callum wore his wax jacket and moleskin trousers, not understanding the necessity of changing clothes to suit the occasion.

Regina was huddled by the fire, a woollen cap tied around her head. Her face was aglow, not just from the heat, but from too much champagne. She smiled at anyone who strayed too close, including Mr MacFarlene, who was making a point of doing so.

The Winnows ransacked the buffet table. It was stocked with everything from lobster tails to sausage rolls. For every bite they placed in their mouths, another morsel was secreted about their persons. Holly suspected they would be on sale at their convenience store by tomorrow morning.

Old Jack sat in a corner, swaying to the music. Big Gregg regaled Arnold with the tale of how he lost his leg. Arnold wiped laughter tears from his eyes and pointed his crutch at his own damaged knee. The Reverend and Bryan were by the sound system, bickering over who might choose the next song. Thrash metal or the soundtrack to *Fame*.

Holly wasn't looking forward to either. She nudged Callum with her elbow. "Are you okay?"

He nodded and sipped from his champagne flute, pulling a face. "I could brew better in an old boot."

"You've seemed a bit off since we got here."

"I said, I'm fine."

Bryan wrestled the CD player from the Reverend's grasp and the soundtrack began.

"For chuff's sake," Callum said, storming off to have a word with the DJ's.

Holly twirled the stem of her glass flute between her fingers.

"I'm sorry your husband couldn't make it," Mrs Masterly said, sauntering over. "We have a lot to thank him for."

Derek's white-tailed eagle was currently in an animal sanctuary in Berwick-Upon-Tweed. Abandoning his efforts to find the Star flower, Arnold had alerted Natural England to the eagle's presence. He had also informed the national press and media. Not to be outdone, Old Jack ran a four-page spread on the eagle's discovery. Little Belton had become a hub for bird-watchers and global conservationists.

The village was busier than ever. Holly had it on good word that the Winnows were attempting to change their spray-painted reindeer into eagles to cash in on their new found status. Thanks to the Little Belton rumour mill, Holly knew the results were less than spectacular.

"We're expecting them to release the eagle in the next two months," Mrs Masterly said. "They're hoping to establish a breeding colony."

"We got there in the end," Holly said.

"And without bending any laws," Mrs Masterly said, raising her glass.

Holly met it with hers. "What about your husband?"

"On to his next project. I persuaded him to let me manage the estate in his absence. It will be hard work, but we have a lot to be proud of here. I'm afraid you haven't got rid of me yet."

"Is he still speaking to you?" Holly asked.

Mrs Masterly shrugged. "He doesn't know what I was up to. How I was trying to undermine him. We girls should be allowed our secrets."

Holly had told Derek about the mixed-up scheme to save the village. After talking for an hour, she eventually found the courage to speak about her feelings. How she felt about Derek, how she felt about Callum. The pain in Derek's eyes was a memory she was unlikely to forget. No matter which way their marriage was heading, it needed to be done.

Holly still believed in the truth.

"I can't share this estate with my husband," Mrs Masterly said, staring into her champagne, "but I hope you might with yours."

"I did invite him, but – "

The doors to the room opened and Derek strode inside, dressed in a black suit and no tie. All eyes were on him. He walked up to Holly, planting a tentative kiss on her cheek.

"I didn't think I would make it in time," he said. "I've been on the phone to the sanctuary and then I got lost."

"And how is our white-tailed eagle?" Mrs Masterly asked. "I want to see her."

Derek pulled on the waistband of his trousers. "They've named her Derek. Apparently, she's a boy."

"Trust you to get that wrong," Holly said, linking her arm through his.

Callum appeared and stretched out his hand.

"Derek," he said.

"Callum," Derek replied with a brief shake of hands.

"I never thanked you for what you did," Callum said.

"Happy to play my part. Even though I didn't know I was playing it at the time."

"This calls for a toast," Mrs Masterly said, tapping a manicured fingernail on her glass.

"As some of you know," she said. "I am the new owner of Black Rock

Manor. We've been through some trials to get here and I trust you'll keep the details of that to yourselves. And that includes the journalists among us."

There was a ripple of laughter and Holly beamed at the smiling crowd.

"My husband promised you prosperity at the expense of our village. I'm offering a different richness, something we can pass on to our children should they decide to stay. I want this estate to be a mecca for nature lovers. Those who don't need flashing lights and merchandise to celebrate where they are. Our theme park is already here, carved into the hills for us to enjoy."

"What about jobs?" Big Gregg asked.

"I have enough money to support your pub until you get back on your feet," Mrs Masterly said. "I've also been informed the Little Belton Herald has been bought from its current owner, who has decided to sell for the good of his health."

Holly sought out Old Jack in the crowd, whispering hurried words into his ear. "You're retiring?"

Old Jack raised a glass. "Don't worry, pet. We'll be fine."

"It won't be easy," Mrs Masterly said, "and I can't deliver the kind of money Arcadia Leisure was promising, but there'll be work for those who want it and a community for those who don't."

Callum raised his hand. "Can I ask a question?"

"Don't worry," Mrs Masterly said. "Your job as estate gamekeeper has been reinstated, as has your house."

"It's not that," Callum said, hooking fingers through the buttonholes of his lapels. "You need people to stay, right?"

Mrs Masterly nodded.

"So, you'll need someone to manage the land and the houses on it?"

"I haven't appointed anyone and that person will have to come cheap, but yes."

Callum pointed at Derek. "He used to work in real estate. I'm told he was good. If you were willing, I suggest you hire Derek."

"What do you say?" Mrs Masterly asked, spinning on her heels toward Derek.

"I would think..." he said, jostling on the spot. "Yes. I can do it. I'd be happy to."

The crowd applauded, the sound so loud it caused a shower of dust to rain from the ceiling. Glasses were refilled and the Reverend turned up the music.

The residents of Little Belton joined each other on a makeshift dancefloor.

Holly pushed her way through the throng. "Are you sure?" she asked her husband.

Derek snatched a bottle of sparkling water from a nearby table. Twisting the lid, he danced out of the way of the froth spraying down his legs.

"I'm sure," he said. "I would like to stay in Little Belton. With you. If that's okay?"

Holly swallowed a mouthful of champagne to cool her racing heart.

"It's more than okay," she said, resting a hand on Derek's arm.

The night continued into the morning. It was a blur to Holly. Champagne and music. Excited chatter and gossip. Friendships rekindled and relationships forged forever. It was only when the sun began to rise that Holly needed some space.

She stood outside, feeling the breeze on her face and the warming glow of the sun. Birds chattered in the trees. Rabbits ran loose in the grass. Nancy's goat strained on its leash, kicking dirt from under its hooves.

"I can see you," Holly said.

A figure on the outskirts of the light walked forward, brushing calloused hands down his wax jacket.

"Thank you," Holly said. "For what you did for Derek."

"Dad would have wanted me to," Callum said.

"What about you? Did you want to?"

"Now he has a job, I think you'll see a difference in how he treats you," Callum said, tugging on the sleeves of his coat. "If your parents can have a long and happy marriage living here, then so can you."

Holly raised a half-smile. "I didn't say they were always happy. This is Little Belton. Not Disneyland."

A deer broke through the rhododendron border of the grounds. It stopped for a moment and then leapt through the bushes on the other side.

"What about you?" Holly asked. "What are you going to do?"

"I have my job back and my home." Callum pulled a tie from his pocket, unwrapping it from plastic sheeting. It was purple and green paisley, oddly suited to his wax jacket and trousers.

"Things change so quickly," Holly said. "Now Derek is employed and it's me without a job. I do the accounts for the Herald. I doubt the new owners will keep me on when they see how little money we make."

"Except there's one thing you don't know." Callum huffed as he struggled to fix the tie around his neck. "I own the Little Belton Herald."

"I'm sorry?" Holly stared at the young man accidentally binding a tie to his thumb. "What are you talking about?"

"I overheard Old Jack talking to Mrs Masterly about it," Callum said, abandoning his attempts. "I stepped in. We all agreed the Herald should stay in local hands."

Holly shook her head, the drunken haze refusing to shift. "How could you possibly buy a newspaper?"

"My Dad was loyal, but he wasn't stupid. He knew the value of his services. The Wentworths thought so highly of him, they paid him a generous pension when they left. I inherited it when he died."

"How generous?" Holly asked.

CHAPTER FIFTY-THREE

Callum folded the tie into a square and handed it to Holly.

"Enough for me to spend my time half-feral on the estate while the grown-ups run the village," he said. "It's why I'd like you to be the editor-in-chief of the Little Belton Herald."

"Wait a minute," Holly said. "Are you saying you're going to be my new boss?"

Behind them, the party was winding down. The music stopped and there were cheers of farewells.

"Actually, no. I bought the paper because I want you to be happy." Callum blew into his hands against the morning cold. "You were waiting for Derek to prove himself. Now he can. You were never going to leave him, but I think you need a chance to prove yourself too."

Guests spilled onto the stone steps of the manor, arms wrapped around shoulders, songs still on their lips. The Reverend held onto Old Jack. Big Gregg swayed in unison with Regina. Catching Holly and Callum in conversation, they respectfully decided to eavesdrop.

Except for Old Jack, who came to the forefront. "I knew all along about what was going on in the Foxglove home and I guessed Nancy would leave Little Belton. It was in her nature to roam. I never said a word, though. I was too afraid." Jack paused long enough for his blue eyes to flash golden. "We need someone like you. We always did. I love my village. Love it too much to question what's happening to it. We need someone difficult."

"Someone stubborn," Big Gregg added.

"Someone to ask the hard questions," the Winnows cried together.

Holly wafted the growing heat from her face. "And that's me?"

"Someone to put principle above profit," Mrs Masterly said, reapplying her lipstick.

"And someone to keep us on our toes," Callum said with a smile.

Holly watched her friends sobering up. They were arm in arm, watching her intently. Something told her they knew about this, that they'd come outside to hear her answer. Like Old Jack said, there were no secrets in Little Belton.

Their smiles twitched in anticipation, their nerves making them fidget.

Derek tapped her on the shoulder. "What do you reckon? It's time for a change, don't you think?"

The sun rose higher in the sky, casting a spotlight on a village that felt like home. The warmth on her shoulders was matched by the warmth of her friends.

Beyond the overgrown gardens of Black Rock Manor lay a forest where ancient trees stood. They were silhouetted against the morning sun and an over-imaginative person might have seen them as figures lurking in the gloom; the spirits of Little Belton's ancestors who had been lost through the ages.

But they were trees, Holly reminded herself. Beings that had stood in the same spot long since before she was born. There was nothing supernatural about them until Holly saw a raven swinging from a crooked branch.

It was Black Eye Bobby fixing her with a stare. Guided by the breeze, he steadied himself and tipped his sharp beak in Holly's direction.

Almost a bow, she thought. Almost a sign of acceptance.

And Holly turned to her friends with her answer.

About the Author

Thank you to those who have helped in the publication of this book. The list is long and varied and I couldn't have done it without any of them. And that includes you, the reader.

If you enjoyed Black Rock Manor, I hope you'll take a few minutes to post a review on Amazon. I would love to hear your feedback and your support keeps me writing.

To post a speedy review, please follow these links

Amazon (US)

Amazon (UK)

Amazon (the rest of the world)

Why not try the next thrilling Holly Fleet mystery? Also available on Kindle Unlimited.

Juniper Falls

Caught in a tumultuous storm, Holly and Callum search for a missing item with a sinister history. Little do they know, they aren't the only ones looking for it.

For anyone interested in updates, promotions or freebies, read my newsletter by joining my mailing list on shaunbaines.org? Your details are secure and you can unsubscribe at any time.

You can connect with me on:

🌐 https://www.shaunbaines.org

🐦 https://twitter.com/Littlehavenfarm

📘 https://www.facebook.com/shaunbaineswriter

Subscribe to my newsletter:

✉ https://www.shaunbaines.org

Printed in Great Britain
by Amazon

74661484R00180